Nine Sisters Dancing

by

Ed Moses

River Boat Books

This novel was first published in 1996 by Fithian
Press, a division of Daniel & Daniel, Publishers,
Inc.

Printed in the United States of America.
Published by River Boat Books, St. Paul, MN.
First printing November 30, 2024

ISBN: 978-1-955823-18-0

for all betrayed children

Nine Sisters Dancing

CONTENTS

* *Note to reader: Chapter Five contains graphic depictions of sexual, emotional, and physical child abuse. Feel free to skip ahead to Chapter Six.*

Chapter One

At Home in the Spring woods, comfortably
alone, Bitch scratched where it itched and
squatted where the urge took her. But when she
visited the Person Place, she went in disguise.
She walked on hind paws pinched in shoes,
half-choked in the woven fibers of the cotton
plant. She bled at the time of the full moon,
wagged her tail, worked like a dog.

A strangeness of the Person Place was that
people lived with unseen Others. As she woke
on this gray mid-March morning, she caught the
familiar spoor of one of them, Dog-Yet-Not-Dog,
who seemingly rolled in apples. She lay still for
a moment, staring up at the underside of the
box spring beneath which she lay. The frame
was not more than six inches high, a funda-
mental design flaw, but Bitch had raised it
on concrete blocks and, with the counterpane
hanging to the floor and a foam rubber pad to
curl up on, she slept in a comfortable den. Only

now the counterpane was disarranged, piled
on the bed out of sight except for two or three
folds hanging down like pink tongues. That was
so inconsiderate. Typical of them, though. She
crawled out and stood up cautiously, naked in
the long shining hair she wore here, creaking
at the knees. The light filtering through the
curtain told her it was almost seven. On the
jumble of bedclothes, a jumble of black lingerie.
Without untangling it she lifted it to her nose
and sniffed—wet fur and old fish. She carried
the dripping black things into the kitchen and
dropped them into the trash. They still smelled.
She picked them out again and, with the sharp
kitchen shears she kept for such purposes, cut
them into square inches and fed them to the
garbage disposal. It choked on straps. Patiently
she worked the jam-breaker button until everything was gone—except the stink, aloft in water
vapor now, clinging to her skin.

By the time she got out of the shower and
into the wrappings which disguised her as
Human and as Woman, the light had changed
and it was too late to eat. She wasn't hungry
anyway, never was, her appetite perpetually
spoiled by the leavings—pizza crusts reeking
of salt fish, sardine and smoked oyster tins,
sugary cereal soaked to paste in gray milk, and
Tastykake wrappers—of the Others. She never
lost weight either, the zipper of her white skirt
straining this morning, and then she realized that

it wasn't hers. It was of some shiny material
like silk, fit her like a second skin, belonged,
now that she put her nose to it, to the One
who smelled of apples. She dragged it off over
her hips and, leaving it pooled on the floor,
scrambled into her own loose white cotton.
Late—how late? The electric clock in the kitchen,
the wasteful purchase of one of the Others,
read five minutes past four. Wasteful because
clocks never worked. Watches, an hour after she
strapped them on, ran backwards. She paced
to the radio on the kitchen counter, willing her
heart to slow, but energy crackled down her
arm and into her fingertips and all she got was
static. She hurled the radio to the linoleum,
wrenching the plug from its socket, and still it
spat and sizzled at her. Bitch ran. Out the front
door and down the steps she plunged, long
lean narrow-hipped Bitch with the gait of an
Irish Wolfhound, each morning into her faithful
square blue car. Only it was not there. She stood
bereft on the sidewalk, long neck swiveling, but
it was not up the block or down the block. It
was gone. Stolen.

Transformed rather, her eyes and then
her nose told her. Square blue to long green,
hip-high on her with the top down. *Chevrolet*
to *Mazda*, a word which did not say *car* to her.
Vinyl to leather, her own doggy hairs and oils
to black lingerie, moist and a little fishy. She
walked up close but did not touch, paws tight

across her belly, and smelled now, from a
discolored patch on the right bucket seat, dark
sweet wine.

With both hands she pawed in her purse,
dumping a plastic bag of dried corn. Her car
keys were gone, replaced by an alien plastic-
girded thing. She tugged at the door, but
it held against her. *Locks have been changed.*
Glanced around — no one watching, and she set
her haunch on the doorsill, lifted her legs and
pivoted, and fell into the driver's seat. Panted.
Now — inserted the key and twisted. Nothing
happened at all.

It was broken. A toy car, not for driving
to work in but for games in black lace. She
scrambled back out over the door, scooped
up what remained of her corn, and with long
measured strides — steady, alert, an Irish
Wolfhound of a Bitch in the obedience ring —
walked the two miles to work in twenty-six
minutes.

She arrived at the school as the bell rang for
first period — late. Twelve-, thirteen-, fourteen-
year-old girls clamored by on all sides, giggle
and elbow and sharp new breasts. Boys with
voices like crows. From the safety of the crowd,
one of them swatted her on the flank. He would
sit in his first period algebra class, erect under
his desk as he dreamed of ripping her clothes
off. Bitch arrived dizzy in the office, breathless,

long nose and her lungs full of pheromones.

Mr. Davis, telephone to his ear as she entered, hung it up and glanced at the clock. "Phone's been ringing."

Bitch wagged her tail. "I'll stay late."

"Grade reports to type in today."

She sat up on her hind legs and begged.

He nodded, turned his back on her and walked into his office. Closed the door.

The clock read 8:27. She set her handbag on the desk, rummaged under the corn for a tissue, finally dragged the bag out and plunked that down too. Glared at the clock. After a few moments the second hand slowed; stopped; backed up. When it had backed thirty times around the face of the dial, she sat down at the computer, which in its turn greeted her with a mad scramble of letters, coherence routed and heading for the hills. She stacked the grade reports at her elbow, entered "Aaron, David," and began. By the time she reached "Baker, Brandon," Brandon had left algebra and was in a stall in the boys' room with his cock in his hand. He had her on her back in nothing but her black bikini panties, kneeling over her, kneading her breasts as she moaned and begged him. In the office she looked up sharply as she felt, yet again, his hands on her breasts and felt him rip her panties off, and spread her legs, and she trotted away into the woods as Coyote, at the desk, took in everything in an instant and entered, in place of the "B" earned in algebra by Baker, Brandon, despite his frequent trips to the bathroom, "C-."

In the woods of the Home Place it is Spring. On this bright morning, pale green leaves cast a light, dappled shade on the forest floor, out of which, in random profusion, flowers bloom: daffodils, daisies, mums, marigolds, asters and roses, and those tall pink spiky ones whose name she can't remember. Bitch ambles along with her head up, testing the air, plumy tail waving. She smells flowers; apples, though there grows in these woods no apple tree she has ever been able to find; blackberries, though there are no brambles; water, though there is no pond or stream or well. Then, in the angle between stone wall and woodpile, she catches a whiff of Rabbit. She breaks into a trot, tail wagging fast now, tongue lolling, and into a full gallop as Rabbit bolts, zigzagging through the trees. She runs easily, tirelessly, her long, arcing strides floating her free of the earth, crushing no petal in her passing. A few feet in front of her, Rabbit darts out into the meadow, and Bitch, head level with the outermost trees, stops.

Rabbit is gone. She sits back on her haunches, stares out across the rank grass of the field. On the far side of it sits a white frame house, a long way away, yet she can see plainly the brown shutters and door, the windows on each side of the door wide open, dull green curtains blowing in the light spring air; through one of the windows a grandfather clock,

brass and dark polished wood, reading five minutes
past ten; sofa in a dim floral print; table with a large
book lying open on it. And that the house is empty.
There is no one in that room or the next or in any
room, nor in the barn or the tool shed or the tractor
shed. In the barnyard no dog or cat, goat or goose or
rooster. Nothing moves except, sharp and swift along
the ground, the circling shadow of a bird. Bitch does
not look up to see the bird. She stands, straining
forward as against a rope; sniffs, but there is nothing
new to smell. Back and forth, just inside the outer
row of trees, she paces, whining. At last she turns
and trots back into the woods, to the angle of wall
and woodpile where, comforted by the scent of Rabbit
and by her own embedded scent, she curls up and
sleeps. She dreams of an empty house. Then in her
dream she dreams.

"Carveggio, Carolyn" was pregnant at
thirteen, though no one but Coyote knew it yet.
Coyote—as Mr. Davis stepped out of his office,
glanced at his watch, the clock, the watch again
with his face petrifying—awarded her an "A" in
Health and Hygiene.

"Why is the clock thirty minutes slow?"

Coyote grinned, showing many white teeth,
and arched her back. She was not now wearing
a bra, having taken it off a few minutes earlier
in anticipation of this very moment, and her
nipples stood out sharply under her shirt.

"Obviously because it doesn't work right."

"It was working fine yesterday."

"So? The day before you die you'll be alive. What does that prove?"

"Would you reset it, please?"

"Only if you'll tell me what it is you find so fascinating about my blouse. Is there a spot on it?"

Oh God help me. Bitch. Bitch!

"That's not my name."

"What's not?"

"What you were just thinking."

"I wasn't thinking anything."

"That I can believe. Now if you care to avoid a nasty sexual harassment suit, just turn your back while I stretch up on my tiptoes to set the clock, which by the way is not part of my job description." She knew without turning that he had gone.

"Late," she yodeled. "Late for your meeting with the Superintendent of Schools, and so . . . it . . . goes." She sat back down at the computer. Two minutes later she stood up again. "Bored, bored, *bored.*"

She went and sat for twenty minutes in the restroom, during which time between three and four hundred early adolescents, the first shift exiting the lunchroom and the second entering, had free access to the unoccupied office. Then from the bottom drawer of her desk she removed a wide-mouthed thermos. It had been there for over a week now, since the last time she had arrived on foot instead of

directly. This she carried into Mr. Davis's office,
which contained in addition to the usual institu-
tional furniture a sofa—primarily for the use of
distraught parents, though one day after school
Mr. Davis had made the mistake of inviting her
to share it with him. She removed one of the
end cushions, and into the nook formed by back
and seat and arm she dumped from the thermos
a raw chicken breast. Already it had a nice tang.
With the edge of the lid she shoved it well down
out of sight, then replaced the cushion. It would
be two or three days, she estimated, what with
the absorbent effect of the upholstery, before
humans would smell anything wrong--though
she herself, breathing deeply, was catching
gamy whiffs. The only question was whether
she'd be there at the right time to enjoy it.

In the outer office again, she took her bra
from her handbag and wiped her pawprints
off the thermos with it. As an afterthought she
slipped off her underpants and wiped with
those too. With thermos and underclothes in her
bag she strolled out into the hall and walked
along until she came to the locker of Baker,
Brandon. No one was in sight; they were all in
their homerooms or at lunch. She placed the
thermos on the shelf in back, where Brandon
would be unlikely to see it, and loped off into
the woods.

*In the Home Place of Coyote it is deep autumn
and deep twilight. The full moon, just risen, shines*

*through a tangle of bare branches. She trots along
through the undergrowth, tan dead fern, laurel,
stump and shelf fungus, until she comes to a
clearing. There she sits on her haunches, testing
the air, but all she can smell is the earth itself. Leaf
mold, rotting down slowly in the autumnal chill.
She howls at the moon, at the distant bird which
flares across its face, but neither answers. And so
she moves on, more slowly now, circling, until she
catches a glimmer of light through the trees. It is the
light of a lamp shining through the window of an
empty house, and fear rises up in her, and with it
hunger. With the hunger comes the smell that draws
her, and so she returns to the clearing, where now
an antlered buck lies dead. He bleeds into the earth
through a round hole in his neck. Coyote can never
remember killing him, though in her dreams she runs
him down the moonlit pathways forever. She dips
her head to his flank and rips with her strong back
teeth, gulps the hot flesh, raises her blood-drenched
muzzle to the cold moon and howls. She devours the
carcass to the bones, curls herself into the ribs of the
skeleton, who is her mate, and sleeps.*

Bitch had always been absent-minded,
losing minutes, hours, whole chunks of days.
So she was not surprised to find herself out in
the hallway, but why was she naked under her
skirt and blouse, and why, as she discovered
a moment later, her sharp nose drawing her,
were her underclothes in her handbag, reeking

of rotten chicken? She ducked into the restroom and into a stall, intending to put them on again. But the thought made her flesh crawl, so she dumped them into the toilet and flushed. The bowl, tightly plugged, filled to the brim—what else had she expected? She dived for them, soaking the cuff of her sleeve, wrung them out, buried them in the trash under a litter of paper towels. Only now, before Mr. Davis got back from his meeting, she would have to go home—walk home, two miles each way, or else downtown and face the smirk of some teenaged sales clerk—for another bra, because if she appeared in the office in this condition Mr. Davis would think she was coming on to him. Not to mention Brandon Baker. She wrung her hands, burst into loud sobs, and went Home. Vixen, emerging from the stall, walked straight into the arms of a woman she had never seen before in her life.

The woman said, "Laurel, honey. What's wrong?"

Vixen said coldly, "Nothing. Why should there be?"

"But I heard you crying. From all the way out in the hall."

"I wasn't."

The woman put the tip of one finger to her cheek. "Tears, no?"

Vixen became aware, to her furious embarrassment, that that was what they were. She glared. "Onions."

"What?"

"Raw onions."

"You don't want to talk about it."

"Obviously not."

"You'll tell Dr. Volker, though? Isn't today
your day?"

Vixen had never heard of Dr. Volker. She
was increasingly distracted, moreover, by a
strange smell from the trash can. Rotten chicken.
What was this place anyway? She brushed past
the woman, out the door and into a corridor
into which materialized all around her a milling
hoard of children. One, a dark boy almost as tall
as she was, paused in front of her and with both
hands began kneading her breasts. Only it was
his eyes she felt. In the red malevolent light of
her glare he turned aside, hands to his stomach.
*Throw up everything you eat for the next three
days—and eat it all over again.*

Then she felt a hand on her arm, drawing
her back into the shelter of a doorway. That
woman again. "Disgusting boy," she said,
"though, Laurel, really." Her fingers, fluttering
at chest height, drew Vixen's eyes downward.
Her nipples stood out sharply against her
blouse. "This isn't like you. Are you all right?"

"I'm fine." She threw back her shoulders and
grinned; without humor, showing all her white
teeth, daring them. Nobody stared.

"I brought you this"—a plastic bag of dried

corn.

"What for?"

"I found it on your desk in the office. I thought you might be about to go without it. But you'll have to go back for your coat anyway, won't you?"

"And where," Vixen said, wary all of a sudden, "did you think I'd be going? With a bag of chicken feed?"

The woman's eyes were round, her breathing shallow and fast. She looked close to fainting. "Pigeon feed. To the park, to feed the pigeons, for your agoraphobia. Laurel, do you . . . maybe need to go to the hospital?"

"No." What was agoraphobia? Suddenly she was suffocating. The shrill cries of the children jangled in her ears, the cries of hounds baying down her trail, and as Bitch caught her weeping best friend in her arms, and held her in a half-circle of solemn little girls, *Vixen trots through the rank dry grass of an autumn field. The full moon hangs low over the house, for it is almost dawn. The house is dark, all is still.*

She stops and sits on her lean haunches, ears cocked. No sound of dogs; only a light rhythmic creaking, as if the house itself, its timbers the wall of its chest, were alive and breathing. In the long slant of light from the late moon, the Hunter's Moon which is gravid with blood, brown grass, red fur, black-tipped tail are all one and all lurid. The light east breeze carries no news of the hunting pack; only of her own hunting. She turns on herself suddenly and with her white teeth gnaws the cockleburs out of her brush, her pride and the hunter's prize. She has no memory of when she last ate, an hour or a night or two nights ago, for hunger bites her even as she gorges, twists her guts into hard slippery knots, wrenches her now to her paws. She drools, smelling apples.

The tree is on the far side of the house, which she circles along the fence row, cringing; yet no one from the house has ever challenged her. Her long nose tells her nothing of the inside of it; it might be a sealed blackness, despite the creaking boards, or simply empty. Still and always she slinks low, a slowly spreading stain of dark blood. Around the corner, the tree at last in sight, she crouches for a moment to look for the bird which perches in it always, on the topmost branch, pale in the eye of the moon. If the bird is there, Vixen is safe: so she knows, though nothing of why she knows.

The bird is there; nothing ever changes; she runs now, floating, leaps into the lowest branches and, her head darting like a snake's head, eats. The fruit is past ripe, sweet still, harsh in her throat. Is that why, that edge of decay churning in her gut, she must now seek blood? She jumps down and out, floating in the moon which during all her gorging has not moved; for a moment her shadow and Falcon's merge, mated, and then she is around the house and into the barnyard, death-dealing. The chickens are roosted on fence rails and the low

*roof of their coop; nightly she rushes among them,
snapping; nightly they squawk, flutter, rise too late
and too low, for Vixen can fly higher. If they flew
treetop-high, still she would bring them down in
jaws which in one motion kill and devour; she bites
their heads off and their stupid eyes, which have seen
all this before but never believed it, watch her eat
them from the neck down.*

    *By the time she's done, the ground will run red
with blood. She will turn, tongue lolling, for one last
look at the house whose closed door, dark, bloody in
the moonlight, and whose shrouded windows will tell
her nothing. Then trot back to the field, no heavier,
gut growling; pause at the mound of her dung to
pass feces, studded with claw, beak, shard of bone
and apple seed. She lives under a tangle of blackberry
brambles in the center of the field. There, against the
dank October chill, she will curl her brush around
her nose, tuck her paws in, and sleep. She will dream
not of apples or chickens or the empty house, nor
even of her hunger, but of the great bird which,
as never in her waking life, takes off from the top
bough of the apple tree. With a light not of the moon
glimmering from his wings, he circles away into the
darkness. She yearns after him, long after he's out of
sight.*

    Under a tree with branches black with rain,
on a damp park bench, Bitch crouched with her
tail tucked under, scattering corn. *Here, pigeons.
Here, stupid pigeons. What is the matter with me?*

The sky oppressed her, yet it was only a city
sky; occluded, hemmed in by buildings. *Does
Mary not know? The other teachers? Of being raped
every day of their lives?*

That was one more thing she could never
tell anyone. That she lived with Others. Fed
underwear to the garbage disposal. Owned
a car she had never bought and could not
drive. Stopped watches, lost days, turned time
backward. Slept under her bed. And most
especially not Dr. Volker, who would think she
was crazy, take her clothes away, lock her up in
a dark room beneath his office. She told him she
was very nervous; had trouble concentrating;
made stupid mistakes at work; could not keep
a boyfriend; disliked open spaces. All that he
found acceptable. He prescribed Valium, which
one of the Others lost or stole before she could
take it, and a daily trip to the park. The pigeons,
milling around her ankles now, grew fat. They
smelled disgusting. Bitch drew her feet up onto
the bench, but that tipped her head sideways so
that, all against her will, she glimpsed tree and
sky. And Falcon, who, circling, wove Bitch and
tree and sky together. She sobbed once, a dry
convulsive catch in her throat, and went Home.
Coyote glanced about sharply. There was no
one in sight, so she tossed corn close and closer
still, until one white pigeon pecked at her feet.
Greedy bird. Stupid bird, and she pounced and
twisted. The neck bone snapped between her

paws.

What she saw now, wheeling toward her
along the ground, could not be. On this sunless
day, the swift shadow of a bird, only not a
shadow. Light against dark. She fled, and in
the second that Bitch saw what it was that she
held in her hands, opened her mouth to scream,
Falcon stooped. One dark fierce eye met hers,
then in a rush of bright wings he was gone and
the pigeon with him. In her hand remained one
white feather. One drop of red arterial blood.
Her scream was the high-pitched, gibbering
squeal of Rat. Rat whirled toward no hole, no
thing, the black heart of space. Fled down and
in, and Wolf stood alone in the park.

She glanced around warily, eyes and
ears and nose seeking. Corn scattered about
her paws, but nothing there to eat it. Pigeon
very strong, a little squirrel. A white feather,
blood-stained. She picked it up and held it
to her nose—pigeon, and under that, faintly,
something strange—sunlight on a bright Spring
hillside, but that could not be. At Home it was
dark and cold, the wind out of the North.

Now she saw, walking toward her along
the sidewalk which wound through the park,
a man with a dog on a leash. She gazed at
it with regret, for it was a fat dog. The man,
who himself was plump, young, dressed as for
office or law court in a blue suit and yellow
necktie, smiled at her. The dog's hackles rose,

it whimpered, turned tail and bolted, dragging hard at the leash. *What?* Over one shoulder from fifteen feet the man, yanked off balance, met the eyes of Wolf. They were deep and calm and cold. They froze him into a place of eternal snow. *God!* Beside his waddling dog, out for a noontime stroll in his leather business shoes, he ran.

Wolf watched him out of sight, then walked to the edge of the park and went Home. *There, through the forests of night everlasting, she hunts the Shadow Deer. North wind whirls dry snow into her face, blinding her. Choking her. On the foggy hilltops she is a ghost wolf. In moonless clearings, in the ghost-light of Orion, the constellation Wolf. She hungers and she thirsts, tongue lolling from her mouth; staggers where the snow drifts belly-deep; bleeds where ice-knives cut her pads, and still she runs. Behind her, calling her down the keening wind, Falcon flies, hunting.*

Underground, in the corner of a cellar behind a rubble of cider jugs, chicken crates, broken wooden toys and moldering books, Rat gnaws. In this darkness, the darkness of a capped well on a foggy winter midnight, cats and rats are blind. In the close air, which stinks of rotten grain, damp stone, decaying wood and paper and her own strong feces and urine, Rat feeds by touch and smell. Her food is rotting apples, the heads of chickens, dry corn. Her drink is strong cider and the damp on the walls.

She creeps out to eat, creeps back to sleep, and never dreams.

The mind of Dr. Herman Volker, a small gray man, was occluded. Bitch as she peered in could make out only shifting patches of fog, lit intermittently from behind or within by a flickering red or yellow glare as of distant heat lightning. It was brightest and reddest when he was angry with her, as he was, she saw, now. Timidly she wagged her tail.

"I really am trying."

Dr. Volker frowned, concentrating on the pipe he lit at the beginning of every session and which therefore she paid him to light, though why should she, considering that the fumes of it made her ill? "No doubt," he said, eyes on the match which he held well away from the bowl until it burned with a clear and steady flame, "you are. You feel you are. Yet something is missing. After almost a year of these sessions, you're not getting any better. What do you suppose is the matter?"

Bitch lay on her back on the floor with her tail between her legs and her throat exposed to his killing bite, and she grinned a doggy grin.

"I don't know. What do *you* suppose is the matter?"

Smoke drifted across the desk and penetrated her nose. "You have not yet entered into the work of therapy."

"I know," she said sadly. "You've told me.
How do I do that again?"

"You have to be honest. You have to be
open." He smiled. Bitch's tail thumped once on
the chair. "You have to trust me with your very
life."

"I do want to. I'm sorry to be so stupid. If
you could just tell me how?"

He puffed on the pipe. Her lungs turned
black and she convulsed on the floor. She stifled
a small cough, ladylike. "Tell me a secret," he
said. The blood drained from her face.

"I don't think," she said. "I'm sorry to be so
stupid, but I don't *think* I have any secrets."

"Now you see, I could have predicted that.
It means you're not being honest with me.
Everyone's got secrets."

What could she say that would satisfy him?
What would be enough but not too much? He
was frowning, not looking at her, disgusted.
He was going to punish her. She cringed. ''I'm
Bitch," she blurted, giving him her true name,
all she had, and, for the first time in forty-two
sessions, she ran Home. *Home is where the air
smells of Spring flowers and earth and sunshine.
Where nothing has ever changed until today.
Something about the angle of the light which she
sees, at first, with her inner eye only. The dappling
of the shadows. She sits back on her haunches,
panting. Sunlight dazzles her, yet she ought, just
here in this bed of lilies, to be in the shade. Always*

*the trunk of the forking tree in front of her shades
her here, but today the sun has risen into the cleft of
the fork. A black shadow flares across the sun. Her
eyes go dark. Her heart freezes in her breast.*

Coyote took in the couch, the diploma
framed on the wall, the little gray man with
the pipe behind the desk, staring at her.
So--somebody was definitely crazy. But not
her. She looked in. His mind resembled the
coiled shit-stuffed guts of a deer lying dead in a
clearing with a hole in his neck.

He said, "What did you say?"

Coyote grinned a wolfish grin, at which the
little man slightly flinched. "What do you think
I said?"

"I think you said, I'm a bitch."

"And am I?"

"That's hardly for me to say. The question is,
why would you think so?"

Coyote arched her long elegant back. Her
nipples stood out against her blouse. The
mind-guts of the little man twitched, grew
turgid, collapsed like a pricked balloon. "Is it
being a bitch to say what's on your mind?"

"Of course not," he said, but his mind
turned the amber-brown of rotting apples, and
she could see and smell the lie.

"Then do you want to fuck me or don't
you?"

"Certainly not!"

"I'm such a hag it never crossed your little mind."

"You're very attractive."

"So don't you like attractive women? Or do you like little boys?"

"What's come over you? You never talked this way before."

"How would you know how I talk?"

"How would I know? Laurel, how many times have you come here?"

"Is that a trick question? You keep records, don't you?"

"You honestly don't know?"

"I forget. It's unimportant. *Do* you like little boys?"

"Why do you keep asking me that?"

"Because I really am a bitch? Because of the way you keep sucking that pipe stem? Wouldn't you rather suck my tit?"

She stood up and began unbuttoning her blouse. The little man stood behind his desk, pipe stem aimed at her, warding. Mind-guts coiled and throbbed, reddened, swelled, burst. A little girl lay there. She was naked, bleeding from the fork of her spread legs. *Coyote ran panting through the forest, frothing at the mouth. In the deep autumnal twilight, she runs in diminishing circles till she comes to the clearing where the deer lies, dead with a round hole through his neck. Coyote's hunger is thick nausea. She edges closer, jaws wide, gagging, and, six inches from her nose*

*in which lingers, still, after all her long passage
through the cold arboreal air of her Home Place the
scent of pipe tobacco, blood oozes from the deer's dry
wound. Now it spurts, carotid pumping it, soaking
the tawny neck and filling Coyote's nose and mouth
with a red spume. She is blinded by blood, drowning
in blood as the deer's legs twitch, his eyes open,
his head rises, and, though he is Red Deer now, his
blood painting him with a red Hunter's Moon which
fills the whole sky, he stands on his four legs and
walks away into the woods. Coyote raises her head
and howls at the moon and the bird swinging across
the moon. Around and around the clearing she runs,
barking and growling and chasing her tail.*

Cat found herself with her blouse half-un-
buttoned, face to face with a man she didn't
know. It was not a new or necessarily a
displeasing situation, but this was such a little
gray mouse of a man. What might she want to
do with him? He was one quick pounce away,
but the desk was between them and already he
looked, without even having got to know her,
ready to bolt for the nearest hole. She undid one
last button, eased one haunch onto the desk,
purred. "Do I know you?"

His stare told her that she knew him very
well indeed. He was one more of the many
details in her life she could not be bothered
to keep track of, then. "I guess I do," she
purred, and went open and naked for him,

paws stroking her inner thighs, belly, breasts;
expecting his hands and hot breath and tongue
on her in turn, but . . . nothing; he backed off a
step, and she closed up snarling.

"Laurel, what's got into you today?"

"Certainly not you."

He turned red.

She had not yet bothered to look inside.
She did now and recoiled at the scent,
overwhelming the tobacco smell in her outer
sense, of burning sulfur. She was in a cave
deep underground, a low-roofed rock cavern
pillared with stalagmites. In and out among
them, dressed yellow-gray in smoke, their faces
painted red by fire, young girls danced. At her
feet ran a narrow red river. It dwindled to a
trickle as she watched, its bed oozy red rock,
sticky brown rock, gray dust; the girls gone
and the smoke and fire gone, and all a stony
silence. So Cat had seen enough with her night-
seeing eyes, and she came back out blinking in
the room light, licking smoke from her fur. She
stared at him, her eyes slits. She said, "You're
going to be dead in six months."

"What? Laurel, you've no right to talk that
way."

"I thought you'd want to know. Put your
affairs in order. Put your mind in order. If not,
forget it. Drop dead on the street for all I care."

He looked for a moment like dropping dead
where he stood, no fun for Cat, who cared

nothing for what she hadn't killed herself.
"Why? Why would you say such a thing?"
     "I say what I see, little man."
     "What you see? Laurel . . . listen. For some
time now I've had a sense that you do somehow
. . . know things that you couldn't know. I
was aware, rationally, that it couldn't be true.
Mentioning it would have been unethical. Are
you claiming, then, that you really do? See
things?"
     Cat glanced in, the merest flick of a glance.
"Melissa," she said. "Known to you as Missy,"
and the face of the gray little man went
bone-white as the blood drained out of it, his
hand went slack and his pipe clunked onto the
desk, his fingers, as at the edge of a smooth
granite ledge above a gorge, scrabbled and
dragged at the desktop, his knees turned to
water and his brain to opaque black ice and he
fell in a heap on the carpet.
     Cat glanced, mildly curious, but he was
not dead. Maybe dying. She looked around
the office, licking her lips, languidly buttoning
buttons. It was pretty barren; nothing took her
fancy except an ebony carving of a woman's
head which reminded her, the narrow feline
skull, of herself. She removed it from the
bookshelf where it sat, flanked by a couple
of nondescript carved antelopes which she
disdained. The solid weight of it, satisfying in
her hand, reminded her of something else to

do, so she walked around the desk to where the
little gray man lay huddled on his side. For he
was after all hers, gray mouse, she had caught
him with a word. His breathing was quiet;
perhaps he had only fainted. So, as she twitched
his wallet out of his hip pocket, she kept her
other paw on the statuette, ready on the rug
beside her. She slipped a sheaf of pretty green
bills into her bag, from which she then removed,
after a little rummaging, a scarlet lipstick. The
word which writhed in his mind, dancing a wet
red dance, she printed in red on his forehead.

He never moved as she gathered her things,
the statuette in her bag now, and stood over
him, considering. She might claw his pants
off, just to see what she'd see, but the thought
bored her. Little gray mouse with his little
white girls, *Melissa, Roberta*, farther back there
was . . . *Mildred*, but that was his mother. Some
black confusion. Her hackles rose, she spat,
stalked hissing out of the office. The waiting
room, formerly the front parlor of the refur-
bished Victorian mansion in which Dr. Volker
conducted his practice, was empty, Bitch's
having been the last appointment of the day.
Cat, on the sidewalk now, looked around.
People on their way home from work hurried
past her, heads bowed against the lowering
afternoon. Where was she? Where was her
darling little car? She couldn't have walked
here, she hated walking. And what time was

it? If today was Friday, she had a date. She
waded ankle-deep into the pedestrian stream,
was jostled by a burly woman, unsheathed her
claws and yowled. "Bitch!" the woman snapped.
Bitch cringed, "Sorry," and the woman snarled
and was gone. Bitch backed into the doorway.
What was she doing, in the middle of a session,
outside Dr. Volker's office? Then she remembered. She had told him her name, *Bitch*, and he
must have become disgusted with her, knowing
her at last for what she was, and thrown her
out.

So she could go home now—a long walk in
the evening chill, and she would most likely
be late for her date—except that she hadn't yet
paid him for the session. He was strict about
that. So just dart in and take care of it, leave
the money at the receptionist's desk, and she
wouldn't even have to see him. That was if she
had anything to pay him with--sometimes she
forgot, and then she had to run home cringing
with her tail between her legs and bring it back
and slip it in the mail slot. *Please*—with no car
and her date with Rick she had no time for
that. Or was it Rick? Her mind . . . But then, as
it turned out, she had all sorts of money. Not
tucked neatly into her wallet, loose in her bag
for some reason, but there it was; she counted
three twenties out into her paw and there was
lots left over, a good day after all, and she
trotted into the building with a light heart and

her tail wagging.

The waiting room was empty; that was
normal. Within, though, something was wrong.
She pricked her ears and caught quick panting
breaths, and the scent those breaths airmailed
to her quick nose was not vapor from the lungs
but blood from the brain, a red mist she could
almost see. So drop the money and run. Run!

Sidewise, dogwise, she edged closer to the
closed door of the inner office, the blood-reek
gagging her. Placed her paw on the knob.
Turned the knob and poked her long nose
inside. Dr. Volker was there, slumped behind
his desk. They stared at each other.

When he spoke his voice was thick, muffled
with loam from his grave: "The session is over."

"Yes. Of course. I just wanted . . ."

She held the bills out in her paw, suppli-
cating. He shook his head. "No. Enough. Just
go."

"All right. Yes," and being Dog and curious,
added "Why?" But being Bitch and courteous
did not go on to ask: is the word *Melissa* printed
in red on your forehead? It had not been there
during their session; surely she would have
remembered. She crumpled the bills into the
pocket of her skirt and, with one last apologetic
wag, trotted back out onto the street.

*In the room which is Cat's Home Place, Fire
burns yellow as the eyes of Cat, red as the hunger*

of Cat, like Cat consuming nothing. She hunts in
the dark cold corners, behind the sofa and the clock
where Mouse's holes are, but Mouse is a memory
of a memory. What breathes out of the holes is
only cold, the killing sigh of Winter. She has spent
numb ages at the holes, like that prehistoric hunter
gathered to Winter's glacial heart, awakened at last
by what she hears only as echo: the scream of a
hunting bird. Tonight she is awake, prowling. The
windows on each side of the door are shrouded, the
curtains, a dusky dark green, drawn close. In the
middle of the floor sits a plain wooden table, onto
which she now leaps. The words in the book open
beside her mean nothing to her--black hieroglyphics
which may not be words at all or even language. The
clock reads twelve o'clock. Is it always twelve here?
She watches, eyes slitted, wondering why she never
before wondered. The pendulum swings right, swings
left, the sole surviving steps of a dance lost in time.
The minute hand edges down the dial, remains
fixed at twelve--could the dial be moving with it?
Yet twelve remains in its place. Cat yawns, licks
her fur, gives it up. She turns to the windows. And
arches her back, spitting, for in the green field of the
curtain to the right of the door, a tree is growing.
Before her eyes its black branches spread, pale leaves
unfurl, buds burst into white bloom; bloom fades,
green apples set, redden, fall and rot, leaves fall,
branches gnarl in the great cold. Then the curtain is
as it ever was. But the signs in the book have turned
red, flickering like fire, dripping like blood.

Bitch trotted along with her head down, nose to the ground. The sky could not hurt her as long as she kept counting the squares of the sidewalk. But if she missed even one, she would be lost, earth and sky pivot on the axis of her craziness and whirl her away into the clouds.

After a time her head rose when she wasn't noticing, her tail rose, and she trotted cheerily, inhaling the misty breath of Spring. For she had remembered that she would no longer have to visit Dr. Volker. Even Mary, who had sent her to him in the first place, would surely not insist. So no more trips to the park, the deep breaths to prevent fainting dragging into her lungs (Dr. Volker had never understood this though she had tried, as delicately as she could, to explain it) a fine spray of vaporized pigeon shit. No more frowns and tobacco smoke and *really, Laurel, how can you expect to get anywhere if you won't open up with me?* Dr. Volker was doubtless a great man in his way, and she had *heeled* and *come* and *downed* and *stayed* for him until she was blue in the face, and what had it gotten her?

Broke, was what. And it was not as if she had not been honest with him. She had told him her name.

So now on Friday afternoons, instead of driving all the way downtown, getting home late and like as not disheveled, her poor head

all full of burrs, she'd be there by ten past four
with plenty of time to spruce up. Unlike this
particular Friday—what time was it? The sun
was down, street lights on, it was late. Mist
filled her nose with cooking smells. Rick might
be there already, tramping up and down the
porch, angry with her. As well he might be,
for she had been forced to tell him that she'd
lost the expensive watch he gave her for her
birthday. *Just like a woman,* and she could not,
though it galled her to be so sly, say *no, just like
a Bitch.* She hurried on doggedly, and there he
was sure enough, sitting, though, not pacing,
so maybe it would be all right after all, on the
porch of the house of which she rented half
the first floor. She could make him out plainly,
though the porch was dark . . .

It was not Rick at all. It was Mary.

Mary stood and waved as she trotted up the
steps but did not offer her a hug, so she must
be mad at her too. She said, "I've been worried
about you. What happened to your car?"

What had happened to it? She glanced
around, as if it might be parked in the shadow
of the porch swing, and then the sight of the
Mazda convertible at the curb brought it all
back. The Mazda's top was down. The beautiful
leather upholstery was going to be ruined. She
ought of course to have gone out at once and
put it up, assuming she'd known how, since
the car was hers in the sense that the key to it

was in her purse, but that would have meant awkward questions from Mary. "It's in the garage."

"Nothing expensive, I hope."

Bitch shrugged, expansive with three twenties in her pocket and more loose in her handbag. "Coming in? It's cold out here."

"Because if Ron Davis has anything to say about it, you're going to be out of a job."

"Oh? Really? Why?"

She fumbled with the key, paws collapsing under her. She lay on the floor of the porch with her head between her paws, whimpering. This always happened. And just when she was feeling good for once. *Why?*

Her den was cold and cheerless. She went around lighting lamps and smelling the Others, apple and wet fur and fish and now, lingering in the moisture-laden air, a cheesy undercurrent. Fainter yet: something cold with scales.

Mary watched silently from the sofa until, finally, Bitch was compelled to stop and look at her. "You really don't know?"

"Of course not. I work hard. It must be some mistake."

"You thought it wouldn't get back to him? Or he wouldn't care, when he's had it in for you from the day you started? That you made a blatant sexual pass at a student?"

"I . . . did . . . *not*. Mary, I'm . . . *nice*. I was brought up to be. I don't *do* things like that."

"Laurel, sit down here with me."

Bitch sprang to the sofa, tail thumping. "You believe me. Don't you?"

"Now listen. This is me, all right? I saw you with your bra off, sticking your chest out at those kids. Look, it's still off. You can see right through that blouse. What's going on here?"

Bitch said sadly, "I don't remember taking it off. Things like that just seem to happen sometimes. So he's really hot about it?"

"He had a call from a parent. He's taking it to the School Board next week, unless you can talk him out of it."

"You think I could?"

"You know our Ron. Maybe you could. Do you want to?"

"I will," Bitch said, "lick his shoes till they glow in the dark. I need that job."

"You shouldn't have to. I hate for you to have to. Laurel—what gets into you?"

"I'm sure I don't know."

"Because I mean you're *so* nice. Mostly. And then you go nuts and screw everything up. Lose jobs, lose husbands . . ."

"Husbands?"

"All right, husband. But isn't one enough? He was a perfectly good one, and they're not so easy to come by."

Bitch had never been married in her life. She fled yelping into the woods. *There it is no longer ten o'clock. It is no longer noon. It looks more like*

*three or four o'clock in the afternoon. She sits on her
haunches in a bed of daisies and howls.*

Cat, with bloody hieroglyphs still flickering
behind her eyes, said, "For heaven's sake. What
are you doing here?"

Mary recoiled. She said, "I just now told you
what I'm doing. See? See what I mean? That's
exactly what I'm talking about."

They stared at each other. But Cat couldn't
be bothered.

She stretched, yawned, purred. She felt good
all of a sudden. "Make yourself at home," she
said, "until my company gets here. When and
who is that going to be, I wonder? Maybe the
magic box will tell."

She prowled over to the telephone table,
elegantly waving her tail, and tapped *Play* on
the answering machine.

*Hey babe, me. I'm gonna be late.
Something came up, so let's just eat in, okay?
Make a steak or something. See you when I
see you.*

*Laurel, I've got to see you. We're still on
for tonight, aren't we? I love you, honey, I
know we can work it out. I love you, bye.*

*This is the Smart Shop calling to let
you know that your check for $153.56 was
returned by the bank. There will be a $20*

*service charge, and please stop in and clear
this up as soon as you can.*

*You haven't forgotten what I promised
you? I haven't.*

*I thought for sure you'd be home by now.
Listen, I made reservations at the Herdic
House, is that okay? They're for seven, so
I'll pick you up a little before that. Love you
honey, bye.*

Cat strolled back to the sofa. "Not too bad.
What time is it?"

"Six? No, that can't be right, it was almost
that when I got here. Damnit, my watch has
stopped. Don't you have a watch or a clock
around here somewhere?"

"They never work right. So pit-of-the-
stomach time, which tells me what? Time to get
. . . my God!"

"What? What is it?"

"What am I doing in this dowdy skirt?"

"Dowdy? It's perfectly fine. Anyway if you
don't like it, why do you keep wearing it to
work?"

Cat unbuttoned the skirt, dropped it over
her hips, stepped out of it. Naked now from the
waist down, she raised the hem of her blouse to
the bottom of her rib cage and slowly, sinuously
revolved. "Nice and thin today? How do I

look?"

"You look . . . Laurel, the curtain's not drawn."

"So it isn't." She walked to the window and drew it.

Sweat beaded on Mary's forehead. "How many boyfriends do you have, anyway? And how many of them are due over here any time now?"

"Come on in the bedroom while I get dressed." She led the way with her blouse still tucked up, tail swaying. Mary followed, her face reddening. "Now where . . . ?"

"What?"

"Where's my sexy black bra? My panties, my stockings, that I bought specially for tonight? They were right here. Damn, damnit, where does everything go?"

"Did you buy them from the Smart Shop?"

"Mm?"

"Never mind. Forget it. What I really want to know right now is, why is your bed up on those blocks?" Cat, rummaging in the bureau, glanced at the bed without interest. "White. White cotton underpants. Yuck!"

She showered them onto the floor. Mary said, "Why did you buy them then? What about the bed? What is going on here?"

Cat gave up on the lingerie. She trotted to the closet, plucked from a hook a pair of black toreador pants, pulled them on over her bare skin. She undid the top two buttons of her blouse, yanked it off over her head, dropped it at her feet. The blouse with which she replaced it was the red of fresh arterial blood. "There. What do you think?"

"It doesn't exactly say Herdic House to me, or are you staying in and cooking steaks for the creep who didn't know when he was getting here? And what about the guy who promised you something? He sounded spooky. Promised you what? Laurel, are you in real trouble?"

"Do I look like I'm in trouble?"

"Not that kind."

She walked up to Cat and caught her by the shoulders. "All I'm getting out of you is evasions, and I'm sick and tired of it. I don't care how many dates you've got, I'm your friend, and I'm not leaving here until I get some answers."

Rat's eyes went red. She chittered and snarled. "Lady, if you don't get your paws off me right now, I'm going to chew your face off."

Mary opened her hands, arms out stiff in front of her. She walked backwards until the raised bed caught her in the small of the back and she sprawled sideways half onto it. Scrambled the rest of the way up and huddled against the wall. Rat was snarling, showing her long front teeth, but she too had backed away. They stared at each other.

Cat said, "What are you doing on the bed?"

"What? What do you think I'm doing?"

Cat purred. "You do look cute in that dress. Why don't you slip it off and get comfortable?"

"You stay away from me! You looked horrible. You said you'd chew my face off. What is wrong with you?"

The doorbell rang.

"Damn, I'm not ready. Be a love, would you? If it's Curtis, tell him I'll be out in a minute. If it's anybody else, tell him whatever. My mom died and I had to go to her funeral."

She turned to the mirror at the back of the bureau and began to brush her long silky hair. Mary scrambled to the floor, jarred by the unaccustomed distance, and with wary eyes on Cat sidled out of the room. God, let it be Curtis. *Her mother died?* Mary knew nothing about Laurel's mother. Nothing it seemed about Laurel herself. She opened the door, and did not have to hear the voice she had heard twice on the tape to know. The navy blazer, the blue and white striped tie, the roses and the diffident smile told her: *this was Mister We-can-work-it-out-at-the-Herdic-House. Not Mister Make-me-a-steak-whenever-I-happen-to-get-here,* and certainly not *Remember-what-I-promised-you?* She went cold, standing there in the bland personal space of the lovelorn Curtis. *Who? Promised what?*

"Come on in the living room," she said. "She'll be right out," and, herself feeling like Laurel's mother, returned to the bedroom. "Tall, blond, doe eyes, real straight?"

Cat's hair was shining. To the red blouse and black pants she had added teardrop-shaped black onyx earrings, matching necklace, red high-heeled pumps. She rubbed her paws together and purred. "That's the one. Just let me at him."

"*Really?* What do you see in him?"

Cat purred. With one paw, lightly, she rubbed her belly. "Lovely food, yum. And . . . "

She rubbed lower. Mary raised her eyebrows. Really? There was more to the man than the bland innocence she'd seen? "All right then. But you be damn careful, okay? Remember what's out there. I'll call you over the weekend." But did not give her a hug. *I'll chew your face off? Slip out of that dress and get comfortable?* She walked out with a nod, feeling wrong about it, but Cat, kissing tongues with Mirror-Cat, paid no attention at all.

She ambled up to him purring, laughing in her throat as his eyes widened at the sight of her. He did not want to be seen with her at the Herdic House, dressed as she was, among men from his law office and women in long dresses. He wanted her naked on her back with her tongue, as it was now, flicking between her teeth. The price of that, as he well knew, was showing her off in public. And food, shrimps and onion soup and red meat in flaky layers of pastry, and dark red wine, and chocolate,

and coffee laced with Kahlua and topped with
whipped cream. She put her paws on his waist,
ignoring the flowers he offered her, and tilted
her head back to be kissed. Her tongue went
into his mouth. She rubbed up against him,
belly to belly, and felt him grow hard. Then she
was dancing away in languorous circles with the
roses in her hand. As she danced she scattered
them — a red flower-drift on the old brown
carpet, all but two, which she held to her two
breasts. "Smell them," she commanded. "Do
they smell nice?"

He bent to her and breathed, his hands
lightly on her shoulders. She laughed. That was
not where they were supposed to be. He understood nothing, he was boring, maybe this would
be the last time for him.

"They smell . . . almost as nice as you."

"I'm hungry. Let's go eat."

But before they had taken two steps toward
the door, the doorbell rang. "My God," he said.
"Who is it? Are you expecting someone?"

"Of course not. I think . . . it must be
someone I thought I got rid of. Who didn't, you
know, like it. Who's been bothering me lately."

"He can't do that."

She glanced up at him with slitted eyes,
laughing in her throat. "But it seems he is. So
I guess, Mister Man, your luck is in tonight.
Come on."

She held her paw out to him, but he didn't

take it. He turned back toward the door, hands
flexing. The bell rang again, twice. Quick as
a cat she flicked a paw under his blazer and
caught him by the back of his belt. "No, love.
Wrong. This is a jealous man. He's been known
to carry weapons. You just go where I tell you.
Where do you want to go anyway?"

"But our reservations. He can't keep us,
what, prisoners in here?" There was a heavy
pounding on the door. "Laurel! Hey babe, you
in there?"

Cat drew close up behind him. Her paw
slipped around to the front, inside his pants,
explored downward. "You want to go out there
and maybe get in a fight? Or go in the bedroom
with me?"

He didn't have to tell her in words. She took
his hand and walked him into the bedroom. As
she closed the door they heard, "Laurel? Where
the hell are you?"

His intent, she knew, was to throw her onto
the bed, drag her pants off, fuck her in thirty
seconds. She'd have none of that. She stood
against the door and, when he reached for her,
snarled. He backed off, whipped dog in a blue
blazer. She purred. Better. "Let's play show
and tell. Take off your jacket and tie so we start
even." He did, fumbling. "Do what I do, now."
She unbuttoned the top button of her blouse,
and watched, tongue flicking, as he worked
with thick fingers. The second button, the third,

and now she opened it, black beads against white skin. Cupped her breasts, her nipples, small red blooms, peeping through circles of thumbs and forefingers. "I'm showing. Now you have to tell. You like?"

"I like."

"Me too. I wish I could suck them. Want to do it for me?"

He nodded, licking dry lips, took one step forward. She held up one hand. *Stay, boy!* He stayed. "I'm way ahead of you. No more till you catch up."

He yanked off his shirt and undershirt, panting.

She nodded. "Better. Very nice. Now watch."

She undid the button at the waist of her pants and lowered them to the jut of her hips. Her finger circled her navel. "You like?"

"I like."

"Nice place for a tongue. Now I wonder, what would I find down here?" Her hand worked down under the cloth. "Mm, nice curly fur. And what's this, all silky smooth, all wet?" The hand reappeared. She raised one finger to her nose, breathed; flicked her tongue out and licked. "Nice. Want a taste?"

"God, yes, please!"

"I'm ahead again."

As he yanked his pants down and his under-pants with them, she trotted away. *The room is quiet. The fire burns brightly. The characters in the*

*open book on the table are black, inert, the curtains
plain dark green.* Snake accepted his tongue,
then took him into her mouth, licking lightly;
led him to the bed, coiled round and about him
and mounted him, her long loose hair brushing
his face; eased him on, drew him back, her
breath hissing between her teeth, through three
climaxes of her own, until it was time for one
last urging and he came inside her.

Then after a time he lay on his back, in his
underpants again, staring at the ceiling, Cat in a
red silk robe snuggled up beside him.

"Laurel . . . "

"Mm? Listen, I'm hungry. I'm starving. Let's
go eat."

"I'm hungry too, but it's long past seven."

"Call anyway. Maybe they can still take us."

When he went, she hopped off the bed
and foraged for clothes. She never seemed
to know what she had lately. But here was a
reasonable long skirt, a sort of tartan plaid —
not her exactly, she couldn't think why she'd
have bought it, but good enough for Curtis. A
blouse — just a plain old white blouse of the sort
people who had to work in offices wore. She
drew the line at the white cotton underwear,
however. She would have to go shopping
tomorrow. She went into the bathroom to dress,
not caring to show herself in her skin. When she
came back out Curtis was dressed too. "They
can take us," he said. "You look nice. I never

saw you dressed like that."

She purred, her mind elsewhere. Her stomach growled. *Shrimps, onion soup, red meat, red wine; chocolate, Kahlua, coffee, whipped cream.* Oh, God. She grabbed him by the hand and pulled. "Come *on.*" On the sidewalk she paused, wondering if she ought to put up the top on her car. But it had stopped raining, a west wind had sprung up, it was a fine, brisk spring evening. "Come on come on come on."

And then after all that, after all she'd done for him, all she got was the shrimps and the soup. For he chose, of all possible moments, the arrival of the main course, the waitress barely out of earshot, to say, his voice wobbling, "Laurel, darling, I can't live without you. Will you marry me?"

For God's *sake.* She spat and went away.

Vixen, who knew the sight and smell of good food when it was right there in front of her, dug in. She was wolfing only her second bite of beef Wellington when the man across the table from her said, "Laurel, please. You've got to tell me. Will you?"

Vixen had hardly noticed him before. Now she glanced up, still chewing. It tasted wonderful. She took another bite; it never paid to miss your chances. The man was nobody she knew, he was hardly prepossessing, what was she doing here with him? Well, obviously--she was eating. He presumably was paying. She

licked her lips and said rapidly between bites,
"Will I what?"

"Laurel! Weren't you listening? Will you
marry me?"

She considered this odd question from
several angles. She didn't want to marry. She
didn't want to marry a man she didn't know.
She didn't want to marry this dog-eyed man in
particular. On the other hand, the beef on her
plate was quickly diminishing, and there was
beef on his plate too, a filet mignon which must
have weighed close to a pound and which he
had not yet touched. "Maybe," she said, eating.
"Why do you want to?"

"Why? Because, Laurel, I love you. Please,
don't you love me? You said you did, so what's
stopping us? Let's get married."

"Just what is it about me you love?"

"Everything. Your mind. Your personality.
Everything."

Vixen grinned a foxy grin, drained her glass
of Burgundy, poured more from the bottle
which happened to be sitting there. "My tits?"

"Well, I mean, of course. You're gorgeous, I
should have said that. Why didn't I say that?"

"And how am I in bed?"

"You're . . . Laurel, for God's sake, this is a
public place."

She speared the last bite of Wellington,
pouting.

He leaned closer. "You're fantastic. I've

never known anyone . . ."

"But that doesn't mean much if you've only known one or two."

"I'm experienced enough . . ."

"You're promiscuous?"

"One at a time! Laurel, why are you doing this to me?"

She regarded him gravely over her empty plate. "I'm teasing, darling. Can't you tell? And I might very well want to marry you, only it's hard to think about it when I'm still so hungry. Could I have that if you're not going to eat it?"

"What? Yes, of course." He passed his plate across the table. She cut into the meat and sighed. It was rare and bloody and good.

"So you will? You said you would?"

She cut and chewed. Hot blood spurted into her throat. Oh good.

"Would what?"

"Damnit, I'm sorry, I didn't mean that. Marry me!"

"I hardly think so, darling. It's true that I'm fantastic in bed but you're terrible, truly wretched. I don't believe I would find it very satisfying."

His chair smacked the floor behind him as he stood. The blood drained from his face. He walked out of the restaurant without a word, blundering into furniture on his way.

Vixen cut, chewed; swallowed hungrily. A waitress hurried up and righted the chair. "Are you all right? Is anything wrong?"

"A small misunderstanding. Could I see your dessert menu?"

She ordered and ate three apple tarts with fresh cream and then, with a happy sigh, trotted off Home. A woman in a black skirt and a white ruffled blouse said to Bitch, "Will that be cash or credit card?"

Bitch looked around the restaurant, which she recognized, having been there with Mary. From how she was feeling, she must just have finished a large dinner. The insides of her thighs were sticky, but it was not the time of the full moon and she could not smell blood. She had no credit card; there had been some confusion about payments and she had lost it. Her handbag was nowhere to be seen. She put her hand in the pocket of her skirt, remembering the three loose twenties—but this was a different skirt. *When had she changed? What was going on?*

With a small apologetic wag of her tail she said, "Neither, I'm afraid." Evidently there had been someone here with her, since the table was set for two. "Was . . . the other person who was here maybe going to pay?"

"He left rather abruptly. You think he's coming back?"

"I'm not sure."

"Excuse me a moment."

She walked over to the reservations desk and consulted with an older woman, similarly dressed. When she returned she was smiling. "It's all right. We have your friend's name and phone number and we'll call him to take care of it."

Bitch lay on her back with her paws in the air and wagged. "Thank you. Oh thank you so much."

"Glad to be of service. Please come again."

"I will. I certainly will."

And then once again she was out on the street, alone at night, miles from home and without a car. She had eaten dinner without remembering it, drunk something that had made her a little tipsy, and *what about Rick?* Had she cooked for him and then come here with someone else? Only cooked what? There was nothing in the house, she hadn't been to the store. Couldn't have been unless she'd walked there too, but it was at least two miles. Had Rick changed his mind and taken her to the Herdic House for the steak she was sure, from the taste lingering in her mouth, she had recently eaten? For a moment, swinging along as fast as she could with her belly almost dragging the ground, her eyes brightened. Maybe he loved her after all.

But he was openly scornful of the Herdic House, a place where doctors and lawyers and college professors ate, and even if he had taken her, things were not so good after all, because there had been a bad fight. If only she'd thought

of asking the waitress the name of the man
she'd been with. Except the woman would have
thought she was crazy. She'd most likely have
been right.

Which did not alter what was true: she was
in love with Rick. If it was Rick in the restaurant,
at least she hadn't stood him up and the quarrel
could maybe be fixed. A little lover's quarrel.
If she went to him wagging, rolled over on her
back with her paws in the air, maybe he would
still like her. If it was somebody else, though—
and she knew, yes she knew that it was . . .

She was in terrible trouble. She trotted on
with her nose to the ground, hackles prickling,
until suddenly she smelled fresh bread. She
looked up and saw that she was standing next
to a bread truck in front of the Acme supermarket, still open. So she could buy the steaks,
run on home and call him, and maybe it was not
too late after all. She herself had no desire to eat,
but she could cook for him and wait on him. She
pictured herself waiting on him in nothing but
black lace underwear. If she could bring herself
to do it, really do it in real life, then he would
like her. Positively he would, and moreover she
had lingerie of that kind, she had seen it that
morning. Then she remembered that she had cut
it up and fed it to the garbage disposal. Her tail
drooped. How could she have been such a stupid
Bitch?

Yet here she still was outside the supermarket,

as if in some strange way she'd been guided. Here was her only chance. She trotted in and straight back to the meat counter. There were beautiful filet mignons displayed there, an inch thick and only eleven dollars a pound. How much would Rick want? Better get lots, enough to serve him for his breakfast if he stayed over. She selected two packages, almost three pounds between them. *She had no money.*

She had no money. Not a quarter for a phone call, to ask Rick, beg him on her knees to come and pick her up and pay for the steaks and she would pay him back. Not a ten-dollar bill for a cab to take her to Rick's place to beg him on her knees to still love her. Not thirty dollars for this beautiful meat she held in her paws but could not have, though it might save her life. She would steal it, then. Three pounds of steak, when look how much they had, for a lifetime of happiness—could that be wrong? If only she dared. If only she knew how. With her tail between her legs she crept Home, *where by this time it is twilight, the trees of the forest black against a pale sky. She howls her misery to Venus, low in the west, to the bird whose luminous track encircles her; nothing answers.*

Coyote felt stuffed. So what was she doing in this store anyway? Still, meat was meat. No handbag, nothing in her pockets? But no one at the meat counter either, for it was after

butcher's hours. Her long plaid skirt was
roomy, gathered at the waist. She stood bellied
up to the counter, slipped the packages under
the waistband--and discovered she had on no
underpants, so what was to keep them from
falling through to the floor? She plunged her
hands deep into her pockets and held them
up through the cloth. Cold, nestled into her
pubic hair, to any man with a doggy nose an
invitation to dine. She sauntered out, daring
anyone to say a word—*Insult a poor pregnant
lady, would you?* Somewhat to her disappoint-
ment, no one so much as glanced at her. By
the time she got outside she felt like she was
being fucked with an icicle, so she trotted
Home quickly. Bitch doubled over at the
shock of the cold. Smells, beef and her sticky
thighs, mingled, and by the time she got to a
dark place, tree-shadow half a block away and
retrieved her booty, her full belly was churning.
If she'd been caught . . . Her hackles rose.

But then she hadn't been, had she? She
glanced over her shoulder, but no one from
the store was after her. She'd done it. Love
had found a way, and now if she could just
get home and call him before it got too late . .
. How late was it? She hadn't thought to look
in the store, which, though, she believed closed
at ten. There might yet be time. She hurried
on, her love-offering clutched in her paws. Not
until she was standing on her porch did she

remember--not only did she have no money,
she had no keys. So it was all in the lap of the
gods. Always she locked the door. Half the time
when she returned it was unlocked. She tried
the knob. It opened. The smell on her thighs
was here too, so strong she could almost see it,
a miasmic drift from the bedroom.

But then there was nothing she needed in
the bedroom, so it hardly mattered. The phone
was beside her, and might he have called and
left a message? She hit *Play.*

Laurel, I've got to see you.

This is the Smart Shop.

*You haven't forgotten what I promised
you? I haven't.*

I thought for sure you'd be home.

*Listen up, bitch. When you stand a man
up you do it in style, don't you? I mean you
think I didn't hear you in there? So here's
a message from me to you, with a little help
from my friend . . .*

*Deeper babe, deep deep deeper! God I love
your cock in me!*

*Just my own special way of saying: Hey,
cunt. Fuck you with a posthole digger.*

Cat's whiskers twitched. The man was definitely mad, whoever he was, but there was no magic in his message. Faked from first to last: Cat if anyone knew what a girl getting fucked sounded like, and that was not it. They were tanked out of their minds, most likely, calling from a pay phone in a bar.

She sniffed at the steaks—smelled nice and she was getting hungry again, having missed out on most of her dinner, but she couldn't be bothered to cook. Nor was she about to hang out alone in this dump on a Friday night. She dropped the frowsy skirt she'd put on for the restaurant—why did her pussy smell like she'd been fucking a dead cow? Threw off the office blouse and got back into the red one and the black pants. She really did have to pick up some lingerie. Money, now—not that she planned to spend any of her own, but *be prepared* was the Girl Scout's motto, and it turned out, when she looked in her handbag, that she had lots. More than she remembered. Keys . . . yes, and so she was ready for her night's hunting. She slipped out, hardly parting the darkness on her way to her little green car. The seat was damp, but she barely noticed. Where, now? There were four or five places on Market Street. The Mazda started smoothly, growled up through its five gears, and in no time, her long hair blowing back, she was there. She cruised. Pete's Place was what it sounded like, a dump. DiSalvo's, Franco's, all

the wops were in the liquor business. Adam
and Eve's . . . she slowed. Had she been there
before? She had an odd feeling—that she'd
been in it maybe more than once, maybe often,
without ever going to it. Once she was inside,
she would remember. If she dared? The hair at
the back of her neck prickled. Her eyes went
green. She was Cat, the hunter. Half a block
down the street she slid the little car into a
space and trotted back.

And now she did remember. Adam and
Eve's with the mural of the Garden. The serpent,
the apple tree, Eve naked but for her long hair.

She looked around. Some couples and
foursomes at tables, three or four guys at the
bar—a working class place despite its name, a
drag in the making, but then one of the men
turned, looked her up and down, another
beside him turned; one of them whistled, and
her hunting instincts drew her to them. Single
one out, maybe the one with the black curly
hair and the mustache, get him to take her
somewhere. A nice late-night menu, music she
could dance to alone, nibbling something nice
while he watched her sway, watched her tongue
flick in and out . . . the other man moved down
and she sat between them. Twisted to face the
one she wanted; he spoke to her in cat-talk, lazy
and cool, so she went naked for him. When she
looked into his mind she saw herself, or not
herself exactly, a loosely assembled collection of

female erogenous zones, spread-eagled, gagged, bound hand and foot to a bed.

It was a picture she'd seen before, but always it had been fantasy. Nothing interesting had ever happened. She tugged delicately at the ropes, expecting them to dissolve like cobwebs, then harder, as hard as she could, her whole body writhing, but they held tight and she was helpless. She mewed her pleasure into the gag, wet with wanting him, tongue flicking as she met his eyes. There was no need for words. They stood. Afterwards she would get him to let her tie him, or do it by stealth when he fell asleep. She would ride him right to the edge and leave him there, leave him naked, bound . . .

As they walked toward the door, a man who had been sitting at a table with a short, dark woman stood up and stepped into her path. He said, "Well, babe. Imagine seeing you here." It was the man who had come to the house when she was there with Curtis, whose voice she had heard on the tape.

To Cat's man he said, "Just wanted you to know what you're getting into here. You better have a can of Lysol and a good stiff brush to scrub your dick off with."

To the seated woman Cat said, "You're the one that loves his cock in you? That's not much to love, is it?" The woman stood and lunged. Cat raked, raising four red welts on the woman's cheek. She fell back screaming. Cat angled with

all ten front claws out. A hand clamped onto
the back of her neck, so she ran Home. Vixen,
hound-stink hot in her nostrils, ducked and
twisted out of the grip. She glanced around
her. To the milling pack she announced, with
bell-like clarity, "I'm going to be sick." And
walked, steady, not too fast and not too slow, to
the sign that said Ladies. Down a short corridor
from there was a back exit; she walked through
it and found herself in an alley. Before she could
reach the street she saw him, blocking her: the
man with the death-stink of Dog.

"You thought I didn't know this way? How
many times have we been here? Shit, I live
here."

Vixen glanced around. The alley was blind.
Nowhere to run, so she ran Home. Bitch said,
"Rick, it's you? You're not mad?"

"Mad? Me? What for? I'm going to beat the
shit out of you for the plain fun of it."

"Honey, no, I'm so sorry. Listen, I got the
steaks."

"Steaks? You crazy bitch!"

He hit her hard on the side of her face with
his open hand.

"I'm so sorry, don't be mad at me, okay?"

He hit her again, backhanded.

"I'll make you a real nice dinner, honey. I'll
do anything."

"You hurt my hand. You fucking bitch, you
hurt my hand!"

Spider crept out and grasped him tight with all eight legs. He pushed at her. She clung tighter. He pried her loose with his knee in her belly. She reached again and he hit her in the face with his fist. She reeled back against the wall. Rat came up snarling with a brick in each paw. "If you take one step closer, I will bite your fucking face off."

He stopped; turned pale and sober. Sweat shone on his forehead. "Crazy. You crazy cunt, you ought to be locked up." He turned away and walked back out toward the street, stumbled on a half brick which he picked up and threw at her. She ducked. When Bitch returned he was gone.

He was gone. Where? He was just now there. She nosed frantically, caught a whiff of him, a fragment of shoe-tread in a dark, wet patch on the pavement . . . it was blood from her nose. She could track him in her own blood. But there wasn't enough, and in a step or two she had lost him. She collapsed where she stood, face in her hands. Her face . . . hurt, her nose and cheeks one dark bruise. She must have been drunk. Walked into something—a door. What was happening? She wanted only to go Home, but it was dark there now. Not like it used to be. What was happening to her?

Finally she went Home anyway, and *curls up tight under the cold stars. Elsewhere, in a dusty corner of an empty barn, Spider spins. Dust motes*

*dance in shafts of August sunlight, wide through
windows, narrow through cracks between warped
boards. A fly drones by, loops into the web, and
Spider wraps it and sucks it dry. She takes what
comes to her. Over the dark place of Bitch and the
dusty place of Spider, Falcon circles, weaving. Soon
now it will be time.*

Cat got in her car and drove home. She'd
had enough excitement for one night. Her face
hurt. She was ready to ease herself down with a
couple of Valiums and go to sleep.

His spoor must have been everywhere, for
he had spent an hour poking into every corner
and drawer, making her place and her posses-
sions his. But Cat was tired, a little drunk, her
cheekbones throbbing. She walked into her
bedroom like an old blind mouse, stopped and
turned too late. His eyes were murky pools,
his face and his hands the color of bleached
bones, and in his right hand he held a long
skinning knife. In his left a thing of red rubber,
brandished upright. A coil of thin rope looped
over his wrist, and all in black like a burglar.
His cock erect, sharply outlined. He stood
between her and the door.

"You thought I forgot?"

His voice was like silk ripping. He was no
one she knew. Nothing to do with her, so she
went Home.

"So now we're alone at last, here's what

we're going to do. You're going to strip yourself
naked while I watch, nice and slow. Then you're
going to fuck yourself pretty good with this."
He held it up, a terrible red thing. "Then I'm
going to tie you to the bed, and you better have
no plans to just lay there. You better give me
a pretty good ride, and beg me pretty good
the whole time, and if you do it good enough,
maybe I won't carve what you are in your face.
Or maybe I will anyway. Are we agreed on all
that?"

Vixen licked her lips. "Hey, lover. It's been
awhile."

His eyes were black. His lips were red. He
smiled at her.

The black hound had bayed her down. He
was going to rip her belly open and eat her, and
she would still be alive while he ate her. She
Falcon
screamed
woke Bear from her deep sleep. Shuddering
and gasping, Vixen fled. Bear growled, shuffled
one step forward and another step. The knife
came up. "Don't move!" She came on. The blade
slashed across, but Bear for all her size was
quick. With one great paw she struck, and the
knife flew across the room. Bone, white stained
red, ripped through flesh. He reeled back. "No!
You bitch, no!" Bitch was not her name. She
came on after him where he cowered against the
wall, with the claws of one paw and then the

other ripped his chest open and his belly open.
He sagged to the floor screaming. She crouched
over him, jaws wide, bit through bone and
nerves and the great vein in his neck, and he was
still. And still she worried at him, dragged him
into the middle of the floor, shook him like an
old empty doll. She caught him by the jaw and
shook, and only when the head ripped free and
she had tossed it away into a corner of the room
was she satisfied. On her hind legs, her head
brushing the ceiling, she stood over him and
roared.

She dropped to all fours, grunting and
snuffling round and about, at last rumbled off
Home, *where it is black as hell, a starless summer
night. There is the well and trees as big around as the
well, whose branches and leaves she has never seen,
whose tops would reach the sky if there were any
sky. She stands against them and rakes them to mark
where she has been. Among the trees no air moves, no
scent of any living thing. From the well about which
she pads, which descends to the roots of the earth,
drifts a faint dry smell whose name is Terror. A black
mist which is all she has to breathe. Some night when
her own name is Terror, the well will draw her in and
she will fall into the darkness forever.*

Bitch must have fainted. When she came to
herself, she was lying on her bed. At first she
was glad to be there, a pleasant surprise since
she couldn't even remember coming home. But
something was wrong. She had hurt her face,

she remembered that from when Rick was so
fussed with her, but down below, her belly?
She raised the hem of her blouse and gasped to
see a long jagged cut, still bleeding. Went faint,
collapsed with her head in her paws. She was
going to die. Bleed to death. She sat back with
her head singing, feverish. Clutched the pillow
tight against her stomach, holding her blood
and guts in. Was that . . . her blood all over the
floor? It lay in dark sticky pools, like the pools
of tar which are full of ancient bones. She saw
the knife on the floor by the wall then, a long
bone-handled skinning knife whose blade, she
knew without fitting steel to flesh, matched her
wound. Cautiously she peeled back the pillow.
The bleeding had stopped. Gazed about with
the round eyes of a two-week puppy: what else
was here that shouldn't be? Rope in scattered
coils like a long thin snake. A red something,
what was it? *Oh . . .* oh. She squeezed her eyes
shut, buried her head in the pillow, her blood a
mask across her forehead.

   She could not stay here in this room as
the room was. She would have to clean up
and throw out, or look for shelter elsewhere.
Or just go. She lowered her feet off the high
bed, skidded on blood, sat down. Up again,
stumbling, head turned from the Thing. There
coiled Rope . . . the better to bind her. Knife,
dark with her blood. Why not just go Home?
But it was dark there. Dark outside, but at least

there were street lights. The night was late and
dank. Go . . . she had her bag with her keys, but
no car she could drive. If only she could learn
to drive it—she was almost going to have to.
She got in, timid car thief . . .why would anyone
buy a car with no roof? Nothing between her
and the sky. If she could just put the top up
even. Were there instructions somewhere? All
cars came with them, they were kept in the
glove compartment. So she would find them;
she would read them by the light of the flashlight that would also be there, she would raise
the top and turn on the radio and drive away.
The glove compartment was locked.

She began to weep. Sat there in the damp
bucket seat crying, at first quietly and then
with great shuddering sobs. She was going to
die where she sat. The man with the Thing was
going to come back for her, and she was going
to die.

Then a quiet voice spoke into her mind. The
voice of a man, but not of the man she feared.
She was safe with it, listening to it.

Simply go Home. Go Home and sleep.

She did not have to ask which home he
meant. Happily, tail swinging, she went. *The sky,
a great vault which does not frighten her here, is
filled with bright stars. She sighs, turns three times
round in the way of a dog, lies down and sleeps.*

Wolf had never driven this car before, so she

sat still for a moment sniffing it out. Then she
turned on the ignition, the lights, raised the top,
started the engine, put the Mazda in gear and
drove off down the street.

It was late, the streets deserted except by
drunks returning from bars. She drove out
of town, navigating by instinct, and then for
an hour down winding blacktop highways.
Woods closed up, fields opened out; she crossed
hills and streams and at every forking, every
crossroads, she steered by a map readable
only in the dark. At dawn she turned into a
dirt lane. Overgrown ditches lined it on each
side; then sagging barbed wire fences, then,
beyond, shadowy dark fields, spiky with last
year's stubble. In a mile or so she came to a
track branching off to the right, a mailbox at
the junction. There was a number on it, but no
name. She stopped the car and got out. At the
end of the track, a couple of hundred yards
back over a little rise, she could see the upper
story and roof of a white frame farmhouse. Its
windows were shrouded by dark green curtains.

A great cold came over her, frosting her
limbs where she stood, her eyes, ears, nose,
tongue, her ovaries in her belly and her heart
in her breast. She crumpled and *runs howling,
howling down the winter pathways of her Home.
The track of the Shadow Deer reeks of fresh blood.
She runs him for a night and a day and a night
again, and she runs him to ground. He lies dead*

*in a clearing at her feet, drenched in blood from the
round hole in his neck. She dips her muzzle and rips
his heart out and eats it, the smell not of deer only
but something else, strange yet familiar, her own
scent almost—Coyote or wild Dog, and she raises her
bloody muzzle to the moon and howls. Coyote, mated
to the bones of deer, rises from her nest in the rib cage
and yowls her reply. The bones rise and flee rattling
into the dark. Vixen pauses in her chicken-killing, as,
at the long ululating wail of Wolf, the front door of
the house opens and spills onto the ground a rectangle
of white light. Sometime between Then and Now the
moon has waned. Bitch leaps up barking, dashes blind
through brambles which catch and snag at her. Rabbit
runs right at her nose, a step too slow this night, and
Bitch snaps, breaks the neck and the scream, and hot
blood spurts into the back of her throat. Rat cowers
back into the dark as the door to her cellar opens,
squeezes her eyes against a rumor of light. Vibration
works through rock, into her nerve endings, inward
to her bones: something is on the stairs. The sky over
Spider's barn turns black, black rain pours through
the roof and rips her web to tatters. An inside door
to Cat's room creaks open, a way further into the
house, but there is no one there. She leaps to the
windowsill and noses her way through the green
curtains. Outside is a winter landscape, with snow
falling. Somewhere in the distance, Wolf howls and
howls, and the snow turns to bloody rain. Bear paces,
hearing the howling, and wind in the trees, and, from
the well, the dry scraping of scales against stone.*

Falcon circles above, weaving
  Winter and Summer, Autumn and Spring
  Night and Day
  Was and Is and Will Be
  together.

An old black pickup truck drove along the lane and stopped, twenty yards short of the little green car and the figure lying beside it. A man in denim overalls and a faded blue work shirt got out, tall, loose-jointed, balding, half a century or so old, his eyes the blue of his shirt. Before approaching he gazed for a few seconds into the sky, then waved, recognizing Falcon, whom he had seen here often before.

He knelt beside the woman, whose eyes, a lighter blue, were open, staring. "Miss? Missy?"

Nothing. Nobody home. Pulse? Strong and steady. Breathing steady. Temperature normal, color normal, no shock, no visible wounds, but nobody home. Sky eyes. He stood, looking over the rise at the green-curtained house. No one in sight. *Which is a good thing, for I believe, Missy, if a man were to come to you from that place, our friend up there would tear his head off. Woman either. Not a good place for you to be, I somehow think, and that you'll not get better till I get you away. How best? More room in the truck, but I wouldn't want to leave your car. Best go in that, then—where? Get you into it first. You wouldn't want a man you didn't know touching you, so I'll ask you to forgive me . . .*

There, now. Sit back, child, and rest awhile.
Forgive me again for poking in your pocketbook.
Some something with your address on it is all I need.
So . . . well, you've come a good way. I wonder just
why? I wonder if Sister shouldn't know about you?
For you're neighbors in that town, and that may be a
sign that needs heeding. But first get you home . . .

You live alone here, then? But ought you to be
alone when you wake up? It would be strange for
you, home and never knowing how. Get you settled,
though, first. Where's the bedroom? Rest on the
couch here while I find it . . .
What happened here? What terrible thing
happened? No wonder, Missy, no wonder you ran,
only why to where you ran?
Surely, anyway, can't leave you here with the
place like this. Law people wouldn't want anything
touched, if they're to get in on it. As they would
surely like to, and have a certain right, only . . . I do
believe what you need most is quiet and healing. That
means a resting place made right again, if it can he
made so. This rug—best take it away and burn it, I
think, and right there goes most of it . . . who could
have shed that much blood and walked away? Here's
a sponge, is there a good stiff brush somewhere?
And still it's stained dark here; this nice old oak is
going to have to be sanded down. Though maybe you
won't he staying here? As for these ugly things . . .
you oughtn't to see them again, but Sister ought, so
here's a bag, plastic, the right covering for them, to

*hide them in. This bed could use changing . . . but
Missy, you don't sleep in the bed, do you? You sleep
under it. Now why is that?*

*Regardless, you'd better come back to yourself
in your home place. Mind your head under the
frame . . . There. Now those pants are so tight it's a
wonder you can breathe in them, but you wouldn't
want me messing with them, so we'll let it go until
Sister gets here. You wouldn't mind me slipping
your shoes off, though. Rest now while I call. You'll
like Sister.*

"You see how her eyes are? If you can see
under there?"

"Yes. And where did you find her?"

"Down the road a little, where Falcon lives.
For a moment I thought she was dead. Then I
saw she'd gone away."

"Gone in, rather. Gone down, under. Close
her eyes."

"Not you?"

"I can talk to her soul to soul, later. You
have the good touching in your hands . . .
There. Now watch her breathing. Listen."

"She's sleeping. Like a little girl."

"And when she wakes, she'll be back."

"But who is she? Who will she be?"

"No knowing. Wait and see."

"You'll wait?"

"Yes."

"How long will it be?"

"Eight o'clock now? Then eight o'clock tonight, maybe. Half the day around."

"I should bring back food?"

"I brought what we'll need. Blackberry tea, bread, Mama's vegetable soup."

"Which can bring the dead to life. What should I do with these things?"

"Mm. Not take them out to the farm. Nothing would grow near them. Not throw them into still or running water. They would poison it. Lock them up in the trunk of my car. I'll put them in the garbage where they belong, to go to the landfill."

"They'll pollute even that."

"But they cannot be unmade. They were made, and are, and so can only be properly disposed of."

"I'll leave her in your safe hands, then."

"How will you get home?"

"Ride with a kindly stranger. Come tomorrow for dinner?"

"If I can. I'll call you."

At eight o'clock that evening, Bitch woke. The room was dim, a single lamp burning in the far corner. It smelled clean, faintly of disinfectant, and of root vegetables simmering: potatoes, carrots, onions, all in a broth of tomato laced with bay. In a rocking chair in the middle of the floor sat a woman in a green gown. Her hair was a shining dark cap on her head, her

eyes brown, and around her neck she wore a
string of lustrous brown seeds. She was forty or
fifty or sixty years old.

She said, "Welcome to your new life. What is
your name?"

"My name is Bitch. Who are you?"

The woman regarded her calmly. Apparently
she knew many people with such names. She
said, "My name is Constance. I am a healer. I
am here to help you."

Chapter Two

Constance's Place, which she will not even allow Bitch to call an office, is nothing like Dr. Volker's. It's underground, in the finished basement of her house. Between five and six o'clock in the afternoon, a narrow ray of sunlight filters in through the single high window. But a wide shelf of plants, a pocket jungle, grows lush under GroLights. In a miniature ocean across the room, tropical fish drift through seaweed and coral. The walls are white, the carpet blue, the low chairs they sit in the green of early spring leaves. They sip blackberry tea and talk.

"How is it that your name is Bitch?"

"It's actually Laurel."

"That's what you were christened and it's how you sign your checks, but when you woke up, Bitch was what you told me."

"I'm sorry. I don't know. I must have been dreaming."

"Have you dreamed before of having that name, or of being what it signifies?"

"I'm sorry, I never remember dreams. It used to make Dr. Volker mad at me."

"Did you know that Herman Volker is dead? He died night before last at his desk, of a massive stroke. You were the last patient he ever saw."

"Oh. Oh, no. I'm so sorry."

"Were you aware of how often you say that--I'm sorry?"

"I'm . . . Shouldn't I say it?"

"There's no should or shouldn't about it, but it might help us learn about you. Do you feel you do a great many things to be sorry for?"

"Pretty much—at work, with my boyfriend. I'm always messing up."

"Tell me about work."

"It's kind of embarrassing. Would you be real mad at me if I didn't?"

"No, you'll tell me when you trust me enough. What about the boyfriend?"

"I sort of stood him up. We had this date, he was supposed to come over for dinner, and I guess when he came I wasn't there."

"You guess? Where were you then?"

"I forget. That's something you're going to find out about me, so I might as well tell you. I have this terrible memory."

"Tell me more about that."

"There's not much to tell. I break dates, like

I told you. I lose things, or sometimes I buy
things and don't remember about it. They just
turn up, somehow."
    "What sort of things?"
    "Clothes and stuff. You know. That I
wouldn't ordinarily buy."
    "But you apparently do . . . extraordinarily?
What sort of clothes?"
    "Like . . . you know, underwear, black, and
things. Clothes. Not real modest. You don't
think I'm crazy?"
    "I'm sure you're perfectly sane. We just
need to learn why these disquieting things keep
happening. What else?"
    "I guess that's about it. Except I can't seem
to wear watches, they stop when I put them on,
which is why I was late today."
    "When you broke the date with your
boyfriend, you said you weren't home when he
came to your house and you can't remember
where you'd gone. What's the first thing you
remember after that?"
    "You're going to think I'm crazy. Do I really
have to tell?"
    "It would be very helpful."
    "You're going to think I was drunk, or high
on something and walked in my sleep. But I
wasn't, I hardly drink at all. I was in an alley
behind this bar."
    "No memory of how you got there."
    "No, I'm sorry."

"What happened then?"

"Rick was there, my boyfriend. I'd bought the steaks for dinner, I wanted him to come home with me."

"What then?"

"He wouldn't, he was mad. Of course he was mad, it was late."

"Is that when he hit you?"

"He never did."

"Then how'd you get those bruises on your face?"

"I fell down. I'm such a klutz, I must have."

"You said it was late, so you must have lost several hours that evening. Does that happen often?"

"I guess maybe it does. I know what you're thinking. Crazy people and drunks have blackouts, so which is she? I'm not a drunk so I must be crazy."

"You're not crazy. Does anyone tell you you are?"

"Just, you know. Rick. When he's mad at me, but he doesn't mean anything by it."

"He sounds a little toxic to me."

"Oh no, listen. He's really a sweet guy, I just drive him up the wall. I drive everybody up the wall."

"Does he call you by your name?"

"My name, Laurel? Generally he calls me Babe."

"Your other name I meant. Bitch."

"No, well. I mean if he's mad, but if you knew me you'd know why. I can be a real pain, can you tell?"

"No, I can't. Who else calls you Bitch?"

"That's about it. Just, I'm such a klutz. If I bump into somebody."

"You have only one boyfriend?

"That seems to have been a hard question. Are you not sure?"

"I guess only one. I better, Rick would kill him. He'd kill both of us."

"But you might have more? Why do you think so?"

"Well, because. You know how I keep forgetting. I was in this restaurant and whoever I went with wasn't there anymore, he must have got mad about something and left, but he'd been there."

"When was this?"

"It was last Friday evening."

"So that was where you were when you were supposed to be home cooking dinner for Rick?"

"I guess I must have been."

"But I thought the first thing you remembered was being in the alley."

"Yes, I'm sorry. I forgot about the restaurant. My life is very confusing."

"Then what happened after you left the restaurant?"

"I bought . . . I got the steaks and took them home. Then I was in the alley."

"And from there?"

"Rick was gone. I couldn't find him anywhere, so I went home."

"You remember going, or you just found yourself there?"

"Just found myself."

"In what room?"

"My bedroom."

"And what did you see?"

"What do you mean? You've been in my bedroom."

"I haven't seen it the way it was when you found yourself in it. What did you see?"

"I don't think I want to talk about it."

"How were you feeling, then?"

"I don't know. Strange. I feel strange all the time lately."

"Had you been hurt?"

"I told you, my face. Where I fell down?"

"But that wasn't all. What else?"

"I had a cut on my stomach. It wasn't deep or anything though."

"How do you suppose you got it?"

"I told you what a klutz I am. I don't really know."

"So what did you do then?"

"I didn't want to stay in the house for some reason. I went and got in the car."

"Where were you thinking of going?"

"I didn't know. I just wanted to get away."

"What happened then?"

"There was something wrong with it. I couldn't get it started. So I went back in the house."

"Then how did you and the car end up sixty miles out in the country where my brother found you?"

"I shouldn't have said I went in the house. I found myself there."

"You couldn't get the car started, but you and it ended up way out of town. How did it happen?"

"I must have forgotten. That must have been it. I told you I do that."

"But you have a clear memory of not being able to start it. Is it your car?"

"What? Of course it is. I've got the key right here in my bag."

"Where did you buy it?"

"At the . . . you know, the place. The car place."

"What kind of car is it?"

"It's little, green, the top comes down. How am I supposed to remember all these things? Why are you asking me all these questions?"

"In order to discover the truth. Did you drive over here today?"

"I walked. You know I walked, it's a nice day . . ."

"It's raining hard. Do you know how to

drive that car?"

"I . . . listen, I thought you were supposed to be helping me. I don't have to stand for this."

"You don't. You may not move from that chair, but you may go. "

In the Home Place it is morning again, the sun shining brightly. Nothing has changed after all, it was merely a bad dream. Bitch trots along happily with her tail high and waving. She will stay here forever. Why go, ever, when the other place has grown so troublesome? To the angle of woodpile and wall she trots, the still center of the circle of Home, where Rabbit lives, from which Rabbit at any moment will leap, her playmate Rabbit . . .

But no one's home. She circles, sniffing and whining. She smells Rabbit. She smells . . . blood. In the scent lies the memory: she killed and ate him. He's gone. Her Place is empty.

Her sides cave in on her ribs. She runs with her hunger driving her, mindless of thorn, bramble, under her paws flowers which, as she tramples them down, wilt, seed, rot into the earth. There is nothing here to eat. If she stays she will starve to death. And then she finds something, a small yellow box, cardboard, smelling of bread and meat. The lettering reads Big Mac. She devours box and all in one gulp. And now she is hungrier than before. Frantically she twists on herself, yelping, must eat, her own bony tail if she could catch it, but it flies from her until at last she tumbles to the ground. Where her scuffling

paws touched, the ground is no longer green with
grass, yellow with daffodils. The heat of her passion
has scorched it black. It resembles the site of a forest
fire.

From behind the cover of the mug she
cradles in her paws, Coyote's eyes flicker
around the room. Jungle, ocean, stranger in
green. From the mug rises the brambly scent
of blackberries. She dips her head and drinks,
heedful still of the woman's calm regard. The
woman's voice is like water over stones, liquid,
musical, with an undercurrent of wildness:

"Who are you?"
"Laurel. We've been sitting here talking and
you don't know?"
"How long have we been talking?"
"Not sure. I don't wear a watch. Don't you
know yourself?"
"What have we been talking about?"
"What is this, some kind of inquisition? You
know perfectly well."
"But you don't, do you? Because you just
this minute got here. Where were you before
you came?"
"Why should I tell you?"
"Because I'm very interested. And I'm the
only person who's ever wanted to know who
you really are. Isn't that true?"
"What if it is?"

"Then you need a friend. And think: if you get tired of talking with me, you can easily go home. Can't you?"

"If I did that, you wouldn't want to be my friend."

"That's not true. You can come and go as you please, and I'll still be right here. Try it and see. But when you return, I hope you will tell me your name."

"You're the one I was talking to earlier? The one who has been called Bitch?

"Did you know that your face is bone white? You look frightened. What happened while you were away?"

"I was so hungry. There was nothing good to eat, I was scared I was going to starve."
"Are you hungry now?"

"No, I'm fine. How could that be?"
"It means your hunger was not of the body. It was some other kind of hunger. What do you ordinarily eat when you're in the other place?"
"I never seemed to need to. It was always nice and peaceful, and I was happy. Nothing ever changed. Now everything's changed, and I hate it. Can you make it be the way it was?"
"I don't know. Tell me what it was like."

"It was so beautiful. Flowers, all sunny, woods. It was spring. And the field, and beyond that the house, but I never went there."

"Tell me about the house. Did you recognize it?"

"I didn't then."

"But now?"

"It was the house I was brought up in. Why didn't I remember?"

"I don't know yet. Why did you never go near it?"

"Because it was empty. Nobody there at all."

"How did you know, from across the field?"

"I could just tell."

"By seeing? Hearing?"

"I'm not sure. I just know things."

"Were you afraid to go to the house?"

"I didn't want to. I'm sorry, that's all I can tell you."

"Think about the place with the flowers and trees, the way it was before it changed. Now think about this place, where you drive around in a car and work in a school. Answer me quickly, which one is home?"

"The other. The flowers.

"I shouldn't have said that. You think I'm crazy now."

"No, I think you're learning to face the truth. Are you willing to dig for more truth with me?"

"Do I have to?"

"Do you want to be rid of confusion? Do you want your life to grow straight and bloom?"

"Dr. Volker never talked like that."

"I'm afraid he wouldn't have, poor man. But my name is Constance. What is your name here, where you work in the school?"

"Laurel."

"And what is it in the place with the flowers?"

"Bitch. It's Bitch."

"And so by telling me that, you've told me you'll dig. In the place with the flowers then, where you were never hungry, always happy, what would you do?"

"What do you mean? Just what anyone does. Run around, chase . . ."

"Chase who? What?"

"Rabbit. I'd chase Rabbit. Didn't I tell you I was Bitch?"

"Chase Rabbit by running on four legs?"

"Yes, how else would I run?"

"So Bitch is what you truly are down there. Female dog."

"Yes. I really am crazy."

"Do you ever actually see your body? In

a pool of water, or look down and see furry paws?"

"No, I never have."

"Then how do you know what you are?"

"I just know. From how I run, fast and low to the ground. And how I can hear and smell things. I think sometimes . . . I can do that here too. I mean hear and smell what real . . . what other people can't. I'm pretty weird."

"You're beautiful—gifted. Is it marvelous, running after Rabbit like the wind?"

"It was. Only when it changed, when it got dark, I was hungry and I did a terrible thing. I caught him and ate him. I'm so sorry."

"Was that a bad thing for a hungry dog to do?"

"I don't know. I'm tired. I'm all confused."

"In the place where you're Bitch, where the empty house is, is there any other person or animal at all?"

"Not since . . . not now."

"Are you lonely there?"

"I never was before. Now I'm so lonely, I want to curl up and die."

"Does being lonely feel anything like being hungry?"

"I guess maybe it does."

"So then, would you like to have a

companion?"

"How? Who? What do you mean?"

"I was thinking, for example, of whoever it was who drove your car, which you never bought and don't know how to drive, out into the country."

"No. I'm sorry, you're very kind, but I don't like them."

"Them?"

"The Others. They play mean jokes on me. They get me in terrible trouble."

"How many of them are there, do you think?"

"I don't know. Going by smell? Three or four at least."

"What do they smell like?"

"Wet fur and rot, apple, cheese, maybe dog."

"Take a minute and use your nose. Do you smell any of them now?"

"Dog. Very faint, but it's there. How could that be?"

"Because why do you think you have all those memory lapses? Who bought the little green car? When you were gone a little while ago, when you were down below starving, one of them was right here. And that's true always. Whenever you're down below, home, someone else is running this beautiful, human, female body."

"That can't be.

"Can it?"
"Truly it is."

"I'm scared. What's happening to me?"
"Would you like me to tell you about the one who was here?"

"All right. How can it get any worse? Tell me."
"She wouldn't give me her name. She tried to put up a bold front, blustered a little, but she was scared too. And she was lonely. What she needs most in the world is a friend."
"No name? Who is she then? What is she?"
"I don't know yet, but from her scent she must be closely related to you. Maybe she's your sister. Would you like me to try to find out?"
"How?"
"Go home again. Either she will come back or one of the others. Either way, we'll learn something."
"But I can't. If I do that... I won't be me."
"You'll be you in your home place, and the body sitting here in this room will be someone else. That's true, but then you've known it in a hidden way for years, haven't you? That you are not the sole owner and proprietor of this body."

"Other people. Normal people. They're not like that?"

"No, but you're not abnormal. You're uncommon."

"This thing that's wrong with me. Does it have a name?"

"It's called Multiple Personality Disorder, but to call it that is misleading and negative. It's an adaptation to something bad that happened to you."

"Something bad? What? This stupid thing itself is the only bad thing that's happened in my whole life."

"How about in your childhood?"

"Dr. Volker kept harping on that too. It was perfectly normal."

"Tell me your earliest memory?"

"I'm not sure. Just playing in the field behind our house?"

"How old were you?"

"Pretty old, actually. Maybe . . . ten or twelve?"

"So you see, a good deal is missing. Some of the others may remember."

"The Others? How?"

"The earliest memory you have is when the body was ten or twelve, approaching puberty. That's when you were born, then. One or probably more of the others was running things before then."

"I don't know. I only know I'm so tired. I have to sleep."

"Yes, it's surely time for that. Go home while I talk with someone else."

"Except Home is terrible now. I don't have any Home. What am I supposed to do?"

"There's a place there where you sleep?"

"The corner of the fence and the woodpile."

"Go straight there. Turn around three times. Tuck your nose under your tail and you'll sleep without dreaming.

"Excuse me for asking, but I don't know you well yet and I have to. It is you? We talked earlier?"

"Of course it's me. Who else would it be?"

"I don't know yet. But you see, anyway, I'm still here, as I promised. Will you tell me your name now?"

"Laurel. Is there something wrong with your memory?"

"Laurel's your name when you're here in the body. But that's not where you really live, is it? What's your name when you're home?"

"I have no name."

"Did you know that the other one who was here until a minute ago scented you? And she was here a long time. Tell me what you smell?"

"Yes, she was here. Dog. It's all over the den where she lives."

"And she smelled Dog too. Is that who you are?"

"I'm not so domestic. Coyote."

"Welcome to my home, Coyote. My name is Constance. Please have more tea, and tell me about your life."

"Why should I?"

"Because our names each begin with C, which is for seeing, because we love the woods and fields, we live on the edge, we thrive anywhere. Because we're blood sisters."

"My life where?"

"Wherever you live, and start where you like."

"I have hardly any life here at all."

"Yes, Bitch has more of that."

"Bitch?"

"Her name when she's home, but she carries some of it around with her everywhere. As you do—with Laurel's nose you smell as Coyote can. As Coyote can, you hear with her ears. What else?"

"What else? Read the horny thoughts of boys. Tickle a bastard's nose with rotting meat. Catch the sun in my jaws in the morning and

bowl it across the sky from east to west. I am
Coyote."

"You are lyrical, and a great joker. I'm afraid
you've made Bitch's life difficult."

"She has no sense of humor, no taste in work
or men, and no more right to this body than I
have. Maybe I'll just move into it."

"Fine. But first, go and talk to Bitch about
it."

"Why would I want to?"

"Why not? She's your sister, and if you
make friends with her, you'll have two friends."

"I wouldn't know how. I live alone, I've
never had sight nor scent of her."

"You've never known her name before. Go
down and call her by name."

"She'd be back up here if I did that. She'd be
nowhere to be found."

"I think not. She's sleeping deeply. If you go
down, one of the others will come."

*In the woods of the Home Place Coyote yaps
Bitch and yowls Bitch, but there's no sight or sound
or sniff of her. She's not here and she never was here
and she never will be, whoever she is or if she is, and
Coyote will hunt Deer alone, eat Deer alone, sleep
alone in the bones of Deer in the autumn twilight
forever.*

Good doggy. Come home with me, good

doggy.

The voice is a high-pitched cackle, right at her tail. Coyote leaps and spins in the air, jaws snapping. Her heart will batter its way through the walls of her chest and spill her life on the ground. An old woman stands there, leaning on a stick.

Nice bone for you in my house, good doggy.

Coyote snarls.

The woman has long white hair, loose down her back. Chicken bones are tangled in it; she reaches around and draws one out, proffers it. It's a fresh bone, Coyote can smell meat on it. More where that came from, good doggy. *Her dress is black, stained green with the guts of frogs. From her chin sprouts a thin white beard.*

Dog is not my name or breed. Name my name.

Your name is Coyote, my love, but we're all one under the skin.

And what is your name?

Don't you know it? Am I so much changed? Look at my eyes.

Constance.

Aye, my love. I am the constant one, above and below.

Who are you really?

That's one question too many. Come home with me?

I can run faster than you.

That you can, my love. Run then, but we will
meet again.

You'll never find me.

*The woman laughs. Her laughter strums
Coyote's bones, makes of her body a music to which
she dances back and away and now in sudden silence
runs. When she turns, the woman is dim in patchy
mist. Now Coyote hears her own heart beating.
But her heart is not safe within her chest. It is
out, above, circling, it is the wing-beats of Falcon,
whose wide arc weaves all things together. Above
the woman now, Falcon hovers, and Coyote knows
without hearing that they have spoken to each other.
If she had gone with the woman, who had nice bones
in her house, bones which would have eased her
hunger, why then she could have heard. Some secret
was spoken which, if only she could have heard it,
would have opened a clear trail through the tangle of
woods. She takes one step back, one front paw poised
in the air. But woman and bird are now lost in the
dark. The moon has risen, higher than she's ever seen
it. She sits on her haunches and howls.*

*At once, from far across the hills, from right
beside her, from within her hungry heart and gut the
howl is answered. It is not Bitch. Something wilder,
that lives in the big deep woods. She has heard it
before. Into the underbrush, brambles snatching her,
blindly she runs. She bursts into the clearing where
the bones of Deer lie, cold and dry and white. No
longer do they even smell of Deer. She creeps up
anyway on her belly, to hide herself in her rib cage.*

But something is there before her. It lies stiffly on
the curved bones, blank blue eyes staring at the sky.
It is naked, arms and legs cruelly chewed, bruised
and bloody. Blood seeps from the fork between its
legs. It is a doll. Its name is Barbie. Coyote howls and
howls.

"Who the hell are you?"
"My name is Constance. What's yours?"
"None of your business.

"You're pretty, though."
"Thank you. So are you. Could you tell me
where you bought your skirt?"
"This thing? Why would you want to
know?"
"You don't like it? Then why did you buy it
and why are you wearing it?

"Maybe I can tell you, then. You didn't buy
it and you didn't put it on, any more than you
walked into my house. You just found yourself
here, wearing it. Does that happen often?"
"Who are you, anyway? I mean your name,
but who are you?"
"I'm a friend of two of your . . . housemates?
The ones you share your house with but never
see?"
"Them. Then I'm not interested in being
here."

"You don't like them? What do they do that's bad?"

"Everything. Steal my nice clothes, cut them to pieces, dress like it's 1940 or something. Screw up my love life. It's a wonder I even have one."

"You do, though? Tell me about it."

"Only if you go first."

"There's little to tell. I live alone."

"That's your tough luck. You get nothing for nothing."

"Well then, suppose I let you look around inside my mind."

"Let me? Try and stop me."

"Go on, then."

"There's nothing. A stone wall. How do you do that?"

"Practice. Now try."

"So? All I saw was a house. Old farmhouse way out in the boonies. And this bird flying around."

"I didn't know about the bird, but I'm not surprised. He's often there. Had you seen him before?"

"Why would I?"

"Not sure yet. How about the house itself?"

"I'm not into houses like that. I'm a city girl."

"Were you always? When did you move here?"

"Who knows? And why am I sitting here

answering these boring questions?"

"Because you sense that they're important.
Where did you grow up?

"It was in that very house, wasn't it?"

"Maybe it was. How did you know?"

"Bitch told me."

"Bitch?"

"One of your housemates. She and Coyote
were here. Can you smell them?"

"Jeez, yes. Dog."

"It's all right. When you're up here in the
body, they're down below. That's how it works.
You never met any of them when you were
down there?"

"Never did, never want to. You're telling me
I'm pretty nuts."

"You're uncommon. So am I. Would you tell
me your name now?"

"I'm Cat."

"I thought you might be—the way you
move, and your eyes are greener than theirs. Is
the little green car by any chance yours?"

"It certainly is. Did any of them mess with
it?"

"Bitch can't drive it. I don't know about
Coyote, but she told me she's not out all that
much. But somebody drove it out to that house,
the one you grew up in, at night without a map.

Was that you?"

"Why would I? It's the back of beyond. Nothing there."

"Could you have found it if you'd wanted to?"

"Maybe. I see in the dark."

"I know you do. So when you're down below, maybe you could find the others."

"I stay inside all the time. There's no way out. Anyway, I'm Cat. I'm scared of dogs."

"Bitch and Coyote are your sisters, though."

"Screw them. That doesn't mean they're my friends."

"You said you stay inside. In the house you grew up in?"

"Maybe. I guess it is."

"Anyone else there?"

"No, thank God."

"Why the thanks?"

"I don't know."

"Did anything bad ever happen in that house?"

"Not that I'm aware of. Just the normal kid stuff."

"Like what?"

"You know. Getting spanked."

"Who did the spanking?"

"Unca. My stepdad. Ma-Ma always had her head in her Bible, so Unca . . ."

"Tell me."

"No, nothing."

"He did something that scared you? You're sure to feel better if you tell me about it."

"Nothing!"

She leaps lightly onto the table. The hieroglyphs are red, shimmering with a cold fire.

"I pushed her too hard, too fast. Who are you, then? Your eyes are almost red."

"Get away from me, lady."

"I won't move from this chair. I won't hurt you. Could you tell me your name?"

"No. I'm going, don't touch me."

"I won't . . ."

"I'll bite your face off!"

"Are you surprised to be here?"

"I'm not surprised by anything. Who are you and what do you want?"

"My name is Constance. If you don't mind, I'd like to talk to you."

"I talk better on a full stomach. Have you got anything to eat?"

"Of course. What do you like?"

"Anything. Meat, chicken, some cider to drink?"

"I don't eat meat. There's cider, though. Nice homemade bread and some comforting soup?"

"Let's try it.

"Yes, it's good. What did you want to know?"

"Your name."

"Laurel."

"That's when you're walking around on two feet up here. What about when you're on four paws down below?"

"You can see inside?"

"Not much. I knew because I've talked to some of the others."

"Others?"

"You're not in this body all the time? You come and go?"

"You know that, so why ask?"

"Then ask yourself who's running the body when you're not. I've met four others—Bitch, Coyote, Cat, and one more who was too scared to tell me her name. But you're not too scared, are you?"

"I'm Vixen."

"I'm not surprised. You're the most beautiful of all of them, and that's saying something."

"Flattery and more soup will get you anywhere."

"Gladly, there's a kettle of it. You're often hungry?"

"Always. That's good, thank you."

"You're very welcome. Yet the body is thin--some would say too thin. Does that mean you're not in it enough to fatten it up?"

"I guess so. Is there more bread?"

"I'll get it.

"Tell me then, when and where was your last good meal?"

"Up here? Some restaurant, how should I know when? A man there had a beautiful steak, and who do you think got it?"

"How did you do that?"

"He was a stupid man—wanted to marry me. I played him along a little."

"I wonder which of them he really wanted to marry? Cat, I bet. No wonder she was mad."

"Her problem."

"In a manner of speaking, but aside from sharing a body up here, down below you're all sisters. What's it like where you live down there?"

"There's the field, the barnyard, the house, behind it the apple tree."

"Anyone in the house?"

"I hope never to find out."

"Why not?"

"Because I steal their apples, kill their chickens. What do you think they'd do?"

"I'm not sure. Please tell me."

"Bang. Dead."

"Is there anyone else around?"

"Maybe hounds. I thought I heard them."

"Tracking you to hurt you?"

"The word is kill. What else do hounds do?"

"So you'd be afraid of Bitch if you saw her?"

"Bitch means dog. What do you think?"

"She's your sister, though. She's very gentle."

"You've never had dogs after you. They run you until you drop in your tracks and then they rip your guts out."

"They've done that to you?"

"I'm here."

"In your dreams, then?"

"I'm not sure."

"The food you eat down below--apples, chickens, does it fill you up?"

"No. I'm always starving. How did you know?"

"Because I know of many kinds of hunger. What do you suppose you're hungry for?"

"More bread. More soup."

"My mother would be delighted. You must meet her sometime. Did you by any chance drive out into the country the other night? In a little green car?"

"No. I don't own a green car."

"It's Cat's. I have to find out who drove it."

"Why?"

"Because there's one of you who desires to

search out the past. But perhaps you would like
to also?"

"No, I'm too tired. I'm finally full. I think I'll
go."

"Just one last thing, then. The man in the
restaurant—was he the one who came to your
house to hurt you?"

"No. It was another man. How did you
know about that?"

"I thought it must have been you or Cat—
you two seem the most sexual. What did you do
when you saw him?"

"Went down. What else?"

"And then? What do you think happened?"

"How should I know?"

"How do you feel, physically?"

"A little bruised here—the face. And . . . it
stings down here. From the knife? I've never
actually thought about what happens to the
body when I'm not in it. But now it seems
it should have been much worse. What did
happen?"

"When my brother looked into the bedroom,
he saw the things the man brought with him,
scattered, and a great deal of his blood on the
floor. There was a fight, whoever came into the
body unarmed against a man with a knife. I
think she came close to killing him."

"Who was she?"

"Another of your sisters I haven't met yet. Very strong and brave and fierce."

"What would have happened if the body had been killed? Would I have died too?"

"I don't know, but I don't think you'd have gone on living down there as you do now. But then, do you want to go on like that forever? Always the same thing, always hungry?"

"What if I don't? What choice have I got?"

"Some things have to happen which will take time. I need to meet all your sisters and earn their trust. I think you all need to meet and make friends down below. Then each of you be willing to come up here and talk with me when I ask, and after that, the talking itself. Out of that will emerge choices."

"Time? It will take half a lifetime."

"Not quite that, but even if it did, think: you'd have the other half to really live."

"You've got nothing better to do with your own life?"

"I've other things, but none better. Healing is my calling."

"I'm glad the body wasn't killed. If you see my fierce sister, thank her for me."

"I will, gladly.

"And who are you? Would you tell me your name?"

"Her name is Spider. She doesn't speak. As you see, she wants only to hold tight and be held. Down below she weaves and catches and eats. I wanted you to meet her. Hold her a little, then I'll send her home."

"She seemed very young. How old is she?"

"You think I know everything? She is as she seems."

"Your voice is deeper than the others'. Your eyes are old and wise. Who are you?"

"My name is Falcon."

"Have we seen you? Circling often over the place down the road, the place we don't name?"

"You had better learn to name it: Death is its name. You have seen me flying guard there."

"Are you one of the sisters?"

"I am no part of Laurel, but never far from her."

"You're not animus then? Are you angel?"

"I am more than you can imagine. Nothing you have a name for. You may call me Friend."

"Then, Friend, how can you help us in this work?"

"Fly circles. Weave together. Name names."

"Can you tell me the number of the sisters?"

"They are nine."

"And which is the one I must speak with

next?"

"Her name is Wolf. When I leave, the body
will be empty. Prepare yourself, then call her
by name. Set her to gathering the others. To
do that, she will need the help of the Wild
Woman of the deep woods. The Wild Woman
has chicken bones stuck in her long white hair.
She has white hairs straggling from her chin, she
wears black stained green with frog guts. Her
name is Constance."

"Why have I not known of her until now?"
"Because you allowed the place down the
road to remain unnamed."
"I have work of my own to do, then."
"And that is the work you have now
undertaken."

Now, with the woman at rest in her chair,
eyes empty as the wide blue sky, Constance
moves quietly about the room. She sets the
kettle to boiling, making ready for tea; tests
with her hand the earth in the pots, adds water
here, there; snips a yellowed leaf; visits the
fish; all the while hums a tune without words,
a song of comfort from her childhood, to settle
her breathing and heart. For a last moment
she stands musing, seeing herself as ancient,
lusty, carnivorous; cackling her fierce laughter.
She touches the seeds at her throat, strokes
her hands down her sides and flanks, settling

the green gown on her body. Now she is ready:
"Wolf, please come."

"Yes, I'm here."
"Your eyes are deep and wild, flecked with
golden light. I think I'd have known you. My
name is Constance."
"I met someone of that name down below, just
now. An old woman. The eyes are the same."
"I am told we're related. Do you know
Falcon?"
"I've seen a hunting bird, always circling, who
might have that name."
"It was the old woman who asked you to
come when I called?"
"I was weary of hunting in the cold, in the
deep snow. She hid herself behind a cedar and
whacked me on the rump with her stick as I
floundered past. First I thought I would rip her
throat, but when I leaped with my paws on her
shoulders, I kissed her face with my tongue.
At that moment I learned what it meant to feel
happy. But she said that the voice I would hear
calling me would be hers."

"Then it was, only I am a great deal younger
and nothing like so wise. Would you talk with me
anyway?"
"She said I would not always have to hunt the
Shadow Deer in the deep cold. What do you want
to know?"

"Was it you who defeated the man with the knife?"

"I can feel where it cut—I felt it earlier, a sharper sting, but I was not there at the time. No."

"Some other fierce sister, then. Could you have?"

"Look into my eyes and tell me."

"Foolish question. But then I'm not my older self. Let's count, then. Bitch, Coyote, Cat, Vixen. One frightened one whose name I don't know, but call her Rat. Then Spider and you out of nine altogether, so there are two more—one fierce and strong, the other, so far, a mystery. You knew nothing of any of them until now?"

"I've never been in this body much. When I have, it's been at times of trouble—almost always with men. I stare into their eyes, and their faces go shiny with sweat, they stink of fear, fall silent, walk away."

"I don't believe the man with the knife would have done that."

"No. Maybe that's why the other came."

"And did what was needed, and then, when you came into the body after that, where were you?"

"In the car. Whoever had been there before me had been crying. My cheeks were wet with tears."

"That was probably Bitch. Let's say that she came into the body in the bedroom, saw

something of what had happened, and she was
frightened and wanted to get away. So she went
to the car, but she didn't know how to drive
it. It wasn't her car, it was Cat's. So she went
under and you came, but why? There was no
man there anymore. There was no danger."

"I don't know. If you're related to the old
woman in the woods down below, you tell me."

"Not closely enough related yet—I can only
guess. I think that what almost happened in
that bedroom corresponded, very deeply, to
bad things that happened to Laurel as a child.
It set up strong resonances, wove now and then
together. And so it was a crisis of a new kind,
and it called you up. What did you think when
you found yourself in the car?"

"It wasn't thinking. I just knew there was
somewhere I had to go. Not where or why. I
drove where the hackles on my neck took me."

"And when you got there, you got out of the
car—because that was where my brother found
the body. What did you see?"

"I saw a house."

"Did you recognize it?"

"It was the house where I lived when I was
born. Only I was quite old when I was born.
Maybe thirteen or fourteen."

"How did you feel when you saw it?"

"I was frightened."

"Did you know what of, or do you now?"

"No. I was terrified. I went under right away."

"Have you felt that way before when you've been in the body?"

"Never. I thought I was afraid of nothing on earth."

"But this, what was fearful about it, came from under the earth. Have you seen that house down below?"

"No. There's only woods and hills and snow, and the Shadow Deer."

"Sight or scent of any of the others?"

"Once . . . How do I tell long ago from not long ago when it's all been the same?"

"If there's a once, there's a not-the-same. Before you drove to the house or after?"

"After. Yes, there was a *not-the-same*. I ran the Shadow Deer down, and he smelled of Dog. But that's all. Where do they live?"

"Cat lives in the house, Bitch and Vixen next to it. Spider and Rat I don't know. Bitch is no deer hunter, so probably you smelled Coyote. We have clues to four of them, then."

"You want me to find them? Go to the house?"

"Yes. You're afraid?"

"Too afraid."

"But brave as well, and do you want to hunt the Shadow Deer forever?"

"How would I even find the house? It must be in some other country. I know every sight and smell in my own, and there's nothing there."

"Falcon can weave those countries together. Perhaps he has already. The Wild Woman will guide you."

"And if I do find them? And remember, there are two we don't even know by name."

"We will have to name and know all in the end, but for now find all you can; try to teach them trust. At first they may be afraid of you, and with Rat and Spider it will be especially hard. But if some of them agree to come up here and talk with me when I ask, I can build stories and fit them together. Each piece will link with two more."

"What will happen when the stories are all told, all grown together?"

"That's better. Not pieces of a puzzle, but living branches grafted into a living tree. Each blowing in its own wind, cradling its own nest, all growing together. I don't know what will happen. Only that we will have to be braver and wiser than we are now."

"But if I go, who will come into the body?"

"Maybe no one. Maybe the Wild Woman has witched them, and they're all sleeping, waiting

for you. No matter, for the body will be safe
here with me."

"I'm afraid."
"I know you are."

"I'm going now."

*The Wild Woman is not there. Wolf prowls in
circles through the mist, in this place like her own
but not her own, a hillside bare of trees, snow soft
and old under her pads. No stars, no moon, only a
pale gray light seeping out of the sky like fine rain.
Wolf's coat turns silver, palely glowing. The circles
dwindle, she twists on herself, chasing her own tail.
Her paws dig into the snow and through the snow
until she is scrabbling in wet black earth. She lowers
her nose to it, sniffs and snuffles, tail wagging. The
rich loamy smell rises to her brain, and she drops
into sleep.*

Bad dog.

*She wakes to the sight of the Wild Woman
leering down at her. Under her belly something
prickles. She leaps up and sees under and around
her, where she cleared the snow, pale green shoots
growing.*

You need to be collared and led?

*In a hand like a claw, the Wild Woman holds out
a collar of bright gold.*

Let me put it around your neck, my love.
Since you can't stay awake for three minutes, I'll
take you where you need to go.

*Wolf backs off, bristling and snarling. The collar
turns into a black hissing snake, coiling around
the Woman's arm. She cackles.* Wise, my love. So
there's something of Wolf in you yet?

How am I to find them?

What can wolves do?

See far, hear sharp, sniff deep. But there is
nothing here to see, or hear, or smell.

What else?

Run forever.

Then—she raises her stick—run!

Wolf runs. She runs downhill through the
mist, which thickens, blinds her, condenses
around her into rain, and she is swimming in
the rain, and the rain is a fast cold river. The
current drags hard, sooty old cakes of rotting
ice nudge at her. A dead chicken floats past,
claws to the weeping sky. Branches and whole
trees. The roof of a house. A little man sitting
on it grins at her, holding out to her a basket
of squealing puppies. That means Dog, but in
the next instant roof and man and pups are lost
in the mist. Then she is across, standing on dry
earth. The sun shines down on a bright cool
morning. She shakes, and where the water flies,
flowers spring up. She has run out of Winter
into Spring, and so trots on, head and tail up,

though her hunger gnaws her. Here she smells
tree and flower, grass, the burgeoning earth,
but of Coyote, of Vixen or Bitch, nothing. She
slows then, wandering, the scents of the season
absorbing her. Here field mouse scurried. There,
vole. Squirrel. Rabbit, and there, leaping out of
an angle between woodpile and fence, is Rabbit,
bounding ahead of her. Saliva flowing, blood a
sweet memory in her throat, she runs. She can
run Rabbit forever. And she may have to. Rabbit
circles and Wolf circles. Rabbit leaps into the
circle of the Wild Woman's arms.

*Oh mighty hunter! Will you now hunt the
mouse, the shrew, the bumblebee? Beware the sting
on your tender nose!*

*Wolf ducks her shoulders, cringing. I was
hungry.*

*Yet before you eat the creatures of these woods,
I will clatter my stick on your dry ribs. They will
dance in the moonlight to that music.*

What then?

*If you can catch Coyote you can eat her. But she
is the fastest dog on earth. You will have to lie in
wait.*

Coyote is my sister.

*And yet you will eat her in the end. To the last
bone you will eat her, and lick the last drop of her
blood.*

How will I find her?
By following your nose.

But there's no scent of her anywhere.
Sniff deeper.

I can't smell her. But I smell stagnant water.
Slimy stone.
And?
Fear. My own fear.
So then? Must I take my stick to you?
If I go there, I will die.
Then die, my love, and I'll have a blind wolf cub
to nurse. I'll nurse her on the broth and blood of
chickens. Too long since I've had babies.

She runs because she is too frightened to
walk, scorching the earth under her paws. The
flowers she crushes wilt and run to seed. Out
of the woods she runs and into a ragged field,
where brambles snatch at her. The sun shines
hot on her head, her tongue lolls out, she
runs through shallow rippling water, a stream
purling over stones; cold and wet on her paws,
but when she dips her head it is gone. Yet she
must drink soon, for she is shaggy pelt and
dried meat, stretched on old dry bones. She
must drink of the water at the place of her fear.
And here it is. She has run it down.

It lies at the center of a circle of earth,
tramped and scorched, where nothing grows.
It is a black hole in the ground. Above the hole
hangs a cold gray mist. And that is all.

On her belly she creeps forward. The water

smell is strong and the stone smell is strong, but strongest is the fear. And still she creeps on, sun hot on her back and earth on her belly, for she must drink or die. She peeps over the edge, and sees, first, her own face reflected in a circle of black water.

The reflection dissolves in a shiver of ripples, and she peers deeper, into a wavering dark cloud. Red eyes and maw, white teeth, but no face, nothing she knows or ever could know, then that too is gone, and from deeper yet she sees colors, milky blues and greens, churning. She lowers her tongue to the surface, fear gagging her. But what she touches and tastes is not water, but blood and offal and rot, and she spits, leaps, hurls herself away across the bare ground and across the field and into the woods, the cool shadow of the woods, and there at her flank is another shadow. It is Coyote, running beside her.

She stops, crashes to a foolish halt, nose plowing the dirt. Shakes dirt off and dignity back on. Coyote, who has trotted a dozen yards farther on, circles back toward her warily. Front paws brace, necks stretch, noses touch.

Sister?

Sister.

Where did you come from?

I was here, running beside you for a long way, but I could not hear you, or smell you, and all I could see was your shadow. When you went to the well, I stayed back and watched. When you lowered your head, suddenly I could see you as you are. What is in the well?

Blood. Shit. Rot. Fear.

Let's run away.

They run until they come to a clearing in the woods, a place in the angle of rail fence and woodpile. Here they stop, panting.

Safe here? What do you smell?

Dog. Strong, fresh, all over everything. Our sister?

We do have one whose name is Bitch. This may be her place.

How do you know about the sisters?

Constance told me. The woman young above in green, ancient here in black. I've met her in both places.

How many of us are there, then?

We two, Bitch, Vixen. Cat, Rat, Spider. Two others no one knows. Nine.

Cat and Rat and Spider cannot he our sisters.

So I thought when she told me, but perhaps if we find them, we'll know them. Bitch first, though. Where can she he?

Hiding, maybe. Our wildness may have frightened her.

So then? If we hunt her down we'll make it worse.

I know how.

Wolf's chest goes down. Coyote's chest goes down. Rumps stay up. Tails wag, and they're off, romping like puppies across the grass. Then, romping across the grass, there are three.

Sisters?

Sisters.

What need can you have of me? You can see farther, run faster, bite harder.

All nine are needed, even Rat, Spider, and the unnamed ones. We need you now to lead us to the house. Vixen and Cat are there.

I couldn't. I'm afraid of the house.

I too. Coyote too. But we must go, or the Old Woman will appear and whack us with her stick, and coil strangling black snakes around our necks.

Is she wicked?

Up above she is Constance, our friend. Here she is ancient and she has her ways.

The house is this way.

I thought it was. It should have been. Everything else is the same, but it's gone. I don't know how to find it.

Look, there it is. There. See the roof through the trees?

Where is it now? It was out of sight for a minute, not more, back there where the ground dipped. And we didn't circle. The sun is right where it was, casting our shadows to our left. But it's gone.

No, it's there.

It can't be. We'd have had to turn almost

completely around, and the sun hasn't moved.
That must be some other house.
    There's only one. Watch it every moment.

    It's not here. It has to be here, but it's not.
Look, it's there.
    Stop, though. We could run till our pads set
the grass on fire, and still not come to it.
    Then what? Wait for the Old Woman?
    We want to not find it. I went to it in the
other world and my fear was bitter in my throat.
Bitch knows and fears it here. But you, Coyote,
have never seen it. You guide us.
    For what? Fear of the Old Woman? I'll eat
her black snakes, gladly.
    For the curiosity I can smell all over you.

    What did she say when you searched for
me?
    She said, smell out your fear. But what is the
smell of a house?

    Of this house? Apples, rotting in the spring
sunshine. Rotting wood, rust, mildew. Chicken
and shit of chicken and blood of chicken.
Almost dog but not exactly dog. Fear.
    Where?
    Not where we think we see it. This way.

    *And now the house hulks in front of them,
windows shrouded in dark dusty green. There are no*

chickens in sight, for all the ripe scent, no rooster or
goose or goat, watchdog or barn cat taking the sun
on the woodpile. The eyes of the house are blind, its
mouth locked tight. It sees nothing and says nothing.

Why do my hackles rise and my paws
tremble? It's empty. No human smell. No one
has lived here in years.
   Cat is in there.
   And if she is? And if we could get in? She'd
climb the chimney from the inside, if we came
on her, sprout wings and fly away as a black
sooty raven.

   She might stay for Vixen, though. If Vixen
went alone. And that was her scent that Coyote
caught, earlier. Almost dog but not dog exactly.
   And for which of us would Vixen stay? Not
you, Bitch. You smell of hound. You, Coyote,
smell too hungry. I will go. Where is the scent
now?
   Around on the other side. Almost masked by
apple rot.

Leaving the others hidden in the field, Wolf
trots off down the fencerow. Let curtain shake
or hinge creak, she will howl away to the winter
country forever. But Bitch was right. The house
is empty. She turns the corner and sees, under a
lean-to against the house, a garden tractor, blotched
red with rust through cracked green paint. On the

*seat of the tractor is a net bag, in which are root
vegetables, potatoes and carrots and onions, so fresh
the earth clinging to them is still moist. They could
hardly have been harvested an hour ago. The scent
from the bag . . . but it can't be, for the roots there
are raw. From the kitchen? But the house is empty.
Is the scent of Constance's vegetable soup. Then is
this the home of the Wild Woman, Constance above
and below, with chicken bones in her long white
hair? Now Wolf smells chicken, not offal or blood or
rot of chicken, but deliciously simmering. And she's
hungry. She's been hungry all her life, but now her
sides cleave to her ribs, her gut growls and gnaws,
saliva fills her mouth as she sees that the back door
is open a crack, and from that crack issue wisps of
brothy steam.*

*Inside that house she will be fed to bursting, and
then she will curl up on the rug in front of the fire
and sleep, and never again go chasing through the
black and hungry cold. She takes a step closer and
another step.*

Stop! They'll eat you in there!

And against the pull of her hunger she does
stop.

Who are you? Where are you?

Vixen. Up here in the apple tree.

Sister?

Sister.

Who's in there? We thought the house was
empty.

It was. It is. I've smelled, heard, seen no one.

But here, look.

Wolf looks. On the ground at the foot of the tree lies a long bloody bone. She sniffs a step closer, and then what bone it is she knows in her own bones, for in her hind leg she feels a deep crippling ache. She cannot run on that leg. They will come, whoever they are, catch and muzzle and bind, simmer her down for their dinner.

When did you first see it?

An hour ago. It wasn't here when I climbed into the tree, no one came, no one put it there, but it was there. It's the bone from my own leg. It hurts. I'm afraid to come down.

Could you run?

The pain eased when you came.

Then jump and run now. We'll go to our sisters,

I smell Wolf, and that's you. Was it you who saved me when I was caught in the other place?

It wasn't. We have to find that sister.

But on your fur I smell Dog. I'm afraid of Dog.

Your sister Coyote runs Deer. Your sister Bitch runs Rabbit. The hounds who run Fox may live in this house.

Your right hind leg is dragging.

I can run on three legs. Run.

As they circle the house, the pain fades, the cooking scent fades, the house is empty.

What was it? How did it happen?

I don't know. But something is loose. Something terrible is loose in this country.

I loosed it when I put my tongue to what was in the well.

No. It was loosed earlier.

When I first went to the house? In the place above, where we wear the woman's body?

The house is there as well?

We grew up in it. Don't you remember?

Who lives in it now?

I don't know. Only that fear lives in it.

Bellies to the ground, sheltered in the high grass and brambles of the field, the four sisters watch the house. The sun shines hot on their backs. Their tongues loll from their mouths. But this is a dry country. There is nothing here to drink.

Vixen, Cat is in the house. Have you seen her?

I've seen nothing. The windows are shrouded.

Would you try to get in and find her?

Never. Why?

Her scent is different, she mews instead of harking, claws before biting, but she's our sister. Did you know the sister who saved you?

I want to go and talk to Constance.

You needn't go, my love. I'm right here.

And so she is, though none of them saw or heard

or smelled her coming. Her stick in one hand, the other a cup for blackberries. The thin white hairs on her chin are stained purple.

Or was it my daughter you meant, who feeds you on roots and tea?

It was your daughter.

Yet your business is here.

I'm hungry. I have to eat.

She proffers her cupped hand. Vixen dips her muzzle and laps up the fruit, sweet and tart and winey.

Better?

Yes.

Then enter the house and return with your sisters.

Sisters?

Three are there.

I don't know how to get in. And I'm afraid.

Are you afraid of trees?

She bangs her stick on the top rail of the fence, once, twice, three times, with a sound like the crack of thunder. At the third blow, the house vanishes. Where it stood is a dark grove.

The hair on Vixen's back rises, her heart batters the walls of her chest. Her knees shake. Her bowels go loose. She looks around at the others, but none will go. It is her place to go. The Wild Woman raises her stick . . . and she jumps, trots off across the barnyard, brush dragging, into the woods. As she passes the first trees, she turns, and there is nothing behind her but trees. She is alone, lost.

The woods are silent. No bird sings, mouse rustles. They smell of leaf and leaf mold, root and bough and acorn. They are dense, tangled, pathless. Trees whose falling ripped their root clusters clear of the earth, roots clutching rocks the size of big burrowing animals, woodchuck or badger, bar her way. Then she hears the baying of hounds.

She scrambles onto a log, jumps for another, vines catch at her and she goes down in a flailing heap. The baying is closer, coming on her from all sides at once. With her front paws she scrabbles at the earth, digging her own shallow grave. At the first touch it opens out under roots, a tunnel Vixen-sized. She dives into the earthy dark. From behind her she still hears the baying, muffled by earth and her own body, then only the scratching of her hard-working paws. From ahead, stronger as she goes, the smell of rotting apples, chicken, mildewed grain, old wet book bindings and paper and stone. And Rat. As the tunnel opens out, as she stands and shakes the earth from her coat, her paws on rough damp stone, the urine and feces, the vomit and sickness of Rat.

Sister?

Rat is here, cowering somewhere in the dark, but there is no answer. Vixen thinks of hunting her here, by nose alone in this black and tangled place, the long yellow teeth of Rat darting in low and meeting in her throat.

I won't hurt you.

I am your sister.

Do you want to live in this foul dark
forever?

*Cat could catch Rat, if Vixen could find her.
Down here there is no scent of her. Yet she lives
somewhere in the house, for Wild Woman said so.
Stairs lead into cellars and out of cellars. The only
way is up.*

*With her nose and her whiskers leading she pads
around the walls. The floor under her paws is a
soggy grit, dust, urine, apple mash, the leakings of
chicken guts. Here there is less air above her--she is
under the stairs. She circles, climbs, toenails digging
into rotting treads, the staircase creaking under her
slight weight. At the top is a door which she nudges
open with her paw, admitting a trickle of gray light.
Behind and below her, Rat rustles and squeaks.*

Come out into the light. The way is clear. I
am your sister.

But Rat is still.

*Vixen is standing in a long hallway, dimly lit,
but she sees no source of the light. It is a tunnel
with white plastered walls, with plain wooden doors,
all closed, on either side. Here she hears nothing,
smells only wood and dust. She trots down the hall,
head up, nose testing each door as she comes to it.
All are blank, dozens of them. The hall has gone on*

for a mile, for ten miles, it goes on forever. How could the house contain it? Then something about the air at her back . . . she turns, and sees that the hall has closed up behind her, at the end of it the door to the cellar, still slightly ajar. But that way leads only back to the tunnel, the woods, the hounds.

She turns to a door on her right, the first or the last she came to, nudges it open, and she is standing in a windowless room, unfurnished, thick with dust. The coil of rope on the floor lies on top of the dust. Someone has left it there in the last hour. She turns to run, but the door through which she entered has vanished. Nothing there but a blank white wall.

Unless she fainted and lost her bearings, for there's a door now on the far side. The room has shrunk or the rope has grown, a thin white snake sprawled all the way across, and she will have to jump over it to get there. She crouches, her fear thick in her throat, for what if it springs at her as she passes, tangling and binding? But she must jump, or die here in this room.

She springs, lands lightly on the far side, pushes open the door. This room is the same as the last. Again the door vanishes behind her. Again it appears in the far wall. On the floor between lies a long bone-handled knife. What if it stabs up into her belly? But she crouches, springs, lands lightly.

On the floor of the next room lies a terrible red thing. Her fear gags her throat. Her blood runs thick from between her legs. Trailing her life-blood she leaps. She pushes the door, finds herself now in a kitchen. Old white appliances, blue formica counter top, round wooden table and chairs. The cooking smell must have come from here. But no one has been here in years. Everything is grimed with dust.

She is no longer bleeding, if ever she was. She stands gathering herself, easing her heart, for now when she lifts her nose she smells, fresh and strong, not more than one room away, Cat. When she feels ready, she pushes on through one more door, and finds herself in a green-curtained room, with a grandfather clock, a table with a book lying open on it, and, although surely it is summer outside, a fire burning.

Sister?

No answer, but one of the curtains moves a little. Vixen trots over, stands with her paws on the windowsill, pokes her head through. Cat is there, staring out through the window, and then they are both staring, for outside it is winter, the field drifted deep in snow.

Sister?

Sister.

Will you come out with me?

Too cold out there.

Where we live it's summer.

We?

The others. Sister Wolf, Sister Coyote, Sister Bitch.

Fine place for Sister Cat.

Yet you're here with Sister Vixen, and you've come to no harm.

Can you read what the book says?
No. It's not even words.
I'd hoped to be able to read it before I left.
There's Sister Rat, down below in the cellar. Only I don't know how to get back there. You could bring her?
Why would I want to?
So we'll all be together. Do you want to live here alone forever? And what is there to eat?
Only that one, up there in the corner, but I can't catch her.
Spider? She's one of us as well. Has she always lived here with you?
For only a little while. After the night when the snow turned to red rain. But nothing ever comes to her web. She hardly moves. I think she's dying.
She first, you after.
It's boring here. I'll go for Rat. You catch Spider if you can.
But there will be no catching her, up there in the angle of ceiling and wall. Vixen hops onto the table, sits with her long ears up. Little Sister?
And after a time, a minute or a day and a night or longer, Spider leaves her web, scuttles across the ceiling, lowers herself to Vixen's head. She spins with the last of her silk a web between Vixen's ears. A fly spirals into the center of the web. Spider sucks,

*drinks, makes new silk. Then Cat appears, with Rat
dangling by the scruff of the neck from her jaws.*

I smell blood.

*Cat lowers Rat to the floor, turns her to her back,
with one claw rakes lightly across her belly. Drops
of bright red blood well up. Rat squeals and chatters
her teeth.*

Mine. She bit me there, deeper than that. I
bear a wound that will scar. My teeth touched
her neck in the killing place. But if any one of
us dies, what will that mean for the rest?

*Cat removes her paw and languidly, with her
rough pink tongue, grooms her fur.*

Sister Rat, will you walk along with us, or
will Cat carry you by your neck?

Don't touch me. I'll bite.

You'll walk, then. Sister Cat, how did you
get to the cellar?

It's only one room away. The stairs are off
the kitchen.

How can we get out of the house?

Out the kitchen door, but Spider will freeze.

Let's go see.

*They walk single file, Vixen leading, Rat
creeping low on her belly between them, back to the
kitchen doorway. The dust griming the kitchen floor
is smooth, unmarred. No one has passed that way in*

years.

This is the wrong way. Are there two kitchens?

How can there be? This is the only door from the living room.

When you passed through before, did you look out the window?

It was deep winter.

The kitchen door stands open a crack. Vixen leads them across to it, their tracks sharp in the dust behind them. Outside stands the apple tree, in high summer leaf. Under it lies a long bloody bone. With her sister between her ears, Vixen hobbles along under the curse of her wound, rotting apples strong and rough in her nose. Underneath that scent she smells, from the gray deserted kitchen, soup simmering. She leads the others around the corner of the house, down the fencerow, to the place where Wolf and Bitch and Coyote are waiting.

You brought all three. That was good work.

Where is the forest?

The moment you entered it, it was gone and the house was there again.

I will not return to that house. What are we to do now?

Gather the other two. But we know nothing of them, not even their names.

Nothing of them, O far-seeing Wolf? Your

eyes are the eyes of a three-day-old cub.

The Wild Woman stalks among them. She puts the tip of her bony finger to the web between Vixen's ears, and Spider runs up it, up her hand and arm and neck, and settles in the white forest of her hair. She touches the toe of her black shoe to Rat's nose, and Rat runs under her long black skirt and up her leg to where her legs join.

These two must come home with me, for they're too young for hard travelling. Aren't you, my loves? And have you, 0 deep-sniffing Wolf, lost your voice as well as your eyes?

Then tell me what I have seen with my eyes.

Your eight sisters.

Spider and Rat, Vixen and Cat, Coyote and Bitch, and with Wolf that makes seven.

Are you thirsty? Where did you smell water?

But there was no water in the well.

Where do you smell water now?

There, close by in the field. But the well was a long way off.

What else do you smell?

Rank and musty. Wild and dark. Fear.

You smell your sisters. What did you see in the well?

Dark. Blue and green shadows . . . Sisters?

0 wise Wolf.

Wild Woman in her gut-stained black dress walks away across the barnyard, enters the house by the front door, closes it again after her.

She lives there?
She lives anywhere.

*In a few minutes they smell, from the house, cold
clean water. Smoke rises from the chimney. Then
they smell soup simmering, potato and carrot and
onion. Bitch lies on her belly in the field and whines.*

I'm thirsty and hungry. In the house is water
and food. If I go to the door and bark loudly,
she may let us all in.
    You say that because of not knowing the
Wild Woman. She will never let us in.
    *Bitch stands, digs a burr out of her tail. Her
tongue is lolling and her sides are caving in. She
trots out into the barnyard, which, all around her, is
littered with bloody bones. Hind paw and forepaw,
rib and breast and back, neck, skull, they shuffle and
scuttle themselves together behind her until they are
the clattering skeleton of Bitch, and they follow her,
casting no shadow in the sun. She runs howling to
the door, stands high against it and rakes it with her
claws, and it opens, catapulting her inside, slams
against the one following. Skeleton Bitch grows
flesh. She sniffs the door and trots back across the
barnyard, now empty of bones.*
    The house is empty. No smell of Woman,
nor water or food. Only dust. Who will lead us
to the well?

No one speaks. Cat grooms herself with her rough pink tongue.

It was I she called by name. I she said had seen them. I will lead us to the place of my fear, but I will not put my head over the edge.

The well is not in the field. They trot on into the woods, in single file behind Wolf, following the water scent and the fear scent. They pass a naked doll with blue eyes, long brown hair, no arms or legs. Rabbit scrabbles away into the thicket on his forepaws only, for his hindquarters are gnawed to the bone. The bones of Deer are bloody, clustered with flies. They travel on, and come to where the trees are blighted, summer leaves turned red and gold, then bare and dead, fallen, rotting under their scrabbling paws. In a bare place beyond, seedlings grow, then saplings, tall young trees, trees whose tops they cannot see. The day grows old, grows dark. A few flakes of snow drift down. They huddle together, whimpering.

Is this the place?

It is nothing like the place where the well was before, but the smell is strong.

Who will go closer?

Cat, you go. You can see best in the dark, and you can climb.

And if I could fly? Why else?

Because you're curious.

Cat slips away through the trees. With her

*night-seeing eyes she sees Mouse in her nest among
the roots, and Owl in his hole in the bough. Against
the blackness of a tree as great around as the mouth
of Well, she sees a deeper blackness. She hears
breathing. She smells a rank wild smell, and her own
fear like a mist around her.*

Sister?

*The reply is a rumble from the center of the
earth.*

I am the eighth. The ninth lives in the well,
where you may not go. Go back now, Little
Sister, into your own country.

I found her.

What is her name?

She is great and black, with a hot snuffling
breath. I never asked.

Who will go next?

*Vixen springs ahead into the trees. She cannot
see as well as Cat in the dark, but the wild scent
first and then the breathing guide her.*

What is your name?

My name is Bear, Little Sister.

Was it you who saved me, when the man
came with the knife and the other things?

I ripped his head from his shoulders and ate
it. Go back to the others, Little Sister. Return to
your own country. You may not pass this way.

Her name is Bear. She bars the way to the
well. Who else will go?

Wolf trots ahead, hackles bristling. She smells only fear, hears only her own breath, sees nothing. Then a scent from deep underground, from a damp cave littered with bones. A breath not hers, the ponderous respiration of the earth itself. A blackness darker than the night, with red eyes.

Sister Bear?

Say what you must, and go.

Was it you I saw in the well?

My shadow. My life is to guard the well.

What lives in it?

The ninth sister.

What is her name?

She has no name.

Was it she I glimpsed, deeper than your shadow?

That is where she lives.

Does she ever come out?

When I sleep. You would not want to be here.

Will you come away with us?

And loose her into the woods? Return to your own place. Does your fear tell you nothing?

When will it be morning here? When will it be spring?

It is always night and always winter.

It was night and winter always where I lived. Yet now I roam through all hours and all seasons.

Bear shows her white teeth and her red maw.

Wolf runs, her heart battering the walls of her chest. Yet never had she known that she could be so brave. The others follow her out of winter and out of night, until they come to a country of open woods and fields. In a woodlot smelling of Rabbit and Dog, they curl up together in the angle between rail fence and woodpile, Wolf and Coyote and Vixen, Cat in the curve of Bitch's side, and sleep.

Chapter Three

Wolf has returned, haunted and restless: changed. And hungry. Eyes piteous at the smell of roots sent Constance in haste to the butcher shop. Now, as Wolf prowls the streets of the city, as beef in a rich wine sauce simmers on the stove, she gazes into the depths of her jungle, musing on the house named Death. Neither she nor her brother has ever seen the house from closer than the road. Neither has crossed the fence line to explore the land, though they were adventurous children and went everywhere else: this though the sober interdictions of Mama, a lighthearted woman and a seer, colored the place with mystery. It was a shivery place to them, the rustling cornfield at dusk haunted with their conjurings, the woods deep and dark like the forests in old stories. And what were they to think of the people who lived there? At a distance they would see a dark man on an old green John Deere tractor, a man in a blue shirt

and denim overalls, what all the farmers wore,
plowing, harrowing, planting, harvesting: what
all the farmers did. If he had a wife they never
saw her, or recognized her if they did; yet they
knew all the other families and all the news of
them for miles and miles around. All Mama
ever said of them (yet on no other subject was
she reticent or evasive) was *They like to keep
to themselves. We will respect their desires.* Now,
pondering the first page of that locked tale, she
feels her heart beat, only it is wings beating.
Falcon, she knows from across the miles, at this
moment is circling the house.

By the time Wolf gets back, hair tangled and
face ruddy from a long walk in a whooping
spring wind, the stew is ready. "I needn't ask if
you're hungry. Eat, and have just a glass or two
of the Burgundy I cooked it in, for the truth we
want is not in wine, and then we'll talk."

Paws thrust deep into the pockets of the
denim skirt she wears (not hers, though it fits
her; Bitch's style or maybe, if she ever got to a
store, Coyote's), Wolf, in somebody's old black
walking shoes, paces.

"Five of us together in the near woods
now — Cat, Vixen, Bitch, Coyote, Wolf. Two, Rat
and Spider, with the Old Woman. Bear in the
far woods, the forest of winter and night. The

other, the one with no name, in the well. And
that makes nine."

"That makes nine, but everyone has a name.
Some part of our work will be to learn it."

"Not mine. I'll never go near that place
again."

"Why not?"

"Fear. I hate being afraid."

"Try looking at your fear. It's a strange
flopping thing that you netted out of the deep
ocean, and at first it seems ugly to you, like
nothing of the earth. But it can't harm you,
because you're safe here on dry land, your own
place where you're fast and strong and canny.
Look at it and name its parts."

"Bear is like none of the rest of us. Not even
Spider, who has eight legs and can't speak. Was
it Bear I feared?"

"Like none of the rest of you, but still your
sister. And you stood and talked with her?"

"Yes, though my legs trembled."

"You know, too, it was Bear who saved
Vixen?"

"So she told us. So Bear is our fierce friend?
Protector? Yet she barred our way to the well."

"Was that where you wanted to go?"

"The Wild Woman sent us there. I wanted to
go anywhere else."

"How did you know that the well was to be
feared?"

"My nose told me. And I had been there alone, earlier. That was when I found Coyote."

"Bear allowed you?"

"I saw her shadow in the well, but perhaps she was sleeping. When she sleeps the thing that lives there, the ninth sister, can get out."

"Tell me quickly what is the heart of your fear. The well, or what lives in the well?"

"I tried. I was going to say quickly, what lives in the well. The well itself is a hole in the ground, with water in it or something that stinks, but what harm can it do me if I don't fall into it? Yet I believe it is the well."

"Good. What is it that stinks?"

"Blood, shit, rot. I put my tongue to it, thinking it was water, and then I ran, and that was when I saw Coyote and she saw me. Before that, running with me, she could see only my shadow."

"Good. Now tell me about the well as you knew it when you were younger, living on that farm."

"There's not much to tell. It was an abandoned well in the corner of the pasture, not the one near the house which we used. Nothing above ground to mark it, just a few rotting boards lying around."

"It was deep?"

"It must have been. The working well near the house is over four hundred feet. But I don't remember looking into it."

"Did you have any feelings about it?"

"I was scared of it even then. Why, though? I was twelve or thirteen at least, the earliest I remember. I wouldn't have blundered into it."

"We'll need to bring your mother and stepfather into this now. What was it you called them?"

"Ma-Ma, though that sounds babyish, doesn't it? Unca. I didn't like calling him that, because we weren't related, but I had to."

"What would have happened if you hadn't?"

"I don't know."

"Did either of them ever say anything that made you scared of the well?"

"I don't think so. Maybe Unca said to stay away from it, but he didn't need to. I wasn't going near it."

"Tell me quickly. Afraid of falling into it, or something coming out of it?"

"Falling into it. Into the dark. Only how could I have forgotten this? Unca liked to tell creepy stories, and he told one about that. Something coming out."

"What was the something?"

"Snakes, I think. A big snake. It was stupid."

"How did you feel about it at the time?"

"I thought it was stupid then, too."

"Did you dream about snakes coming out?"

"Not that I can remember."

"What were the other creepy stories about?"

"Things with long teeth and red eyes that lived down in the woods. Stupid."

"Were you afraid of the dark?"

"I liked the dark. I used to run around the place at night whenever I could. Only not near the well."

"So the story about the snake coming out of the well was scarier than the others?"

"No. Of course not. I just didn't want to fall in."

"You ran around at night whenever you could. What did you mean by that?"

"Just that Unca kept me pretty close—why not? I was a wild kid."

"But what's wrong with a thirteen-year-old girl wandering around in the woods?"

"He said I was ....."

"Was what?"

"I don't like to talk about it. It's stupid. Rutting."

"Did he have any reason to think that? Any boys in your life?"

"No, how could there have been? He never let me off the place."

"Except for school?"

"But I just went and came home. I wasn't involved in 4-H and those things."

"Why not?"

"I was shy, I guess. Ugly. And I wasn't allowed."

"You just said three things. You were too shy to want to join in, you were too ugly for the others to want you, Unca wouldn't have let you anyway. Which was it?"

"Maybe I knew I wasn't allowed, so I talked myself into not wanting to."

"Who gave you the idea that you were ugly?"

"Nobody had to. All I had to do was look in a mirror."

"But did anybody?"

"Unca. And he was right."

"He told you often? When would he do it?"

"How do you mean?"

"When he was mad at you? Out of the clear blue sky?"

"Maybe when he was tired from working all day. He'd say he shouldn't have to look at me on top of everything else. I'd have to go to my room."

"How did you feel about that?"

"What should I feel? That was just the way he was."

"How do you feel about it now?"

"It was years and years ago. I don't feel anything."

"Are you aware that you're stunningly beautiful?"

"No. I'm Wolf. The concept doesn't apply."

"You said Unca wouldn't let you go out

at night, wouldn't let you do things at school. What happened if you disobeyed and he caught you?"

"Nothing awful, if that's what you're getting at. He never hit me or anything. I'd lose things, or have to spend time in my room."

"Did he just tell you to stay there, or did he lock the door?"

"Locked the door, he had to. I was a wild kid."

"What would you lose?"

"You know I can't even remember? It seems like dolls, but I would have been too old for dolls."

"Did you have any physical contact at all with Unca?"

"No, he was distant. Like most men back then."

"How about between him and your mother? Do you remember them hugging and kissing?"

"Are you kidding? Ma-Ma wasn't into that. She worked and she read the Bible."

"How did she react when Unca called you ugly?"

"I don't remember that she did. It was really no big thing."

"Did it bother you that she didn't react?"

"No, because I *was* ugly."

"Did she participate in the discipline?"

"She couldn't, I was too much for her to handle."

"She said that or Unca?"

"She'd shake her head and say it, and then Unca would do whatever he had to do."

"How about hugs and kisses from your mother?"

"You're talking like I was a little girl. I was a teenager, too old for that."

"You're basically saying, then, that your mother was absent. She provided your physical needs, and that was it."

"I guess so."

"Are you in touch with her now? Any idea whether she or Unca still live on that farm, or whether they're alive or dead?"

"No idea. Couldn't care less."

"Were you aware of yourself as Wolf from the beginning? You were a human girl who went to school with other children, but you were Wolf under the skin?"

"That's how it was always."

"You never told anyone?"

"Of course not. They'd have thought I was crazy."

"But you yourself didn't think you were?"

"I didn't think of it like that. I knew I was Wolf, and I liked being Wolf. When I went under and lived in Wolf's body, and was Wolf all the time, I was happy."

"Before that, though, were you aware of being different? That you were carrying a big secret around?"

"I might have been."
"How old were you when you went under?"
"Fifteen or sixteen, I think."
"And how old—I mean how old was this
body—when you started visiting again up
here?"
"I'm not sure. Grown up, but I never had
any reason to wonder."
"As we sit here now, looking back on it, do
you have any particular complaints against your
mother and stepfather?"
"I was a wild kid—don't you remember I
was Wolf? They did what they had to do."
"Did they love you?"
"Ma-Ma must have."
"Why must?"
"Why? Because she was my mother."
"What about Unca?"
"I told you, we weren't related. I'd just as
soon forget him."
"Suppose you had a child you loved very
much, and you knew she loved to roam the
woods and fields at night. And in the corner
of one of those fields was an open well, four
hundred feet deep. What would you do?"

"I'd board it up."
"Tell me how you'd board it up."
"I'd drive heavy stakes at each corner, deep.

Build a frame around it with two-by-fours. Nail two-by-fours across it with long nails."

"Your child would be safe, because you loved her. Were you safe when you were a child?"

"I wasn't going to fall into it. Wolves don't do that."

"Wolves are hunted. Driven into the deep woods. In what other ways were you not safe?

"For what were you hungry?

"Were you hungry for love?

"For someone who knew your name?

"Wolf darling, you're safe here with me. You could even cry here."

"I think I want to cry. I don't seem to know how. What's wrong with me?"

"Nothing, darling. Nothing. Let me hold you for a little while.

"This work we're doing, it's hard. It hurts. And more to do, but not now. Go down, send Coyote. Sleep."

And she traces the damp track of Wolf's tears on her shoulder. Blinks back her own tears.

"Coyote? Is it you?"

"You don't know me?"

"You resemble your sister Wolf, though your eyes have a humorous glint in them. What happened to Wolf's body when she came up here?"

"It lay still. We thought she was dead. Then the Wild Woman came and stroked her neck, and told us she would be born again from that death."

"When you yourself return to your body which is now lying still, you will find her alive and changed. But then you will be changed as well. Tell me, how are the others?"

"Bitch goes about whining and wagging her foolish tail. She tried to follow the Wild Woman home, but the Wild Woman chased her away with her stick. Cat has climbed into the fork of a tree. Vixen sits at the foot of it, grinning up at her. Yet I think they are whispering secrets."

"Has anyone ever told you to keep a secret?"

"I keep them without being asked. Why give away something for nothing?"

"Then what will you take for a secret?"

"That stew I smell cooking?"

"Done."

"It's good. I hid a raw chicken breast in the principal's sofa, and I hid the bottle I brought it in in Brandon Baker's locker, because his dirty mind was all over my breasts."

"That's a good secret. How did you know where his mind was?"

"I can see into it. They think they're prize stud dogs and I'm a bitch in heat. But I'm Coyote, and I'll pour lye into their milk, and then they'll know about heat."

"You sound angry. Who else has made you angry in your life?"

"All men in rut, which means all men."

"Why did you happen to use that particular word, rut?"

"It's in the dictionary, isn't it? Why shouldn't I use it?"

"But it's not very common, at least in town. Who else have you heard using it?"

"Nobody. You're getting boring."

"Let's play a game, then. Look into my mind and tell me what you see."

"A tall blue-eyed man, a farmer."

"That's Brother. What now?"

"A white-haired woman. She looks like the man. Like both of you. Like . . . the Wild Woman of the woods."

"That's Mama. And now?"

"Falcon. Circling. How could that be in your mind?"

"I'll tell you in a minute. What do you see now?"

"A pale man with dark hair. On a green tractor. Who told you about him?"

"Wolf told me, but do you think he'd be so clear in my mind if I'd never seen him myself?"

"How?"

"How is it that Brother was the one who found the body you're wearing, when Wolf drove it out there and left it, in her terrible fear, and no one else came into it? We were your next door neighbors, a mile on up the road to the north. Brother and Mama live there still."

"You knew him? Unca?"

"I saw him from the time I was about twelve. But I never met him, never spoke a word to him. So you'll have to be the one to do the telling."

"Does he still live there?"

"To this day, I believe, though he no longer farms. The fields are leased out."

"Then he could have died or gone away. He must have. It's been years and years."

"But then why would Falcon be flying guard around the house, this very moment as we speak?"

"Who is Falcon?"
"Your guardian."

"And Ma-Ma?"
"Still there as far as I know, though no one

sees her. Do you want me to try and find out for certain?"

"All right. How?"
"Wait here a few minutes, and I'll tell you.

"I talked to Mama. She says they're both there. She feels the emanations. If either of them had died or left, she would know. She's a seer."

"So I could slip out there late at night with rags and gasoline. I could burn the house down with them in it."

"Yes, you could do that. Then people would want to know who did it, and they'd find out that your mother had a daughter and track you down and ask you questions. And the others would know what happened, now that most of you are together down there, and who knows what some of them would say? Then you would be defined as insane, and confined for the rest of your life in a mental hospital, or sane, and spend the rest of your life in prison."

"Not worth it."
"Not for Coyote, no. Not for Wolf, the far-ranging free spirits. But please tell me why you want to do it."
"Why would anybody? I hated them."
"Both?"
"Unca. Ma-Ma was hardly worth it."

"Tell me about Unca."

"Nasty little jokes, that's all there is to tell. He set traps for me. He thought it was funny."

"What kind of traps?"

"Mean ones. A bucket balanced on my door, only not water in it. Do you know how awful pig shit is? On your head? Then I'd have to clean it up. I was the one that spilled it. Or a thin wire stretched across the top of the stairs. Or oil in the shower stall, right where I'd put my foot."

"No wonder you're angry. Did he claim to have a reason for what he did? That you'd been bad, or provoked him?"

"Sneaky little bitch. That's what he said. Because I'd try to play back on him, only then he'd punish me. It wasn't fair."

"It certainly wasn't. How did he punish you?"

"With his belt. So I stopped trying. It hurt too bad."

"Did he do anything else to you?"

"Wasn't that enough?"

"Any at all was too much, but we need to know everything. Did he touch you with his hands?"

"I already told you. He used his belt."

"Did you tell your mother when he did bad things?"

"What for? He said it was to teach me a

lesson. Bring me back to Jesus, he said. She believed him."

"How old was this body when you were born into it?"

"Ten or eleven."

"And when you left it and went into your Coyote body?"

"Twelve or thirteen."

"So let's say you were there, he was playing these tricks for two years. Quickly now, what was the one worst thing he did?"

"The hunting."

"Tell me about it."

"Not much to tell. It was just rabbits and things, but I hated it."

"You went along on these trips?"

"Oh no. I'd have been in the way, but he'd bring them in. Soft and furry and dead. You know how girls are."

"Had you seen any of these animals close up when they were alive?"

"Not especially. Who can get close to a rabbit?"

"Coyote can. What else did he hunt?"

"He'd shoot anything that moved. He divided the animal kingdom into game, like rabbits and deer, and pests. Rats, crows, hawks . . . "

"Coyotes?"

"I don't remember."

"I think you do."

"All right, yes, there was one. He hung it
on the fence, right where I could see it from
my bedroom window. It hung there and rotted,
dried up, I can't remember him ever taking it
down."

"So maybe, before he did, you went down
into your coyote body?"

"Maybe."

"Could that have been part of the reason
why you did?"

"I guess it could."

"What is it that you yourself hunt, as
Coyote?"

"Deer."

"Why is that?"

"Why not? What else would Coyote hunt?"

"But you said Unca hunted deer."

"I didn't."

"You said that to him everything was either
pests or game — like rabbits and deer."

"Well, so. It was just a way of speaking."

"He shot everything that moved. And I
know how many deer there were around there. I
lived there."

"Stop that. It's like, it's like now you're
hunting me."

"Did you hear what you just said?"

"I said to lay off."

"It wasn't 'You're hunting *me*'—as opposed
to hunting deer. It was 'Now *you're* hunting
me'—you too. Who else has hunted you?"

"Nobody. You made that up."

"Coyote dearest, don't you know what we're
hunting here together, the two of us? Secrets.
Think of them as . . . blind white worms,
squirming around in a cave somewhere, in
the dark, way down deep in your mind. They
give off poisons that make you feel weak and
confused and scared. So what we need to do,
the two of us, is put on our rubber boots and
gloves, take our big bright flashlights, our
buckets and our nets, and go down there after
them. Net them, carry them back up here and
look at them in the sunlight. Watch them shrivel
and die. Don't you want to do that with me?"

"I'm too scared."

"Of course you're scared—it's dark down
there. Too scared? I doubt it. Want to hold
hands?"

"Maybe we'd better."

"Can you tell me now about the deer
hunting?"

"It wasn't that. Even he didn't call it that.
It was, he said anything on his land belonged

to him. It was harvesting. He'd set up a salt
lick down by the pond, a hundred yards from
the back porch. The buck would come every
evening at the same time. He had the rifle
mounted on a tripod."

"How long did this go on before he did his
harvesting?"

"He didn't . . . It was more like grocery
shopping. Let me know when we're low on
meat and I'll get you some. It went on for a long
time."

"You had a freezer? There was no special
reason not to get it over with?

"I'm sorry, I couldn't hear you."

"I said, he knew I loved the deer."

"Yes. So he strung it out because he enjoyed
watching you suffer?"

"He said . . . oh God. That if I was good
enough . . . maybe he wouldn't . . . "

"Poor darling. It's all right. You're safe now,
safe here with me.

"Can you try to tell me what it meant to be
good enough?"

"No, I . . . I can't tell you anything right
now. I'm so tired. Could we do it some other
time?"

"Yes, dearest. Go now, send Bitch. Sleep long
and deep."

But Constance, with apologies, leaves Bitch alone with her tea mug for a time. She goes up into her little living room and stares out the window into the thundery twilight, arms folded tight across her chest, shuddering.

"What's it like down there for you now, being with your sisters?"

"I don't know. Not so lonely, but strange. Funny."

"You don't look terribly amused."

"I'm sorry, I should have been clearer. I mean, there's all of us down there. And only this one body up here."

"You've been worrying about what's going to happen because of this work we're doing? What would you like to happen?"

"I don't know. Only I don't want to die."

"Of course you don't, but why would you?"

"Because that's what Vixen said. She said you would decide which one of us was best. Something about the survival of the fittest. And you would kill off all the others, and then that one would live all by herself in this body, all the time. Vixen said she would be well-adjusted, whatever that means, but I'd think it would be lonely."

"And how would I go about killing you off, even if I wanted to?"

"The Wild Woman is you down below,

Vixen said, and she's a witch. She'll catch us and
stuff us in her oven, and when we're cooked
she'll eat us."

"And which of you in Vixen's opinion will
be the lucky survivor?"

"She didn't exactly say. She grinned, though.
See, I think she sees me as a threat to her? To
her chances, because I'm the one that's been
out the most? And so if she can get me nervous
enough, if I come up here and act real nutty . . .
Am I? Right now?"

"Hardly. I hope you can believe what I'm
going to tell you now, because without trust
we're not going to get anywhere. I have no
intentions of killing anybody."

"You don't?"
"Absolutely not."

"But then what's going to happen? It's
gotten so strange down there, there's something
scary walking around. And up here, I never
know where I am from one minute to the next."

"Tell me first about that scary something."

"Nobody's actually smelled or heard or seen
it, but there are signs. Bloody bones and dead
dolls."

"That does sound scary. How are you all
managing?"

"We've been staying close. Vixen says,
anyone who goes off alone will never come

back."

"Vixen sounds like quite the rumor-monger, but staying close makes sense. You asked me what's going to happen--is it reassuring to know that I have very little idea?"

"Was that a joke?"

"Not at all. I'm lost in the woods, and even when I find my way out--do you think I think I'm God? You nine must work out your own fate."

"But how can we? If each of us wants control of the body all the time?"

"Is that what you yourself want? You said it sounded lonely."

"I'm not sure. What are the alternatives?"

"There's the something scary wandering around down there—it's going to have to be identified, stared down, dealt with one way or another. Then there's getting Bear to join the rest of you and make friends, and the other, the ninth sister, whose name we don't even know. We need all of you on good terms. A little squabbling is inevitable, the sort of thing Vixen's been doing if it were toned down a little, but basically, the nine of you would need to be sisterly. You'd take turns coming out for different purposes—for example, you might go on holding the job if you're best at it, but with the others helping instead of sabotaging you. You'd all be communicating all the time, and with that, with the energies and talents of nine instead of just one, you could have a fine life."

"That sounds good. I vote for that."

"Only it might not work out that way. One of you might become progressively more powerful and simply absorb the rest--something like what Vixen was saying, but accomplished on your own. And that too could be healthy."

"That wouldn't be me. Maybe it would be Wolf. I hate the sound of it."

"Would you fight if it started to happen? If you felt yourself fading?"

"How could I? I'm only Bitch."

"But best adapted for city life?"

"I'd hate it. I wouldn't want to. But what if one of the others decides to just take over?"

"I've heard no interest in that from Wolf or Coyote—it never even came up. Vixen might want to, but I'm sure she's not strong enough. I'll talk to her, though. It's important that you stay separate and strong while we go after the scary thing in the woods. After that, we'll see."

"I'm sorry. But what will we see?"

"There is one more possibility. A union of all of you. Still nine, at the same time one. Laurel, one woman, yet Laurel with the strength and wisdom of nine."

"How could that happen?"

"I don't know. I know only that if it does, Falcon will have had . . . a wing in it."

"Who or what is Falcon?"

"I would have said your animus, a powerful element in your psyche which can face down ogres. But he said he was no part of you, so he is your guardian angel, only what does that mean? He is a Being of Light who loves you. A mystery, beyond our understanding. There are no words for him."

"You keep saying *he*."

"So I experience him, as I experience my brother as he. He is of that good clan of brother, father, grandfather, husband."

"I wouldn't know. I've never known any men like that."

"Later I'll take you out to meet Brother, only to appreciate him you will have to make yourself ready. Tell me about your name--Bitch."

"It's just my name, when my name isn't Laurel. Like the Others' names."

"Yet it has, as opposed say to Coyote, a certain feeling about it. Does it affect how you feel about yourself?"

"Why should it? It's what I am."

"And how did you happen to become what you are?"

"I don't understand. How does anybody?"

"For example, let me tell you about a girl who lived on the farm with Ma-Ma and Unca. She might have been about twelve, a crucial time for a young girl, and she loved animals,

as many girl-children do. Unca shot a coyote
and hung it on a fence where she had to see
it, and when she went under and took on her
animal body, that's what she was. Who she
was--Coyote, your sister. So I'm wondering why
you are Bitch."

"Oh. Well, I guess he called me that a lot."
"That was very bad. In itself, it was not as
bad as what he did to Coyote. Can you tell me
more?"
"I'm sorry. I want to help, but I really don't
remember anything."
"How old was this body when you first
came into it?"
"About . . . ten?"
"Yes, that fits. So now, what happened
during the two years or so you were in it to
cause you to opt out, as the others did? To give
up being conscious up here, in this world, and
go underground as a real female dog?"
"I don't know. When you think about it it's
pretty weird, isn't it?"
"Actually it makes sense. It was your way
of adapting to stress, of sealing off wounds the
way a tree does. You went into hiding, only
what were you hiding from?"
"I'm sorry, but nothing. I had a perfectly
ordinary childhood."
"Tell me quickly then, what is your happiest
memory involving your mother?"

"It's hard to come up with just one."

"Tell me any. Or as many as you can think of."

"When she used to read to me?"

"What were some of your favorites?"

"The Bible."

"That was your favorite book? What else did she read?"

"I guess that was about it."

"What parts did she read?"

"Pretty much just straight through."

"Did you find any of it boring?"

"No, why should I?"

"Any of it disturbing?"

"Of course not. It was the Bible."

"Do you ever read the Bible now that you're grown up?"

"I hardly need to. I practically know it by heart."

"Do you own a Bible?"

"No."

"When she read to you, where were you in relation to her?"

"I'm not sure I know what you mean."

"Were you sitting in her lap?"

"Of course not, I was much too old for that. She'd be on one side of the table in the living room, and I'd be on the other."

"Quickly, what's your worst memory of your mother?"

"I'm sorry. I don't have any."

"Were you allowed to express your anger when you were there?"

"I don't think I had any to express."

"Would you say you were happy?"

"Yeah, sure. It was a neat place to grow up."

"Did your mother ever hug you?"

"I already told you, I was too old for that."

"Did she ever touch you at all?"

"Why would she? I was a good kid."

"So when I said *touch*, you automatically assumed I meant in the sense of hitting or punishing. Why is that?"

"I'm not sure. Because she certainly never punished me."

"Did Unca punish you?"

"No. I was a *good* kid, I keep telling you."

"What's your best memory of Unca?"

"When he'd go out in the woods and he'd take me with him."

"Out walking? Or hunting?"

"He might take his gun along, but not really hunting."

"Didn't he always take it along?"

"Maybe so. What difference does it make?"

"What did he shoot with it?"

"Just wild animals if he happened to see any. Rabbits."

"Did that bother you?"

"Why should it? We needed them to eat, we were poor."

"That's the first I've heard of that. Did being poor bother you?"

"We had enough."

"For your birthday, for Christmas, what gifts did they give you?"

"I told you, we were poor."

"Poor child, none at all?"

"We were poor. It wasn't their fault."

"Did you have a tree at Christmas? That at least would have cost them nothing."

"No, we weren't religious."

"Did you hear what you just said? Your mother read you the Bible until you almost know it by heart, but you weren't religious?"

"I meant we weren't religious like *that*."

"Like what? You didn't celebrate the birth of Christ?"

"Of course we did."

"Then how?"

"I told you. My mother read to me from the Bible."

"Anything special for that holy day? The Christmas story?"

"I don't guess so."

"Going back to those outings with Unca, would you be walking behind him, beside him, or ahead?"

"What difference does it make?"

"For one thing, if you ran ahead he'd have had to be careful with his gun, wouldn't he?"

"I don't understand what you're getting at."

"Were there any near-accidents with the gun? Or times when it went off in your ear and scared you?"

"Unca was very responsible."

"But you didn't answer my question."

"I'm sorry, I don't remember. Which must mean there weren't, because you'd remember something like that, wouldn't you?"

"Maybe. On these outings did Unca talk to you??"

"Sure he did."

"What about?"

"How could I remember? It was a long time ago. Just, you know, teasing. He'd tease me in fun."

"For example?"

"Like he'd say if I was running all over, you're sure a long-legged little . . ."

"Bitch?"

"But he didn't mean anything by it. It was just his way of talking."

"Did it bother you?"

"Why should it?"

"Did he talk to you often about your body?"

"That's a funny question. I don't think he ever did."

"You said he called you long-legged."

"Oh, that. But that was because I was."

"The two of you were out there in the woods by yourselves, talking and having a nice time. Did you have any secrets between you?"

"Why would we?"

"They wouldn't be bad secrets necessarily. Anything your mother wasn't to know about?"

"No. It's wrong to keep secrets."

"Who told you that?"

"Both of them. There were no secrets in our family."

"So if they asked, you had to tell them your private thoughts?"

"It never came up. I never had any to tell."

"But how would they have known that without asking? Did they ask?"

"I don't remember. What difference does it make when I never had any?"

"Do you have any private thoughts right now?"

"I don't think so. Am I supposed to tell them to you if I do?"

"Only if you trust me enough to do it freely."
"I can't think of any, anyway."
"Quickly please, fill in the blanks in what I'm going to say to you. For example if I were to say 'Apples are blank,' you might say 'Red.' Ready?"
"Go ahead."
"Ma-Ma was blank to me."
"Good."
"Unca was blank to me."
"Good."
"I had a blank childhood."
"Happy."
"The favorite thing I had was my blank."
"Puppy."
"Even though I had a happy childhood, sometimes I felt blank."
"Lonely."
"When my puppy died I felt blank."
"Sad. How did you know she died?"
"I guessed. How did it happen?"

"It was all my fault. She was supposed to be in the kitchen, but I let her out and Unca thought she was a fox. She looked like a fox. It wasn't his fault."

"Why did you let her out?"

"To go to the bathroom."

"What would have happened if she'd gone in the kitchen?"

"We'd have had to get rid of her, of course. You can't have a dog that has accidents."

"And after that was one of the times you felt lonely?"

"Well, sure. Why wouldn't I?"

"Why indeed? Did you have any friends at school?"

"Oh no."

"Why so definite about it? Why wouldn't you have?"

"No special reason. Just because I was different from the other kids."

"In what way different?"

"I guess . . . it's hard to say this. That even then, I was Bitch. So my friends wouldn't have been people, would they? They'd have been dogs. Only after Foxy died, I never had any. That's why I was lonely sometimes."

"Tell me about Foxy."

"What's there to tell? This little mixed-breed dog, I don't even know where she came from. Maybe she was a stray. She was brown and she had white on her tail, like a fox. She'd get so excited to see me, her tail would go round in circles. She'd . . . Why are you doing this to me?"

"Bitch dearest, you said you were too old for hugs when you were ten. Do you think you're too old for one now?"

"Maybe . . . not."

"Go down now, send Vixen. Sleep.

"Are you hungry again by now? There's some stew left."

"Hungry, bored, suppose I took the body out somewhere? How would you stop me?"

"I wouldn't even try. Was that how you got into such terrible trouble, because you were bored?"

"What trouble?"

"You know what trouble. 'Thank Bear for me if you see her.'"

"You don't have to do that now. I did it myself."

"Did you indeed? What did she say?"

"That she tore his head off. Bloodthirsty lady, old Bear."

"Good thing, too. Where does Bear live?"

"In the back of beyond. Hardly social, old Bear. Way back in the big deep woods, by the well where the other one lives."

"What other one?"

"You know. The ninth sister."

"So the way to the well lies through Bear."

"You might as well say, on the other side

of the great water. You'd sail off the edge of the world first."

"Yet the world is round. We can sail till we come to the far shore."

"Then climb the highest mountain in the world, and still not be there. I'm not messing with Bear anymore."

"Tell me about this man who attacked you. Was it someone you knew?"

"A slight acquaintance, you might say."

"Why did he do it?"

"Why? You, a woman, you can ask that? He was a creepy-crawly worm from the black swamp. That's what those things do."

"Yes, but my impression is that you were rooting around in there. Did you do anything to stir him up?"

"Nothing. Played with his head a little, who doesn't?"

"Turned out to be dangerous."

"Turned out I can handle myself."

"Not exactly so. Can you count on Bear to be there every time?"

"Why not?"

"Because in the winter she sleeps deep?"

"No matter. Falcon wakes her."

"Really? Tell me about that."

"I heard him scream as I went down, and Bear came. So now I'm going out, and I won't be back till late."

"Go ahead. I'll be here."

"You're really not going to try and stop me?"

"Of course not."

"Maybe I'll stay long enough to eat. I'm hungry, and I don't seem to have any money."

"I'll gladly lend you some."

"No need when there's good food here."

"I hear you've been saying I'm going to kill all but one of you."

"So? You say you're not?"

"Dearest Vixen, if you think I'm a mass murderer, why are you sitting here with me eating my stew?"

"Why not? Why die hungry?"

"Are you scared of dying?"

"Who isn't?"

"But I mean dying soon, as a result of this work we're doing."

"Maybe I'll get lucky. I'm a born survivor."

"Oh? What have you had to survive?"

"You know. Like the snake from the black swamp?"

"You said 'worm' last time."

"Worm, snake, what's the difference?"

"How do you feel about snakes?"

"The long skinny kind that crawl around on the ground? I've never met any socially."

"What about when you were a kid on the farm? There are garters around there, black-snakes, even a few copperheads and timber rattlers."

"Don't remember them."

"Anyway, I have no intention of killing any of you. But in return for my mercy, I would like you to tell me why you're hungry all the time."

"I guess I have a rapid metabolism."

"You've also got rapid answers, don't you?"

"Sharp as a fox, that's me."

"Did you get enough to eat as a child?"

"Sure, why would you ask? It was a farm. We grew food."

"What would typical meals consist of?"

"Stuff from the garden—corn, potatoes. A lot of chicken, and ham, they slaughtered pigs every year. Really, what are you getting at?"

"You sound anxious, but you needn't be. Vixen dear, from the look of that plate, I believe you were deprived of something basic as a child. And we need to know what it was. Did your mother or stepfather take away meals as punishment?"

"I guess so, but it was certainly no big deal. All parents do that."

"How do you know?"

"I'm not sure, but I know it's true. Maybe Unca told me."

"And do sharp foxes believe everything they're told?"

"So maybe he didn't. Maybe I read it somewhere. Why is this such a big deal?"

"Because digging for the truth is always a big deal. And foxes are good at digging, aren't they?"

"If there's anything worth digging for."

"Well? Is there?"

"What do you want to know?"

"Tell me about losing meals. What would you have done?"

"Basically it was accidents. I was a hyper kid, always running around and into stuff. So if I'd break something, like I'd get going too fast when I was setting the table and drop a plate? Ma-Ma's nerves couldn't take that. Big trouble."

"Was that an issue in your house? Ma-Ma's nerves?"

"Yeah, I had to be quiet all the time, and you know how kids are. What you would call a normal generational conflict?"

"Yet my brother and I were rowdy, and we dropped things, and we were never deprived of a single meal."

"You were lucky."

"Yes, we were. Did you ever lose more than one meal in a single day?"

"Unca used to say, I don't know what's going to slow you down short of starving you to death. But he was kidding. Anyway, I had ways of getting around it."

"Tell me."

"Well, it was like . . . I couldn't get anything out of the kitchen because Unca kept track of it. He'd know, I found that out. So I'd sneak out in the garden after dark and take stuff. Or apples off the tree."

"Did he ever catch you at it?"

"Sometimes he did."

"What would happen then?"

"It was sort of a game we'd play. Only not exactly. I'd see him at the back door, he'd call out to me. 'Any foxy little thief in the apple tree, better climb pretty high and hide pretty . . .'"

"Vixen, what is it?"

"What happened? Why am I on the floor?"

"You fainted. Your eyes went blank and rolled back and you slumped over. Stay still a minute till you're better."

"But I never faint. I don't do that."

"What you were saying about what Unca said--it loosed some big memory. What was it?"

"Not a memory. I heard them right behind me, right here in the room. You didn't? I must be going crazy."

"Heard what?"

"Hounds."

"Running after you? To hurt you?"

"Kill. Tear and kill. What else do hounds do?"

"Have you ever heard them up here before? When you were in this body?"

"Never. Always down below, never here. What's happening to me?"

"What's been hidden for all this time is stirring around down there. You're getting leakage into your conscious mind."

"My God, how do I jam the plug back in? What are you doing to me?"

"Bringing you to consciousness, to a new birth. Vixen dearest, we've got to pull that plug all the way out and look at what flows. Tell me again what he said."

"Any foxy little thief in the apple tree, better climb high and hide good."

"That wasn't quite it. It sounded different."

"Close enough. It wasn't what he said, anyway, it was what he did. I'd have to stay in that tree all night."

"All *night*? How old were you?"

"Eight, nine."

"What would happen in the morning?"

"Nothing. They'd be eating breakfast, but I'd know it wasn't for me. Just hike on out to the road to catch the school bus."

"Lunch at school?"

"Are you kidding?"

"You must have been pretty hungry. Had you done something pretty bad to deserve it?"

"I spilled milk on Ma-Ma's Bible once. Was that it? Defaced the holy word."

"You must have been pretty scared. What happened?"

"No more milk for me until I paid for it. I don't know how long it took. In fact I don't remember ever getting it paid for."

"How would you have earned money to pay for it?"

"I don't remember."

"You had a pretty hard time of it, didn't you?"

"Not so bad. There were good times too."

"Pretty rough on a little girl, depriving her of milk. If you got any milk at all from your mother's breast, I bet it was pretty cold. I bet it was pretty sour."

"*Why do you keep saying 'pretty'?*"

"Vixen, do you hear the hounds?"

"Yes, goddamn you, they're here!"

"When else did you hear them?"

"When the snake came, when he came to rape me, he said . . . "

"What did he say?"

"I better give him a pretty good ride."

"And where had you heard that word before?"

"Who knows? It's a common word."

"But commonest on whose lips? Of all the people you've known?"

"You don't have to ask, do you?"

"Who was he—the snake?"

"Thing from the swamp."

"Dig deeper. Who was he really?"

"He was Unca."

"*Was* Unca? Not just like him?"

"That can't be. Unca must be sixty by now. He can't have been over thirty."

"Can't be. But it was?"

"How? What could it mean?"

"Vixen darling, it means that what the snake threatened to do to you made you feel, at a very deep level, just the way some of the things Unca did to you made you feel."

"That makes no sense. All he did was send me to bed without my supper."

"I'm afraid he did a great deal more than that."

"He can't have."

"Suppose he were to walk into this room right now? How would you feel? What would you do?"

"I'd go down. Send for Bear."

"Just as you did when the snake came. Well then?"

"But why can't I remember?"

"Because, darling, it hurts too much to remember. Only, over the long journey of a lifetime, it hurts worse not to."

"I'm scared. What should I do?"

"How do you feel about being where you were, in the woods with some of your sisters?"

"Scared. Scared to death. There's something bad in those woods."

"Then I think . . . can you get to the Wild Woman's house?"

"I don't know. How would I find it?"

"I think Falcon will guide you."

"But what if she won't let me in? She wouldn't let Bitch."

"Tell her I sent you--or you won't have to, she'll know already. She'll let you in, knowing this is the time of your need. You'll eat well and sleep safe there."

"Thank you."

"You're more than welcome, dearest. Send me Cat.

"You look angry."

"Why wouldn't I be? Stuck down there with a pack of bitchy dogs."

"Bitchy meaning how they act, or that they're female?"

"How they act because they're female. Cunts."

"Your sisters."

"So you say. Why should I believe you?"

"Vixen got you out of the house."

"Who said I wanted to go?"

"I understand you were talking with her."

"Best of a bad lot. What am I supposed to do, go off by myself and go crazy?'"

"I thought cats liked to be alone."

"Not this one."

"Who do you like to be with?"

"Take a wild guess."

"Well, let's see. Was it you who had the dinner date at the Herdic House the other night?"

"It would have to be, wouldn't it? Who else has that kind of taste?"

"In restaurants, or in men?"

"Are you kidding? Restaurants."

"So what was the problem with the man?"

"The poor dear fell head over heels in love. Wasn't happy with what he was getting. Wanted me to marry him."

"And what was he getting?"

"For the line of work you're in, darling, you strike me as dense. He was getting me."

"In bed?"

"In bed, on the kitchen table, bent over the back of the sofa—why limit oneself?"

"Then I presume you don't limit yourself to one man?"

"I take what I like, darling. And what I like, every man is equipped with."

"What do you do about birth control?"

"Trust my good luck, and why not? It's never failed me yet."

"I'm not so sure it's luck. The body changes physically depending on who's in it--Wolf's eyes are amber, yours are green. So if you have sex and go under, and Bitch, who hasn't, comes up . . . "

"The spayed bitch system of birth control— what a wonderful idea! Could we patent it?"

"I'm afraid it's not practical on a large scale. I also don't think Bitch is spayed. She's interested in men too."

"Creeps. I may have met one or two of them. But I bet you anything she's a virgin."

"That's probably true. Tell me, do you climax when you have sex?"

"What kind of crazy question is that? Of course I do. Why else would I have it?"

"Do you always, even if the man is too quick?"

"Always, darling. Without fail."

"Before the man, with him? Both?"

"Both. Once is not enough."

"Besides intercourse, what do you like doing

with men?"

"What else is there?"

"You're the experienced one of us two. You tell me."

"You mean like tying each other up?"

"Yes, have you done that?"

"They just like to think about it. They don't actually do it."

"But there are other things I'm sure men have wanted to do with you. Tell me about those."

"They like to suck my tits, and stick their fingers in my cunt, and fuck me."

"What else?"

"That's it, darling. What else is there?"

"Would you look into my mind and tell me what you see?"

"Boy, you've got a dirty mind."

"What did you see?"

"Woman kneeling, naked, with her back to me."

"What else?"

"There was a guy with her."

"And what did she have in her mouth?"

"I couldn't see."

"You could see very clearly. What was it?"

"You know."

"I do know, but I want you to tell me."

"I can't."

"I know you can't. You can say *cunt*, you can say *fuck*, but you can't say *cock* or *prick* or *penis*. Can you say any of those words even now?"

"Of course I can. I just don't want to."

"Have you ever seen a man's penis?"

"Of *course* I have. You think I'm some spayed bitch that does it in the dark?"

"Held an erect penis in your hand?

"In your mouth?

"Had a man come in your mouth?

"What does semen taste like?

"What does a penis feel like inside you?

"Dear Cat, is it true that you know nothing about any of that?

"Is it true that you're a virgin just like Bitch?

"You lead right up to it, don't you? You're both excited, all ready to go, but just before the last of the clothes come off you go down, and someone else who is not afraid to say *penis*, see *penis*, take *penis* into her—she does all that, carries it through, and you come back for the cuddling afterwards. Because what you truly desire is not sex, of which you are deathly afraid. What you desire is love. Dearest Cat, isn't all that true?"

"How could you have known? When I didn't even know myself?"

"I had already guessed."

"Then you're smart after all. Who is she?"

"She is the ninth sister, the one who lives in the well which Bear guards. And Bear guards it with vigilance, so that she gets out only at moments of sexual consummation. At such times the pressure is too great, and Bear, I think not knowing what she's doing, turns her head away or sleeps. When the moment has passed, your sister returns to the well, you return to the body, and all is as it was."

"Do you know her name?"

"From something Vixen said, I believe her name is Snake."

"I hate snakes. Loathe them. They scare me to death."

"I'd be mightily surprised if they didn't."

"But she's our sister? One of us?"

"Your sister, as is Rat. As is Spider, and all the rest."

"The rest I can live with. Dogs, but I can live with them. Spider is just Spider, in her web by the ceiling. Rat I caught, and she bit me, her fur tasted sour and earthy, but I can live with her. But Snake. So cold, all coiling."

"Coiling and shining, shimmering in the light. If ever we see her in the light."

"I hope I never do. I want things to be like they used to be. Live by myself in my own little room, and sleep."

"Forever and ever?"

"Sort of like being dead, I guess."

"Sort of."

"So what else do you want to know?"

"Tell me about your childhood. How old were you when you were born into this body?"

"Five or six? I think."

"Tell me about Unca."

"What about him? He was okay. He used to play hide and seek with me."

"Who'd be it?"

"Funny question. We'd take turns."

"And what happened when you caught him? Or he caught you?"

"Well . . . nothing. We'd play another round. I don't know what you're getting at."

"Did Unca ever touch you?"

"He'd hug me, swing me around--you mean touch me wrong?"

"That's what I mean."

"Nothing like that. I liked Unca a lot better than Ma-Ma. She never touched me at all. Just

sat around reading her Bible. Is that why there's
an open book in my room down below?"

"I imagine so. Can you read anything on the
page it's open to?"

"It doesn't even look like letters—just
squiggles. Why is that?"

"How old did you say you were?"

"Oh . . . right. That's how they looked to me
then?"

"I presume so. Cat, when I asked you about
Unca touching you, you were in a terrible hurry
to change the subject."

"Was I? I guess it just happened to happen."

"If Unca were to walk into this room right
now, how would you feel?"

"Fine . . . I guess."

"Well then, suppose we take a drive out
there. I'll drop you off and you can visit with
Unca and Ma-Ma, and I'll go see my people and
pick you up afterwards."

"They still live there?"

"They do."

"I'd want you there with me."

"Why is that? Wouldn't a stranger get in the
way of your reunion?"

"You're not a stranger!"

"I'm glad, but even so?"

"Maybe I don't really want to do that.

Ma-Ma was such a cold fish, who cares about
her?"

"What if we could arrange it when just
Unca was there? Your mother must go to town
sometimes."

"I don't think I want to."

"Why not?"

"I don't *know* why not. I just don't."

"Who do you think taught you to be terrified
of sex, and penis?"

"I guess that's just the way I am."

"Nobody's born that way, dear Cat. If you
come to it at the right time, the right way, sex is
a natural function."

"I don't know, then. It was a lonely farm.
Maybe somebody came . . . "

"A stranger, once? I doubt if that could have
done it. And you're uneasy about seeing Unca.
And the others have told me terrifying stories
about him."

"I don't want to hear them."

"No, I don't think you're ready for that. But
I think you can begin to face the truth. What do
you think that truth is?"

"He did touch me wrong?"

"Good for you, dear Cat. I'm certain he did,
not once but many times."

"But why can't I remember?"

"Too much pain. When the time is right,
when you're strong enough, we'll drag it all up
and look at it."

"What happens now?"

"Maybe you'd like to stay up here and walk
the body around for awhile—but stay away
from men?"

"I never want to see another man."

"At least you need a vacation from them.
While you're doing that, I'll rest a bit. Then,
when you go back down, go to the Wild
Woman's house—Falcon will guide you—and
send me Rat. One more question before you
go, an easy one. Did Unca or Ma-Ma give you
sweets?"

"That's funny. I can't remember them doing
that at all. Why do you want to know?"

"Because Rat is very young."

"Is that why I love chocolate?"

"Cat dearest, it's one more reason why all of
you, in your different ways, so deeply hunger."

Constance has forgotten her intent to rest
or forgotten how. She paces in her long green
gown, pausing at her jungle, her ocean, but this
night they cannot hold her. After awhile she
goes up into the kitchen. She puts a disc in the
player she keeps there; then, dancing lightly

to the fifth Brandenburg Concerto of Bach, she rolls up her sleeves, puts on her white canvas apron with "I've Got a Steak in Public Radio" in blue across the front, gets out flour and baking soda and eggs, butter, sugar, vanilla, chocolate and walnuts. Soon there is a mingling in the air, the sound of cookies baking with the smell of the harpsichord: a work of art in mixed media, by Constance.

When Cat gets back, wind-swept and ruddy-cheeked, the cookies are piled on a plate in the downstairs room. She grabs a pawful and stuffs. And so when Rat comes, her paw too is poised above the plate. There it remains for an agonizing time, uncountable seconds.

"Those are for you, dear Rat. Have all you like. There's cider there too."

"Why would you bake cookies for me?"
"Because I thought you would like them."
"Why would you care if I did?"
"Because I feel friendly toward you, dear Rat, and I'd like to know you better."
"You can't say dear Rat. Rat isn't dear."
"I think this one is. This one is very special. And maybe hungry?"

"How do I know they're not poisoned?"
"How foolish of me. Of course you would need to know that, because of the terrible way that people treat rats. So how can we make

sure? Let's figure it out together."

"You could eat some first."

"I would be glad to, Rat dearest. I've
been working for a long time, and I'm hungry
myself."

"But what if you had certain ones picked out
that you knew were safe?"

"That would be very clever. I'd never have
thought of it, even if I'd wanted to harm anyone.
But listen, here's an idea—you pick some out
for me to eat. Take them from the bottom, the
middle, anywhere. That way, you see . . . "

"You couldn't guess where to put the good
ones. Take these."

"They're delicious, if I do say so. Is anything
better than a fresh chocolate chip cookie? Now
you?"

"They're good."

"Have some cider? It's the last of the
season, still fresh and nice. "

"You first."

"Yes, and see—the glasses are clean and
dry. Pick which one you want, and I'll take the
other."

"The cider is good too. What is this going to
cost me?"

"Not a thing, Rat darling. Chocolate chip
cookies and cider are every child's birthright."

"What do you mean by that?"

"You ought to get good things just because

you're you. You don't have to earn them."

"You do. Yes you do. Everything costs."

"In some places that's true, but not here. Here the rules are different."

"What are they?"

"They're simple. You see the plants, the fish, the books on that shelf? Those are things that I like, and no one's allowed to harm them. But then you wouldn't want to do that anyway, would you?"

"I don't guess so. Why would I?"

"If you were very angry?"

"But I'm not."

"What if, by accident, I did something that scared you?"

"Like what?"

"Suppose I came up to you suddenly, when you weren't expecting it, and put my hand out to touch you."

"I wouldn't like that. I'd bite your face off."

"Rat dear, you're so smart--you followed another rule without even knowing it. And that is, we make our feelings clear to each other. You've told me unexpected touching is no good for you, so now I know not to do it. But suppose I put my hand on the table like this, palm up, right next to the cookie plate where it's been already. And then asked you, would you like to put your hand on mine?"

"What if you grabbed it?"

"Then I would be breaking another very important rule, which is no touching except friendly touching, and friendly touching only by permission."

"I could always pull away."
"Of course you could. You're much taller and stronger than I am."

"I guess I am. Then why aren't you afraid to be alone with me?"
"Because you're my friend, Rat dearest, and friends don't hurt each other."

"You can have my hand."
"Thank you, dearest. Could I hold it gently?"

"All right, but how do I tell you when I want you to let go?"
"Pull back just a little, and I'll know—try."

"Yes, that was good. I didn't even have to pull that hard. Let's try again, only this time, I let go when you pull back.

"It was easy. I could tell right away. But how do I know it will always work?"
"It will always work with me, and you find that out just by trying. It's safe to try, because you're stronger, remember? We can even hug,

if you're willing, and if you don't like it then
just push me away. Only not too hard, because I
don't want to fall down and hit my head."

"That was all right. It wasn't scary. Could
we do it again?"

"Of course, dear Rat. That's what we're here
for."

"But what if I got scared all of a sudden and
hurt you?"

"I don't think that will happen, but it's a
chance I'm prepared to take."

"Why? That doesn't make sense."

"Because how can I make friends with you if
I don't get as close as you're willing to let me?"

"I don't know why you'd want to."

"Because, dearest Rat, you are lovable."

"Oh no. No, not me, you're thinking of
somebody else. I'm Rat."

"Nobody, when you were first born into this
body, ever told you they loved you?"

"Of course not. Don't you get it? I'm Rat."

"You're Rat, *and* you have silky brown hair
and beautiful brown eyes, *and* you like chocolate
chip cookies and hugs, *and* that makes you
lovable."

"What do you want of me?"

"The cost again? There is no cost. I want you
to talk to me if you feel like it. I want you to

not talk to me if you don't feel like it. I will love
you either way."

"What would we do if we didn't talk?"
"Have some more cookies. Look at the fish.
Hug."
"Let's do that for awhile.

"I like the fish. What kind is that long
skinny one?"
"He's a moray eel. His big cousins in the
ocean eat anything that swims near enough."
"Do they coil around them like a snake?"
"Just bite, I think—also like a snake."
"Is their bite poison?"
"No, but it's strong, and their teeth are
angled in—whatever they get hold of is dinner."
"He's kind of scary."
"He's only a foot long, and he's swimming
around behind thick glass, and he'd die right
away out of water. Are other things that get
hold of you and won't let go . . . scary?"
"Not things."
"People?"

"You never finished telling me. You said
you would always let me go if I told you to,
and anyway I could make you because I was
stronger. But what if it was somebody else, and
I wasn't?"
"Are we talking about now, or when you

were little?"

"Now?"

"Something like that happened to your sister Vixen. A bad man tried to hurt her, so she went down and Bear came. Bear fought the man and drove him away. And that is what you would do. If you're in the body and you're threatened, go down at once and stay with the Wild Woman where you're safe. It's no business of yours, at your age, to be fighting people. It will be taken care of."

"Funny you mentioned her. I was scared of her at first. Thought she was a witch."

"Many do. Have you had any troubles with witches?"

"How do you mean?"

"Well, for example, did your mother seem like a witch to you?"

"Not exactly."

"Do you know the story of Hansel and Gretel?"

"Yes, that's why I thought that. About the Wild Woman."

"Was your mother like any of the characters in that story?"

"The wicked stepmother."

"Why is that?"

"I don't know exactly. Was that a bad thing to say?"

"No, because it was true. That's exactly who she was like."

"How do you know?"

"Your sisters told me. She gave them no love, did nothing to protect them, so we can be sure she was the same with you."

"Protect them from what?"

"Dearest Rat, this is hard for me to say and hard for you to hear. From your stepfather. From Unca."

"Really? He wasn't so bad. He read to me."

"What did he read?"

"Fairy stories, like what we were just talking about."

"All right, let's do that too. Could you tell me about Hansel and Gretel, just the way you remember it?"

"I'd have to know which one."

"There was more than one?"

"The one when I'd been good, and the one when I'd been bad. Except I was pretty much always bad."

"Tell me that one then, but just quick. Tell me the ending."

"Where the witch eats them up? Only if I was real bad, she'd hurt them first."

"And what did you do that was bad,

darling?"

"I don't remember. Can you believe it? I don't remember at all."

"I can easily believe it, dearest. Because you did nothing bad."

"I didn't?"

"No, nothing, never. You were an innocent little child. Would you like me to hold you?"

"Yes, please."

"Would you like me to tell you the story as it truly goes?"

"Yes, please."

"Once upon a time, at the edge of the forest, there lived a poor woodcutter. He had two children, a boy and a girl, and their names were Hansel and Gretel . . ."

"And was the witch truly dead, burned to ashes and gone forever?"

"She was, darling."

"And they truly lived happily ever after?"

"Yes, dearest."

"It's a nice story the way you tell it. Is it true?"

"It's true, every word."

"I feel so sleepy."

"It's been a long day for you, dearest Rat. Have the last cookie if you'd like it, and go home to the Wild Woman and sleep. But first, if you would be so kind, ask her if Falcon will bring Spider up here."

"I'm Rat, ugly and dangerous. I carry germs, everyone hates me. If I'd be so *kind*?"

"You're Rat, beautiful, clean, gentle, and I love you."

"You gave me cookies with no poison in them. I'll ask Wild Woman."

"Spider is here. I am looking through the eyes of this body as through windows at the world you see. You could say that she is perched on my shoulder, looking also."

"Is there anything I could do that would make her happy?"

"Just now she is well-fed and sleepy from her time with Wild Woman. Watching the fish soothes her, and that's why I'll stand here while we talk."

"What can you tell me that I need to know?"

"Nothing, I believe, that you haven't learned for yourself."

"What is that, then? They lived with a woman who was no mother. She was an Ice Witch, a blasphemer with a cross of white frost where her warm red heart should be. Her own

child froze to death in her womb and she stole a
child and offered her up on her altar of ice to be
tortured and murdered. And she was tortured
daily for all the years of her childhood, out of
a satanic hatred whose aim was to break her
mind and spirit. And a black lust which meant
to eat her alive. And yet she was not broken and
did not die. She carries scattered memories of
mental torture, but none of rape. Snake holds
those, and the way to Snake is through Bear.
Without those two, I believe we can go no
farther."

"And then?"

"Bear first. Can you bring her?"

"If I brought her by force from her work,
guarding the well, it would break her mind."

"Wild Woman, then?"

"She does as she pleases. She lives by no
laws but her own. Have you forgotten the
meaning of her name?"

"So it will have to be one of the sisters. Wolf
or Coyote."

"Wolf is afraid of Bear."

"And Coyote runs fastest, is trickiest, moves
easily between the near and the far woods. Will
you send me Coyote?"

"What you want her to do will be difficult
and dangerous. The woods down below are no
longer safe. And she herself is sleeping deeply,
and when she wakes, the wounds the two of
you opened will bleed. I don't know if she has

enough blood in her now for long running, and so I will not send her. But when she wakes, I'll ask her."

And the fierce far-seeing eyes, the amber eyes of Falcon are gone. The eyes that remain are the blue of the empty sky. Constance sits with her head bowed into her hands, grieving; desiring only sleep, too weary even to pray. In a little while she does pray. *Let me conjure the strong medicines, the cunning tools. Why else was I placed on earth?*

"Coyote dearest, here you are after all. Sit quietly and share tea with me for awhile."

"That's not what you wanted me for."

"It is, just not all of what I wanted. Did Falcon tell you?"

"He said I had no blood to spare, and you were not to shed any. What you could want me for other than bloodletting made me curious, so I came."

"Then I'd better tell you at once, so you can say yes or no and be done with it. I want you to fetch Bear to the others, and get her to come up here so I can talk with her."

"We all went to her before. She can't be fetched. She might kill whoever tried."

"She could hardly do that, dear Coyote. Aren't you the fastest of all the dogs? And she wouldn't chase you far from the well, anyway."

"So I go on a long walk through the woods with nothing to eat, come near the well. Bear stands high as a tree, growls loud as thunder, I run back again with nothing to eat. What's the good of that?"

"I was thinking you might persuade her to come with you by means of a trick."

"And what might that be?"

"You would devise it, Coyote dearest. Aren't you the cleverest of them all?

"Which is hardly saying much. But I'm too hungry to think of tricks."

"That problem we can easily solve. What would you like?"

"Steak, red in the middle. Baked potatoes with both sour cream and butter. Asparagus. Red wine. Whatever was on that plate."

"And all that you shall have, only first we'll have to go to the store. Shall we go together?"

"I'd rather stay here. I feel safe here and I need to rest. Only hurry back, or you'll return to a fish tank with no fish in it."

"Coyotes eat fish?"

"I eat what I can find, and still, always, I am hungry."

"First we will feed the hunger of the body, Coyote darling, and then, and I hope it will not be so long now, the hunger of the soul."

Coyote comes into her body, rough-furred, prick-eared, long-striding, in deep twilight in a wood she has never known. How is she to know which way to travel? She turns full circle, seeing only trees, hearing only wind in trees, smelling only the whiteness of old bones. There is no one way. And so abruptly, without thought, she simply goes. Her going starts something else moving, bones clicking and clattering together, leg and hip and rib, spine, shoulder, neck, skull, the Shadow Deer up and running behind, beside, ahead of her: a whole rattling boneyard announcing her name.

Something hears. There is something heavy abroad now in the woods, its footfall masked first by the lighter cacophony of Deer, by the trip-hammer pounding of the heart of Coyote, then for a little time by Coyote's fear of her fear.

It is nothing at all.

It is everything at once, the beating of the heart of earth.

Wild Woman, come to guide me on my way. Shall I stop and call her?

It is nothing.

A nothing whose feet drive the breath out of earth's body. Drive blood in fountains out of earth's heart.

The thing that rapes and renders dolls.

She runs in the dark. Whatever it is can see in the dark, for that is where it lives. She is the fastest of all the dogs, but this is no dog, and she will never outrun it, for it is walking behind her on its legs like tree trunks and growing

nearer. It will trip, catch, bind, stab, crush.
Devour. For she has just now remembered. Has
known it all her life.

And knows therefore the one trick that may
stay it, remembering *I am Coyote, the smart one*—
if she can find what she needs in time. And the
forest gives it to her, a tree with two trunks,
split at the ground. She stands between.

As she goes still, Deer goes still. All goes
still, and then the heavy tread three trees, and
two trees, and one tree away. And a flash of
white, rising almost to the treetops. It is the
bones of Deer, in a hand too dark to see in
the dark. Flung splinters of white bone shine
like shooting stars, mark her, one catching hot
in her fur, she springs away as the looming
darkness lurches into the vee of the trunks,
and, for just the moment she has to have, hangs
there, the tree creaking, shaking to the tips of
its twigs, while Coyote, the fastest dog, runs
for her life. There is a great thrashing, a shower
of leaves. One lands on her back, extinguishes
the bone-spark. Coyote, the cleverest dog, lies
down in a little hollow. She is mottled gray and
formless, silent and without scent, disguised
as the raw material of creation. It is quiet now,
the stalker's quiet. Then the great thudding
footfalls, receding, and the quiet of earth at rest.

She goes on with no heart for it, tail
dragging. She is lost, wandering in a place
where all she knows of the trees is *hard on the*

blundering nose, cold, smooth, every one alike.
Hungry again—nothing to eat. Thirsty—nothing
to drink. Blind. On she goes for a minute, for
hours, for the remaining days of her life. Until
at some time she hears a snuffling growl ahead
of her, and she sees a shadow darker than the
darkness, and that is Bear.

The well lies ahead. You may not pass this way.

*I am your sister, Coyote. Come away from this
dark place. Return with me to the morning country.*

*My place is here and only here. I may not go,
you may not stay. Go now, Little Sister.*

*I'm afraid to go alone. There's a terrible thing in
the woods. Come with me.*

*I know of that thing, and I too fear it. I have no
strength against it. Little Sister, run fast.*

Coyote turns and trots back into the woods.
A trick? What is there here to play a trick with?
Is she supposed to conjure one out of the air?

She sits on her lean haunches, throws back
her head, and howls. The moon appears, borne
swiftly in the talons of Falcon. Falcon drops it at
her feet, where it rolls, wobbles, falls flat, splat-
tering her with silver light.

She picks it up in her mouth, leans it on
edge against a tree. Stands near it, casting her
long-legged shadow on the ground. When
she picks it up again, Shadow remains there.
Lightly she breathes her wailing, yodeling cry
into it, then, as Shadow yodels, runs fast with
the moon. With the water-scent of Well now

strong in her nose, she circles, making seven
more loud Shadows. That makes eight, but the
ninth is quiet. The ninth is Coyote with the
moon hidden in her mouth. Off somewhere
in the distance she hears Bear crashing about,
growling and cursing. But curse all she likes, it
does her no good, for Coyote has come to the
well.

She sticks her head over the edge and looks
down, but she can see nothing; so she takes the
moon out and holds it over the water. Now she
sees the head of Coyote, with the silvery disk of
the moon in her mouth. And deeper, a long way
down toward the center of the earth, a wavering
luminescence, blue and green. That is Snake. But
she has no desire to see if Snake will come up.
Instead she holds the moon out over the water,
one side down and then the other, then on edge,
turning it in her mouth with her clever tongue.
Now it is stained blue and green, the colors of
Snake.

Bear knows she's been tricked by now.
Coyote hears her coming. She runs, rolling the
moon on its edge ahead of her. Thus she leaves
behind her the shining blue-green track of
Snake.

She runs a long way into the woods, her fear
growing in her. What will Bear do when she
learns the truth? But that is nothing. She can run
faster than Bear, but *if Bear can follow, the Other
can follow.* So at last she has to stop. She hangs

up the moon in the branches of a little bush,
hides herself behind a tree, and waits.

She does not have to wait long. First she
hears Bear snuffling along the trail. Then smells
her strong wild smell. Then sees her, a humped
black shadow in the moonlight. When Bear sees
the moon, she stands on her hind legs and roars.
She swats the moon with one great paw, and it
flies into the sky, splintering as it goes. The sky
is filled with stars.

Little Sister, are you here?

I am here, Great Sister.

*Why have you done this thing? Snake must be
loose by now.*

Are you afraid of Snake?

*I remember her coiling around me and
swallowing me in her great jaws. Yes, I am afraid.*

You cannot return her to the well.

Out is out. She is loose in the woods behind us.

Then why did you think to follow her?

*Because I thought, what better way to die? I have
no life now.*

*Your life is with us, Great Sister. Come with me
now to the morning country.*

Why should I?

*Talk to Constance, our friend in the Person
Place. She will tell you.*

*I have no friend, and I care nothing for my
sisters. I will come because, now, one place is like
any other.*

And so they walk along through the starlit woods, but before very long they hear the thudding footsteps behind them.

Run, Great Sister.

But Bear cannot run as fast as Coyote, who thinks: *It will catch her first, take a long time to eat her, and may sleep after that; so I will get away.* They run, Coyote slowing to stay with her sister, thinking: *How can I be such a fool, having no more tricks for either of us?* The ground behind them shakes. Bear can run no faster. *Go,* she cries, *Little Sister, save yourself,* and *Go,* Coyote thinks, as bushes crackle, trees bend in the storm overtaking them, as into the clearing behind them lurches a great booted foot. They run, trip, tangled in a swathing darkness, netted in a night which suddenly is warm and smells of old frog. For they have run into the black skirt of Wild Woman.

Ogre, do you think to harm my daughters?

The forest is silent.

Wild Woman picks up Coyote in one hand and Bear in the other, puts them in her pockets, and carries them home.

Bear paces in a blackness she draws around her. It is a dark water which laps at Constance's feet. Out of it Bear's eyes burn red.

"It was you who did this. Sent Coyote to trick me."

Bear is dangerous, and Constance is alone with her.

"It's true. I needed to talk to you."

"And now Snake is loose."

"What does it mean, that she's loose?"

"Nothing to you. Why should it? But see what your meddling has done. She will hunt us down one at a time in the dark and swallow us."

"Even you? She must be a mighty Snake."

"Snake can swallow the world."

"Then how, for all these .years, were you able to keep her in the well?"

"When she wanted to come out, she came. And went back in again. She lived in the well. Now she lives in the woods."

"How do you know?"

"I know."

"But have you seen, heard, smelled her? Heard even a rumor of her?"

"You think she's stayed?"

"You said yourself that she came out when she wanted. But just now there is nothing to draw her out."

"What would draw her?"

"Snake is the sexual energy belonging to this body. You didn't know that?"

"I've seen her only through deep water—a writhing of blue and green coils. Snake is terrible."

"And beautiful?"

"I would not want to get close enough to see."

"She lives in the cold depths, in the dark. I'd like to bring her out into the sunlight and talk with her."

"She has no voice but the scraping of scales on rock. She will not come out and she will not speak."

"You sound proud of her."

"I have lived with her all my life. No one can know her as I do. Certainly not you."

"Then I'm glad you're here to tell me about her. Could she swallow the Ogre?"

"What do you know of him?"

"He takes different forms. One was that of the man who was going to hurt Vixen."

"That was just a man. I killed him with one blow."

"He hurt you first with his knife?"

"A little cut, here. Nothing."

"Yes, across your belly, just where a surgeon would cut to lift a baby out. Does it still sting?"

"A little, and what does it matter?"

"I want to be sure you know what body you're in. You see your hands, your arms? You could not kill a grown man with one blow."

"I did, though."

"I think you got the knife away from him somehow and cut him with it—there was blood all over. Only during that fight, you lived altogether in the body of Bear, with her great strength and wildness. That was how you were able to win. Also, why you thought the man was dead."

"But he was not the Ogre."

"Why do you think not?"

"Because I'm still alive."

"Ah. But up here, you see, the Ogre is diminished. Not twelve feet high, but six. Still dangerous, but if you're savvy, go armed and alert, you can avoid or defeat him. It's the Ogre down below we have to think about. What if all of you fought him together?"

"What if nine ants fought him together? He'd crush us under his boot and that would be the end of us."

"We'll have to think of something else, then. But Wild Woman's not afraid of him."

"Wild Woman has strong magic."

"Yes, and I wonder if we could borrow some of that somehow? Only, Bear dearest, for magic to work, you have to have all the ingredients. We're missing Snake, and she is important. I don't think we can get any farther without her."

"Nevertheless, I will not go into the woods to be crushed by the Ogre. I will not go into the well to be devoured by Snake."

"I wouldn't want to either. Where is your home now, down below?"

"I have no home. I stay in the clearing by the woodpile, with the others."

"The Ogre doesn't come there?"

"Wild Woman lives too close, I think. But we hear him at night. He's growing bolder. All the deep woods are his, and the edge of the near woods."

"Then we need to beat him back, chain him up, cut off his hands and feet. To do that, maybe you all need to see him as he is in this world. You will see that he's small."

"He's alive still? Here?"

"Sixty miles from here, by paved roads almost the whole way. Would you be afraid to go and see him?"

"But what of the others? The smaller ones?"

"You and Wolf would be with them."

"I believe I am afraid."

"Of course. Yet you defeated the Ogre when he was armed with a knife."

"But there was no one there to say, *Thou shalt not kill.* I could strike him down and be done with him."

"Who used to say that to you?"

"Ma-Ma. And the other one."

"What other?"

"Commandment. Honor thy father and thy mother. Would Ma-Ma be there?"

"I'm sure she would."

"Then I won't go."

"Maybe you've been too long alone, guarding the well. What if you went back down and talked it over with your sisters?"

"I still won't."

"And there's one other thing you might do together, all eight of you. Search the house."

"What house?"

"Where Unca and Ma-Ma and you used to live. Where the two of them still live up here."

"What good would that do?"

"You might find something of interest. Treasure has to be searched for."

"Does anyone live there now?"

"That's something you'd find out."

The eyes turn empty sky blue. Constance closes her own eyes, covers them with her hands.

First Bitch leads them, trotting through the woodlot where only a few pale violets bloom. In a hundred yards they will come to the edge of the woods, the house then plainly visible across the field. Only the woods go on. There is no field and no house.

So Cat leads for a time, since she if anyone, having lived there, ought to know her way back; and Vixen leads with her head high, testing the air for the scent of apples; and Wolf

for sight, and Coyote for trickery, slipping up
on it by running from it; Rat on Wolf's back
for hunger, Spider on Vixen's head for blind
wanting; but Bear trails always, shuffling along
at the back edge of sight, and none dare ask her
to lead. They search for days and nights and
days, wandering in woods which none of them
know. There are no signs of the Ogre, or of Wild
Woman or her house, and the sky is empty.

    None of them can say when they first
noticed the change. A slight wavering mistiness,
not in the air but in the quality of solid things
around them. Trees shimmer as in the first light
of morning, yet the sun is high, dappling the
ground at their feet. The light spreads out, rolls
smooth; a cloud must have crossed the sun, but
it is not that, the sun is shining through leaves
grown translucent. Wolf looks back at Bear and
sees, under her black coat, ripples of red which
are muscle, flashes of white which are bone.
And so, when she looks forward again, with
the house. She cannot quite see through the
walls, the door, the dim green curtains, but it is
only a matter of angles. Nor can she say if the
barnyard is boneyard, a litter of upright articu-
lated skeletons, chicken and hawk and crow, rat,
fox, dog, and deer, or if they are clothed in flesh
she cannot see. She herself, front paws and flank
and tail, is Wolf in rough gray fur; but Coyote
ahead of her is mostly bone. Coyote's eyes are
empty of all but fear. Her voice is thin, for there

is not enough air between them to carry it.

Should we run?

We'd be running bones, and what after that? What then?

Here is what we came to find. What else?

She leads them across the boneyard. And now she hears, they all hear, a thin milling commotion of chickens, the bones moving around them, skulls ducking to peck at earth like brown foam. Flanking bony Coyote, the bones of Deer. Nuzzling the knobby white neck of Bitch, the cold white nose of Dog, or Fox, Vixen-sized. They will never get to the house. If they do, there will be nothing left of them weighty enough to push the door open. Wolf's paws are sinking in something she can't see which is swallowing her, water she never learned to swim or breathe in; she chokes, raises her head for the howl that will sound her passing, and sees, sun glinting off each feather, off beak and talons and golden eyes, Falcon circling in the blue sky above them. Falcon cries once, and twice, and three times, and the earth comes together under and around them, Coyote's fleshed and furred self snaps into being, with just that sharp-edged clatter which freezes everything that creeps or runs or flies in the forest, a rifle bolt loading a round into the chamber . . . and they stand all together there in the barnyard, among scattered dry bones.

*Did you hear that? He's in the house. He'll shoot
us if we move.*

Then he'll shoot us if we don't move.

Wolf leads the way to the door. From inside
the house there is no further sign. But the door
is locked and solid.

Bear?

Bear walks up to the door, rears tall against
it, smashes it down. They stand there looking
into the kitchen, which is clean, shaded except
for a shaft of light which trails along the gray
tiles of the floor. Hanging on the wall next to
the window is a wooden plaque saying *God
Bless Our Home*. The room smells of the kindling
stacked in a crate next to the stove, of ashes, of
bread. Someone was baking here an hour or two
ago, someone cleaned, wiped the flour-spills off
the countertop, hung up the rag she used over
the sink, and went away, leaving no other sign.

Wolf leads the way in—guiltily wondering,
in this place they have broken into and are now
invading, if she's leaving paw-marks on the
clean floor. The others crowd in around her.

What do we do now?

*Explore the rest of it. Who will go first into the
next room?*

I will. I lived there.

Cat on her light paws stalks through the
open doorway into the living room, looks
around and returns.

No one is there, but a fire is burning and the book is open on the table. The clock is running. It says twelve o'clock. Everything looks as it did, and I heard nothing except the fire crackling, but I smelled blood.

Wolf leads, puts her front paws on the table (her claws will scratch it), looks at the book, sees not even words. She looks at Coyote beside her, who, far from being careful, is raking the polished wood as if to dig a hole in it.

What are you doing?

Leaving my mark. What's the good of coming here, otherwise? We all ought to.

Wolf scrapes once, lightly. Pain jolts from her pad into her paw, her shoulder.

Splintery?

No. I don't know. Can you read the hook?

I wouldn't even know it was writing.

Nor I, but why not? I could read perfectly well when I lived here.

Did you ever have a chance to read that hook?

I had heard about the Song of Solomon somehow. Somebody giggling about it at school. I went down late one night to look at it. I was curious.

And?

The pages were glued together.

Coyote barks her laughter.

Do you smell the blood?

Over there behind the couch.

They go and look, crowding up behind some of the others, Cat, Vixen, and Bitch. It is a brown-haired plastic doll, in red blouse, white skirt, shiny black shoes. Her hands and face and clothes are stained with moist dark earth. Her skirt is tossed up around her waist, her pubic hair matted with blood. Her eyes are blue, blank as the sky.

Whose was she?
No one speaks.
Cat?
No.
Vixen?

Maybe she was mine.
Where did you get her?
I don't know.
They never gave us gifts. Certainly not gifts like that.

I think my father sent her.

You knew our father?
I didn't know him. She came one day. I think he sent her. That was all.
How did she get like this?
I don't remember.
Where else should we go?
Up. The bedrooms.

But at the foot of the stairs, Coyote stops them. *What do you smell up there?*

Pig?

Filth of pig. Stay behind me.

Two steps below the landing *Rat?*

From her perch on Wolf's back, Rat has seen. She leaps to her work, biting with her teeth like yellow chisels, and the taut wire, ankle-high, snaps and springs aside. Coyote now leads them down the hall and into a large bedroom. It has two bureaus, a rocking chair, a bedside table and lamp; a big brass bed made up neatly with a white counterpane, and a bolt on the inside of the door. The smell is strong, but its source is not here. All but Spider gag on it as they walk on down the hall to a second room, its door ajar inward.

Careful. Bear?

With her deft paw, she hooks the reeking bucket from the top of the door.

You know where it goes?

Bear carries it back to the other bedroom and dumps it on the white bedspread. Coyote laughs and laughs.

Safe to go into the other room now?

Never safe, but we can go.

They crowd in. It is a cell with one bureau, a straight chair, a narrow wooden bed. The bolt is on the outside. The hackles on Wolf's neck rise, raising Rat with them.

I remember when he put that on. Bear?

With a single blow, Bear smashes the door.

Good. What else do we need to see up here?

Bathroom.

Coyote leads them. The fixtures are plain white porcelain, the floor gray tile like the kitchen floor. A thin brown towel, a little damp and sour, hangs from a rack. Someone has used this room within the past few hours, leaving no scent of himself. But there is another smell, out of place in a bathroom. Coyote sets her front paws on the rim of the claw-footed tub, then down inside. They skid out from under her, so that for a moment she hangs flailing by her belly on the edge. She scrambles back out, raises a paw and sniffs; then drags the towel down and scrabbles on it with both paws.

Oil. I should have remembered.

Where are they? What if they come back and find us here?

There are eight of us. Bear is with us. And we need to search the cellar.

Unca will have his rifle.

He's twelve feet tall.

He's the Ogre. What if he's down there?

Then we'd better not all go. Rat, you lived there. Will you come with me?

No. I'm afraid. I'll stay in the kitchen.

Who, then? Coyote?

I'm afraid too, but I'll come.

Bear, watch over your little sisters in the kitchen.

The stairs are thick with dust. No one has been down here in a long time. Even with the door to the kitchen open, it is too dark at first to see. Wolf descends, dusty air harsh in her lungs, with Coyote behind her. They stand at the bottom together breathing the smells of Rat's home, rotten grain, paper, cider, stone. And something else.

Wolf?

I'm here.

There's someone down here.

How do you know?

I can smell her fear. In the blackest corner of this place, she's hiding from us.

She?

She's small, huddled. Displaces little air. Who else but she?

One of us?

Smaller. Younger.

Laurel? Little Girl?

From across the cellar they both hear her now, whimpering. A little light has seeped in, disclosing old barrels, rotting wooden and cardboard boxes. In one or behind one, Little Girl is hiding.

Coyote, you go first. You're smaller, younger.

Coyote noses her way across the room, Wolf following. The whimpering is louder. *Quiet, oh quiet, Little Girl. Is that any way to hide? If we meant you harm?* They find her in the blackest comer, too dark to see, but she shines a little with her own light. She is naked, wounded between her legs, thighs and belly caked with

dark blood. But her eyes are not empty sky blue.
Little Girl?

Her eyes are brown. She cannot speak, but
there is someone in there.

Coyote leans forward. Her tongue goes out
to wash the grime from Little Girl's face.

As it touches, Little Girl vanishes.

On the instant the cellar is gone. The house
is gone. They are standing under a bright
vaulted sky, the eight of them. Falcon circles
eight times, screaming his harsh cry. At the
junction of the ninth circle he wheels away,
ascends into the eye of the sun, and is lost to
their sight.

Chapter Four

Wolf paces the floor, six long strides from jungle to ocean and back again: awaiting the birth of something. In the instant of that birth, a dry rain of leaves falls. Ocean freezes; light into dark; and the limbs of Wolf, blood in her heart, tear in her eye. What remains is the howl in her throat, silence of the night before time.

So Constance finds her, stilled. She pauses at the doorway, then walks up softly, puts a light hand on her shoulder. And Wolf shakes a little, tossing her fear off her; now she can move and speak again, but her fear is a red mist in the air.

"You needn't tell me what he said."

"No?"

"'Gladly will we welcome the prodigal daughter.'"

"The connection was bad and he spoke low, but yes. Those words exactly. You heard with your inner ear?"

"With the hearing of Wolf. But who would have thought Wolf could be so afraid?"

"I would, dearest. Knowing her as I do."

"What was it like, talking to him?"

"We were both terribly polite. When I hung up the phone I was shaking."

"Did you sense anything wrong about him?"

"He'd had no contact with you in twenty years, he knows what he did to you—and he's going to see you today. Yet he was quite, quite calm. Dear Wolf, everything was wrong."

"I'm surprised they have a phone."

"Maybe they have family that calls them. Maybe they order clothes from L.L. Bean."

"Impossible. Both, either."

"Yet they wear clothes, and they are not widely known in town."

"You're saying they're ordinary? Just like anyone else?"

"Of course not. Hitler wore clothes. I'm saying to expect they'll be heavily disguised as ordinary."

"They'll deny everything."

"Yes, and not only that--they'll cast blame on you. Perhaps you will be the unmanageable and ungrateful daughter, they the long-suffering and forgiving parents. We went into all that before I called. Do you still want to go?"

"They'll say worse than that. They'll say I'm crazy, and Constance, how am I to know I'm not? Who, knowing me as you do, wouldn't think so?"

"Some would understand you as I do: that your bravery, your honesty, your sanity run strong as a great river, deep as the ocean. Because many indeed would not, we will keep our fences up. But, dear Wolf, your mother and stepfather have a powerful motive to deny what is true: to save themselves the pain of guilt. What would you accept as proof that your memories are real?"

"There can be no proof. They're just memories. Could I take them to court and win?"

"Probably not, but that's just law. Not truth or justice. And truth is an open well-shaft, four-hundred feet deep, and a young girl who haunted the woods and fields at night."

"Would that well still be there?"

"Why not?"

"You can get to it without going to the house. It's out of sight of the house, down the hill at the edge of the woods."

"And so? Are we ready?"

"You'll do the talking? We'll take turns coming out and just listen?"

"As we planned."

"They'll think we're morons."

"They won't know you're *we*, and, Wolf dearest, you look fiercely, disquietingly intelligent."

"But when it's Rat? When it's Spider? We're all completely different."

"Only to one who knows and loves you all."

"Do I look all right?"

"You look strong and beautiful."

"You know what I've been wondering about? The telephone. I was a teenager, I ought to have been on it by the hour, but I don't remember it at all. Could they have hidden it?"

"You were a prisoner, dear Wolf. Incommunicado, solitary confinement. Those details are going to be coming back, because you're strong enough now to live with them."

"They did all that to me, and to the others, and then they just went on with their lives. Can't anybody do something about that?"

"No, dearest. It's the way of the world. But I hope you will understand, by the time we're done, that they live in a hell of their own making."

"Small consolation."

"That depends on how much you know about hell."

"Can you go there and come back again?"

"The heroes of the old stories did it routinely. That's why they were heroes."

"Then we'd better go."

When they open the door to a raw March

morning, mist shrouds them. Constance drives
her small green car with the heater and the
headlights on, the whole way out. Then when
they get to the approach road, and stop where
Wolf stopped the other time she came—when
they get out and look, shivering in the damp,
they can't see the house. Wolf stares and stares.
Makes no move to get back in and go on.

"Wolf? Is it still you?"

"I really am Wolf. Standing here disguised
as a city lady, but I'm Wolf, and I want to howl
and howl until the fear of God enters into them.
Am I crazy?"

"Perhaps you are a prophet of the Lord,
thought to be crazy by all but the Lord."

"Small consolation when they put me in a
cage."

"And so, dear Wolf, be careful whom you
trust—your city lady disguise would fool
anyone. Where is the well?"

"Drive a little farther, to where the angle of
the woods meets the road."

To get into the edge of the field they have to
scramble across a ditch and through the strands
of a barbed wire fence. Both are wearing boots,
blue jeans, bulky sweaters, like mother and
daughter out for a routine country ramble—
their boots mud-soaked within a few steps. "If
I'd walked into the house like this, big trouble."

"Do you care? Now?"

"Part of me does. I want to march in there and say to Unca, 'See, I'm a woman—you can look but you can't touch.' To Ma-Ma, 'See, I'm a lady, more than you ever were, and screw you.'"

"You seem angrier at your mother."

"Don't you ever stop doing that? Stuck in the mud, all tangled up in the thorns, and it's like we're still back there with the fish."

"Sorry. It's a hard habit to break."

"I guess it's true, though. Why?"

"How much do you remember about Unca? Still just what you told me?"

"I remember . . . "

"Wolf, what is it?"

"I can't say. I can't let myself, not here. Constance, I think we're getting close to the well. I can smell it."

"What is its smell?"

"Water with something rotting in it. Something that wandered into it, or was thrown into it, and died. I don't want to go any closer."

"Is that it? By those old boards?"

"It must be. You go."

Constance walks on alone. The well shaft is six feet across, stone-lined as far down as she can see. It is wide enough, deep enough, dark enough to swallow any human life. She kneels, breathes of the long column of stale air; listens, but it is her inner ear which hears a thin cry.

What if there were other children?

She looks around for a loose rock, sees none, picks up instead a spongy remnant of two-by-four and drops it down. Nothing. Yet it must have struck something, somewhere. There are limits to how deep you can dig a well or would need to. Someone could come with dump trucks and fill it in, burying whatever is down there forever.

Yet her work is not burying, but raising into the light. She glances back to where Wolf now sits, arms around her knees, in the wet grass. She is fifty feet away at least, and that is as close as she's going to come. What happened to her here? And how is it possible to know, from fifty feet away, that that's still Wolf? If there's no one there, if it's sky-blue eyes she sees . . . She hurries back, paying for her haste with a stab-wound in her thigh.

"Wolf? It's you?"

"Who else would be so foolish? What's at the bottom of it?"

"Darkness. Maybe earth, maybe water. Maybe bones."

"What else?"

"That's not enough? Everything you fear. We'll come back with a long, strong line, with large barbed hooks, we'll drag it all up."

"It will eat me alive."

"It lacks that power in the sunlight."

"Sun never shines here. I'm cold. I'm afraid."

"As soon as we're done up at the house, we'll go see Mama and Brother. They'll warm us up and cheer us up."

"If we're done. What if they keep me there? What if they won't let me go?"

"They would have to keep me too, dear Wolf. And aren't you Wolf, with sharp teeth and fierce eyes?"

"I don't know who I am. Afraid of dying there, yet I must go. What should I do?"

"Hold my hand. You are not alone. And there, look" — in the sky up the slope from them, right on the horizon line, a swiftly flowing arc of golden light.

The house squats on its hilltop, dark green curtains drawn. There are no chickens in the barnyard, no geese, goats, cats or dogs. On the roof, a large satellite dish antenna.

"That's new. They watch television?"

"Most people do."

"And what would Unca do for entertainment, after all? Now that I'm gone."

"Are you ready?"

"No. Come on."

They walk side by side in their muddy boots to the steps. Up five creaking steps to the porch, empty except for firewood stacked against the house. Not even a chair to sit in, but then it's still March. The boards creak under their feet;

they must have been heard by now, but from
inside there comes no sign. And no car or truck
in sight. Can they have gone for the day? After
the prodigal daughter is welcome, played so mean
and cowardly a trick? *What a relief . . .*

Wolf crosses the porch, Constance now
a little behind. There's no bell, no knocker,
nothing but a plain jute floor mat, on which
she scrapes her feet with some care, then sets
her fist to the door—once, twice, three times.
As Constance is thinking *damn, thank God, they
really are gone,* the door swings open.

The man standing there, Unca, is not quite
six feet tall and wiry. He is wearing heavy black
work shoes, polished to a dull shine; clean
faded blue jeans and a flannel shirt, a Stewart
tartan, which could indeed have come from L.L.
Bean. His mouth, wide and thin-lipped, is set
in a slight upward curve. Roman nose; masked
dark eyes, black-browed; black hair still thick,
cut short above ears set out a little from his
head, as if permanently cocked for listening;
skin pale, one shade removed from death's-head
white. His hand, which he now extends to Wolf,
is narrow, long-fingered, too smooth for the
hand of a working farmer, and pale as well.
He might be sixty years old, but for sixty he is
insufficiently lined. Almost anyone would call
him handsome.

Wolf stands there stiffly, ignoring the hand.
But she will not brush by him to get inside,

fearing contact and unwilling to turn her back
or even her side to him. Finally the man, clearly
Unca though everyone seemingly will have to
take that on faith, lowers it with a wry smile.
"I never expected you were coming here to be
friendly," he says, his voice soft, a dry tenor,
not a countryman's voice (can this really be the
man Constance has seen plowing?) — too clipped
and final for that, a voice for closing off and
closing out. He walks ahead of them, beckoning
them over his shoulder into the house. It would
be difficult to testify — in a court of law — that he
has not, if not exactly warmly, welcomed them.

The room so precisely matches the one Wolf
and the others explored, she is astonished to see
no claw marks on the table. To smell no blood.
Except that the place coalesced around the tall
clock and the fireplace; now it is dominated by
the television between them. It sits on a dark
wood cabinet which contains a DVD player and,
below that, closed doors with keyholes. They
look locked.

She walks up close to the table, circling to
the far side to have something between her and
Unca, eager to examine the book which lies
open there. But when she stretches her hand
out to touch it, "Careful," Unca says. "Mother
wouldn't want you losing her place." And the
voice, no louder or more urgent than before,
freezes her hand; she can no more extend it
than thrust it into fire. At the same time she

thinks *Mother? He calls her Mother?* And then
remembers that he always did. So this really is
Unca, the man who certainly, though she has
no recollection of that yet, put his cock into her
when she was a child. She backs away from the
table, first registering the word in bold print
at the top of the page: *Deuteronomy.* "Mother's
bringing tea," Unca says. "Just so's we're pretty
careful not to spill any, we can set around the
table here."

  I'm not drinking your tea. But when Constance
sits down in one of the four hard chairs,
arranged two on each side, she hastens to claim
the one next to her, so they will be in what?
Negotiating teams? Two on each side, with the
Bible between them. It's not a negotiation. It's a
trial, only who is being tried? No: it's a game,
the sanity of Laurel against . . . nothing. In
which, whoever else loses, truth will lose.

  Here is Ma-Ma now, stabbing the door open
ahead of her with one stiff arm while balancing
the heavy silver tea service with the other.
The tray and pot shine brightly, obscuring the
woman behind them, who must have begun
polishing soon after Constance called—for
surely they are not in daily use. Ma-Ma sets the
tray on the table, closes the Bible—knowing her
place apparently, at least not marking it—carries
it across the room, and sets it on the mantel. The
gesture, for Wolf, snaps new details of the room
into focus. There is nothing else on the mantel,

no pictures on the walls, no fire in the fireplace.
The room is cold.

Ma-Ma now returns, walking in her hard
black shoes with the tight steps of one long
enjoined to silence, and pours pale tea into
brittle Havilland cups. She looks ten years older
than her husband, her hair iron-gray, pulled
back in a neat bun, flesh fallen, shapeless under
her dark blue dress. Her mouth is a straight
pinched line, her eyes a watery blue—rimless
glasses on a chain around her neck, presumably
for reading. It is not evident that she cares to
see anything else, certainly not the two beautiful
women who are her guests and who occupy the
space directly in front of her.

"Daughter has been kind enough to honor
us with her presence," Unca observes. He has
taken the chair opposite Wolf and is leaning
forward with his elbows on the table, cup
cradled between his hands. "And this I take it is
her medical advisor, Doctor . . . ?"

"My name is Constance. I'm a therapist, but
not a doctor."

She meets his eyes steadily, waiting for
something to happen—for him to blink, look
down or away, but instead he smiles and his
eyes gleam with sexual complicity. So now she
must close him off coldly, like tightening her
lips against an intrusive tongue, declare him
her enemy at the outset, or slip aside, which she
does by picking up her cup and sipping from

it. It contains, in essence, tepid water. Until that moment she had considered adding, *I'm also your neighbor.* But the ditch-water taste on her tongue has pulled up, by some trick of rejection or compensation, the tastes and smells in her mother's kitchen, and she knows it's not true. She won't give him that word, with all it means to her, for an accident of geography — any more than *lover* for the fit of male body with female. She glances over at Wolf, only it's not Wolf any longer. She doesn't think it is. Something about the sardonic set of the mouth suggests Coyote. And what did Coyote say she could do? *Read the dirty minds of boys* . . .

He's cold. Solid ice. The room up there is cold. I couldn't be there any longer.

"I must have misheard," Unca says. "I'm getting to be a pretty old man."

He doesn't look it. Constance wishes suddenly she had told someone where they were going, wonders if Bear could or would fight back if she had to, in this place and against this man, who surely would do anything to protect himself.

But if Coyote or any of them should feel her to be afraid of Unca, that would be the end of it. They would crawl home, lie down with their heads under the covers, and wait to die. Then suddenly, as if from some source outside, the steel comes into her. She feels beating strongly in her heart the bright-eyed fierceness of Falcon.

Blandly she says, "We won't keep you long from your work. My family are expecting us in any case."

"I'm retired. Farm work's pretty much of an ordeal for a man my age."

"What do you do with all that free time?"

He nods at the television. "A hundred-eleven channels, is it? Remote control and an easy chair. What more could an old man want?"

"DVD player, too."

"Toy Mother got me. Never got around to getting any discs for it yet."

Constance glances at Coyote. Some kind of tremor, a disturbance in the field between them. Unca is lying and Coyote knows it. There are discs in that locked cabinet that he wants no one to know about.

She says, "We'd better get on to what we came for. Can we agree at the outset that all of us seated here have a common purpose, which is the healing and ultimate well-being of your stepdaughter?"

"I can't say I see what she needs to be healed of. She looks pretty healthy to me, and always did, and was, as long as she was here. But surely we wish her well—don't we, Mother?"

Ma-Ma, seated a little away from the table with her hands folded in her lap, nods at the teapot.

"Then we might start with the issue of this long separation. You've had no contact with Laurel during the past twenty years?"

"Her choice, not ours. As you see, she's always been welcome."

"But what might have caused her to make that choice?"

"Pretty strong-willed young girl. Always was, from the day I first knew her. Mother will tell you, from birth. Mother almost died birthing her."

"In what way was she strong-willed?"

"She was defiant, Miss . . . ?"

"Smith." Her name is not Smith; Unca knows it and she knows he knows. Coyote briefly, mirthlessly grins.

"I'm sure, Miss Smith, you are aware of that admirable dictum, children should be seen and not heard. Which from what I see on the television is not widely observed, the result being that this country is in pretty sad shape. I have no desire to say anything painful to either of you, but Laurel was a defiant child. Her back-talking her mother, in particular, was constant and intolerable."

Constance looks past the teapot at Ma-Ma. "What's your feeling about that?" Ma-Ma nods, an abrupt, startled jerk of the head. "It's true." Her voice is thin, scratchy—little used.

"Then how did you respond to this

defiance?"

"All that is needed for child-raising, Miss Smith, is pretty sure to be found in the Holy Word of God. Or don't you agree with that?"

"What did you feel applied in particular?"

"Did you come here with the idea of making me out to be some kind of monster, Miss Smith?"

"We came seeking the truth. Are there any child-raising precepts in the Bible which are monstrous?"

"I mean, has Laurel given you the idea that she was beaten?"

"That she was punished severely in a variety of ways. Did that include beating?"

"But now what would you have had me do, Miss Smith? The child was uncontrollable. Reason had no effect on her. So I spanked her with a light switch as the Good Book enjoins and as the occasion demanded. Spare the rod and spoil the child, and she can consider herself pretty fortunate that as a God-fearing man that is all I did."

"For how long did you discipline her in that way?"

"From when she was little. The bad blood from her father came out early, Miss Smith. Until she was a big gawky girl and it got to be too much trouble to catch her. Which I regret even now. Had I done more of my duty by that child, I doubt she'd be setting here today. But I had a farm to work."

"What do you mean, the bad blood of her father?"

"Of a wild man who ran out on his wife and little child. That blood spoke out loud in her."

"You kept on spanking her, but evidently it wasn't working. Did you think of trying anything else?"

"You're not speaking in good faith, Miss Smith. She claims to have been *punished severely in a variety of ways,* if I recall correctly. I don't know if I exactly need to have my lawyer present here, but I'm pretty sure I have a right to know what I'm being accused of. You can just lay it out on the table."

"All right. At times you deprived her of meals for a full day or longer as punishment for accidents?"

"Not accidents. It was like having a hurricane in the house. I may have sent her up before supper, once or twice."

"Did you lock her into her room?"

"Now how else could I get her to stay?"

"You used to shoot deer for venison?"

"You've got papers from the Game Commission in your pocket now? Certainly I did. There were times, otherwise, we'd have gone pretty hungry."

"How did Laurel feel about that?"

"She wept big tears, Miss Smith, and then she dug right in."

"Did you tell her that if she was good, you'd let the deer go?"

"There were times, I was so worn down I'd have said about anything. But not that—we needed the meat. Not that I'd have been taking much of a chance."

Out of the corner of her eye, Constance sees just a flicker. Vixen now, she thinks.

We were bad, he says. He never did but what he had to.

Did you look inside?

It was dark. I saw ice stained with blood. That was all.

What if it's true what he says? Bad then means crazy now.

Wait. Wait.

"Did you play with your stepdaughter?"

"I earned our bread by the sweat of my brow, Miss Smith. My time was pretty limited."

"But did you when you had time?"

"She was not what I would call a playful child. You need to understand that. She was off by herself."

"What did she have to play with?"

"Have I given you the impression that we were rich? She had what was on this place. She had the apple tree in back to climb."

"Books?"

"The school provided those, and Mother

read to her out of the Good Book. We were,
Miss Smith, and we are, a simple Christian
family."

"What about friends?"

"She may have had them at school, though
she was wild there as well. We received
complaints from her teachers and principal. It
was shaming."

"Did she ask to bring friends here?"

"She may have, but that was not a privilege
she had earned. I can see she's fooled you, but
you'd better open your eyes, Miss Smith. She
was a pretty bad girl."

We were bad. We were bad. That's all he says.
Does Constance believe him?
She must. She has to.
We are crazy then.
What did you see inside?
Blood. Ice. Bloody footprints in the ice.
Wait.

Cat now, and
what can I do? What of the truth can I give
them?

"Would you say, then, that Laurel had a
loveless childhood?"

"I would say, Miss Smith, that she never
wanted our love. She was a perverted child in
that way. So we coped as best we could, and
we passed God's love on to her through prayer.

What else could we do?"

"It never occurred to you to seek counseling?"

"Laurel was our own burden. Our cross to bear."

"What were the circumstances of her leaving home?"

"One day when she was eighteen, she simply announced that she was going, and she went. How could we stop her? She was of an age to make her own way in life."

"Where was she going?"

"She didn't say. Why don't you ask her?"

"She went without money?"

"She had money."

"Where did she get it?"

"Now where, Miss Smith, does any pretty young girl get money?"

"Would you explain that?"

"I dislike to with her setting here. It's pretty painful, even yet."

"You're implying that she got it from men in return for sexual favors."

"Which I never meant to come out. Better it hadn't. I hope she has repented of that sin."

"How long had it been going on before she left?"

"Longer than I like to think, even now."

"And where did she learn to act like that?"

"It was born in her, Miss Smith. It was bad blood. It was the devil working in her."

"When did you first become aware of it?"

"This is not something I would ordinarily speak of in Mother's presence, Miss Smith. It's painful to me. But perhaps it's something you need to know, so you'll be aware of what you're dealing with. The devil drove her to perverse ways with animals since she was pretty little."

"Then you yourself were the devil. You sexually abused her from the time you came into this house until she left it."

Unca stands, hands white on the table. He is eight feet tall, looming over them. ''I'd better hear that lie from her own lips."

The eyes of the figure across from him are golden, piercing, But there is no answer.

"As I thought. I've seen on the television about people like you. Did you fill her head with filth

Constance made the memories. They were never real. He says.

Be quiet. Use your eyes. What do you see?

for the money? Or purely out of mischief?"

Blackness writhing

"How old was she when you first had intercourse with her?"

ten feet tall and in his hand

"May the Lord forgive

fire that gives no light

the two of you. I don't believe I'm up to it."

"Think before you lie again. What's in the television cabinet?"

"Leave my house."
"Pornographic videos?"
"Get out."
"Children? Animals?"
twelve feet tall and he wields in his hand
"Out."

as

*Cat descends, drowning in a flood of filth which
pours down with her, naked children, ponies, dogs,
a reeling, flailing darkness fading, translucent now,
afterimage*

rope   knife   red fang

as

Falcon stands, golden eyes flaming

"For your pride, for blasphemy, for the
heat of your lust and the cold of your lies, for
the evil you have done this child and never
repented, you will abandon one another as you
abandoned your daughter and God. One will
die screaming in the redness of fire, the other
silently in the blackness of ice. You will burn in
hell and freeze in hell with the gate wide open
before you, and there you will remain until the
day when the earth is unmade."

and

Ma-Ma stands
"The devil! Satan is in her! Look at her eyes!"

and

Unca stands
"Satan
right arm warding
get thee hence!"

and

Falcon catches Constance by her hand and walks with her around the table and through the kitchen, out into the clean chill of early Spring, not looking back even when they hear the door snap shut behind them.

And it is Falcon who gets into the driver's seat of Constance's car and holds his hand out for the keys. Constance gives them to him, and he drives down the approach road, turns onto the county road, and stops. He gets out, leaving the keys in the ignition, and leans against the door. Constance joins him. The fog is thinner now, but it has clustered around the house, of which only the roof is visible. Constance cannot see even that much, for her hands are over her eyes. After a little while her shoulders shake, and she is weeping. Falcon puts his arm around her shoulders and waits.

"It was terrible. The most terrible thing I've ever known."

"Yes."

"But what else did I expect? Why did I bring them?"

"Because they had to see for themselves."

"Where are they? How are they? What are they doing?"

"Wolf has led them into the well."

"Wolf? But she was terrified of the well."

"She still is."

"What will they find down there?"

"Memory. Terror. Grief. Anger. Death. Life. What else?"

"Will you be staying here? In this body the whole time? How long will they be gone?"

"Longer than you can imagine. No time at all. I will not be here. Soon they will need me."

"What of the body when you go?"

"It will sleep. When Laurel returns, she should wake in a safe place."

"My old room at home? Mother and Brother will be there, even if I'm not."

"The love there will help her."

"You said . . . When Laurel returns. But what of Wolf and Coyote and the rest? They're my friends."

"Wait. Go on with your work, but as you

can, be solitary to prepare yourself. It will be a time of great sorrow and great joy."

Constance cries for a long time, broken-hearted in Falcon's arms.

When she draws back to arm's length, Falcon's fierce golden eyes meet hers for a last long moment. Then he is gone. The eyes are empty, sky-blue.

Constance guides Laurel, who walks as in her sleep, to the passenger door of the car and settles her inside. She drives to her childhood home and leads her into the house. Mother is there in the kitchen. Her other name, as Constance knows when she sees her, is Old Woman, so nothing need be said. They lead Laurel into the bedroom where she will stay, undress her, then into the bathroom where they wash her with warm water. They rub her dry and put her to bed naked, in Constance's childhood bed between clean white sheets. Over her they spread the quilt which Mother made for her before she was born, with the golden sun high in the sky, and that is for fire; white birds against the blue, and that is for air; a silver river curling across it, and that is for water; green shoots seeking their home in the light, and that is for earth. There Laurel lies through spring and through summer, the time of growth; through autumn, when apples ripen; winter, when green things rest; and into the season of awakening.

The blackness of the well has leaked into its water. Wolf, forepaws braced on the rim, can see nothing. If she stays long where she is, the blackness will rise around her and she will live in it, carry it with her wherever she goes, for all of her life.

We'll die down there.

It is Coyote, beside her now, the other six hanging back. They touch noses. They are sisters, and they love each other. Wolf remembers the words of Old Woman. *You will eat her to the last bone, and lap the last drop of her blood.*

Up here we'll not-die. Which is worse?

If I could think of a trick.

Here, Unca hides behind the walls of his lies. They are stone walls three feet thick. How could you trick him? But below . . .

Below, the Ogre is twelve feet tall, his heart is stone, he thinks only of killing. How could I get close enough to trick him?

But at least you could get close enough to die.

That much I believe I could do.

So, Sister?

If you go, I will follow. What of the others?

They heard Unca's lies or they have been told. None of them want to not-die. They will come.

Coyote sniffs at the water, if that it is what it is. Snake ought to be down there somewhere, but she cannot smell or see her. The blackness

swallows light, eats seeing. The ooze she smells
is the stuff of old night, of the time before time.

Well then?

And Wolf goes into the well.

It sucks her down and in like thin mud or
quicksand. Then after that first plunge there is
no more falling. She floats where there is no *up,
down, mass, extension, a not-place* where her eyes,
her ears, her mouth and nose are filled with
no-thing, only there is no *where,* no *full* since no
empty, or *before, after, because* or even *and.* There
is only cold, which is *absence.* It is the *not-being
of uncreation,* and Wolf is *there, not-there,* breath
and blood stilled.

She is standing on the ground. She is
breathing, her heart beating. Then Coyote beside
her. Then the others, *not-there* then *there* in
no-time's passing. Coyote says to her:

What was it we passed through?

*I know only that we did not carry it down. I'm
not cold. But did we go down?*

*We went into a well, and now we're somewhere
else. That will have to be called down. What is this
place?*

Look around you. You know it as well as I do.

For they are standing in the familiar
woodlot, in the angle between woodpile and
fence. It seems to be late spring and late
morning, the sun dappling the earth around
them through pale green leaves. Then the light
grows smoother and cooler as a cloud crosses

the sun. By the time it passes, the shadows have moved. It is getting on toward noon.

It's real, then? It looks like the upper world.

If that is so, the house stands on the other side of the field—over there beyond the trees.

We're going to the house?

Why else did we come?

We could live quietly in this wood.

Not-live. And you think the Ogre never comes here? And . . . Sister, do you remember who is in the cellar of that house?

Little Girl. So we've come to get her out?

What do you think? Is that cellar any place for a child?

The Ogre and his wife will he there. Both of them. She's almost worse.

There are eight of us.

Eight or eighty, what does it matter? I'm afraid—not of dying. Of something I can't remember, and so it has no name.

And yet? Are we going to the house?

Coyote looks at her, around at the others, who are all standing quietly. Rat is riding now on Bitch's back, Spider between Vixen's ears. She trots ahead quickly to the edge of the woods. The house is there, across the field, which in the bright sunlight hums with bees. Blackberries are in bloom. She sits back on her haunches and howls.

Then Wolf joins her, and the others add their voices, barking, yapping, yowling, squealing, all but Spider, who has no voice. In one breath they stop. Everything has stopped. The whole world is silent.

Now they know we're here.

Now they know.

But it is not from the house that their challenge is answered.

From under the tall arcing brambles, from in among the high grass, they hear a rustling. Then, along a wavy forty-foot line, in languorous undulations advancing, grass and bushes move—not as in a high wind; displaced by something denser than air. Then a long, broad, scaly back, dusky-dark, green and blue shimmering. Out of the field now the head rises ten feet into the air, the mouth gapes wide. The teeth are white, the flicking tongue is red. And the obsidian eyes and the hissing breath freeze them where they stand, for this is Snake, their sister the great Serpent, come to dinner. In the throat of Snake, Bear will be like Rat, Rat like Spider, Spider like the flea that lives on Bitch's belly.

From out of the eye of the sun, Falcon plunges. Screaming he stoops, talons to the neck of Snake, and rises with Snake dangling. Once only he circles, glides low, lower, to the height of Wolf's head, and drops Snake into the grass among them. She is six feet long, black with iridescent highlights like the back of a grackle. She whips away under a bush, coils with her head up and facing them, hissing.

It is Coyote who says: *Don't be afraid. We won't harm you. We're your sisters.*

Snake only hisses.

Do you speak?

Will you come with us?

It seems a long time, but the sun has hardly moved, it is almost noon now, when she uncoils and crawls out among them.

Now we are all nine.
Nine or ninety . . .

It is Wolf who leads them into the field, Coyote at her shoulder; Bitch with Rat, Vixen with Spider, Cat in a close group behind; then Snake, and Bear trailing. The barnyard when they reach it smells of chicken, and there are one or two in sight, scratching idly in the dust. The house itself, dusky curtains drawn against the noon sun, tells them nothing.

They know we're here. They can't be afraid. Why don't they come out?

Tell them again.

Wolf howls. The air around the house trembles, but there is no other sign.

Can we get in?

We got in.

Not into the same house. Bear?

Bear leads them to the door, rears up, smashes her paw into the solid oak. Once, twice, three times, but it stands.

Not that way.

They walk all the way around. In back the apple tree blooms as it has every spring in memory, but the door there is locked, the door into the cellar is locked, the house a fortress against them. They return to the front and stand in a milling little group. There is no way in. Coyote is out of tricks. What are they to do?

Then Vixen says: *Spider will go in. There's room for her under the door.*

She told you? She doesn't speak.

In this place she can, or with all of us here she can. She spoke into my ear. She will go.

But what can she do?

She can see, and tell us.

Vixen walks to the door, lies down, lowers her head. None of the rest see Spider go in. She scurries up the wall to the ceiling, across to the doorway into the living room. Then she can see. And the curtains covering the front windows vanish, and they all see. Ma-Ma is seated at the table, reading her Bible. Unca is seated on the sofa with Little Girl in his lap. It seems to be cold in the room, for Ma-Ma is wearing a sweater and Unca a heavy flannel shirt, and there is a low fire burning, but Little Girl, who might be three years old, has on only a white summer dress. She snuggles against Unca, cheek pressed into the rough shirt, as he strokes her shoulders, her neck and arms, her belly. He raises her skirt and they see that she is wearing no underpants; and he strokes her legs and up between her legs, raping her. She squirms in his lap. Ma-Ma never looks up, not even when Unca shudders, catches Little Girl tight by her hips and grinds her against himself; nor when she cries out, because that hurts; nor when after a long sigh, a stillness, he pushes her away so hard she stumbles and falls, and she cries out her anger.

From outside the windows they howl and bark and snarl their rage, leap at the glass, batter it with snout and paw until their blood flows, but it holds, never cracks or even vibrates, all harm turned back against them. Little Girl runs sobbing from the room. Ma-Ma sits like stone. But Unca stands, head cocked, listening to something faint and far away. Then the wall between them vanishes.

They fall silent and back away from him, cowering. He steps out into the yard, plunges his hands into his pockets and stands there looking at them. His face darkens. His lips spread into a thin smile. He says, "You've been a bad girl, haven't you? I'm going to have to punish you pretty good."

Chapter Five*

Once upon a time there was a little girl. She lived on the Place with Ma-Ma and Unca, and she wanted to be Little Girl. And for a season, so she was. When she danced in the meadow, Bramble scratched, Bee stabbed, Nettle stung, but still she was. Well with his damp breath shivered her, calling her face and her name. When she walked in the woods, Root tripped and Cedar clutched. When she rode in the lane, Dust choked, Mud splashed. In the barnyard Goat butted, Cow nudged, Goose pecked. Sun burned, Frost froze, and she bled at the knees and grew. Still she was. She was. And then Spider weaves his shadows on the wall.

In the sharp light cast by her bedside lamp. Eight long wriggling writhing things like worms not legs. There in the center a round pulsing

---

* Note to reader: this chapter contains graphic depictions of sexual, emotional, and physical child abuse. Feel free to skip ahead to Chapter Six.

darkness which is
Spider's body and
a darkness bulging from it with two dots of light
his head and eyes and
a thing like a stick
his fang
What is fang?
Sharp tooth to poke you.
Why?
Because Spider is hungry.
Why?
Because Spider's belly is big and round just look
it is big and round on the wall sucking up the light on the wall.
What does he want to eat?
Little spiders eat flies they catch them in their sticky webs and suck their insides out but big Spider eats
What?
Bad little girls.
Am I bad?
Let's see what Spider thinks. Face feels good. That's your fingers.
It's Spider's feet.
It's your fingers.
Bad little girls contradict is your mouth bad?
Is it?
Spider has to see are your lips bad? Tongue bad? Teeth? Teeth that bite are bad. Lips that suck are good. Suck Spider's legs.

What's that?

What does it taste like? Did Spider give you candy?

You did.

Bad little girls contradict. Who gave it to you?

Spider?

Good, and who's that on your chest?

Spider?

Who's on your tummy?

Spider. Tickles.

Bad little girls are all wiggly and giggly. Know what Spider does to them?

What?

Webs them all tight so they don't be wiggling. Sticks something in their mouth so they don't be giggling.

What in their mouth?

I'll show you.

It's big. What is it?

Something you don't have. Only Spider has it.

You're not Spider. You're Unca.

Bad girls contradict. What does Spider do to bad girls?

What?

Webs them up tight. Sticks a big thing in their mouth to quiet them.

What?

Open your mouth like a good little girl, and I'll show you.

Was that good?

Candy is better.

The candy is inside it. See the little hole in the

*end? I'll rub it against your tummy, and the candy
will come out.*

Doing it too hard. It hurts.

You have to do it hard. There!

It's all sticky. It doesn't look like candy.

Bad little spiders contradict. Taste it.

It's not candy.

*Good little girls do as they're told. Take some on
your finger and lick it off.*

No.

*You never say no to me. Ever. Ever. What is
this?*

Like the other thing.

The thing the candy came out of?

Yes.

Smart little girl. Know its name?

No.

Fang. What happens to little spiders who say no?

Don't know.

Fang stabs them dead. Where does he stab them?

Don't know.

*Stupid little spider. In their mouth, that's where.
All the way down their throat, and down through
their belly, and out . . . right . . . here. What do you
think happens then?*

What?

*All of your blood pours out. Your insides pour
out, all black and oozy. Right out of that little hole
where you pee. Know what happens to a spider when
its juice gets sucked out?*

What?

It dries up and blows away. Open the window and toss you out. Wind takes you, sticks you on the highest branch of the tallest tree. There you hang forever. Open your mouth.

Why?

Bad little spiders ask why. Good little girls do as they're told. Open it.

That was a little nip from Fang. Do you want any more?

No.

You say No thank you, Unca.

No thank you, Unca..

That's a good little girl. But you hurt Fang's feelings. Stroke him with your hand, kiss him, make nice to Fang. Don't you want him to be your friend?

Yes.

Of course you do. Go on, stroke him. He won't bite you.

Good. Now put your finger in the candy on your belly, and put your finger in your mouth. Like I told you a long time ago.

Not candy.

Fang is angry. What happens when Fang is angry?

Bites?

And we don't want that, do we? So how can we make Fang happy?

How?

Stupid little spider. We say Spider candy is good.
When can I have some more?

When?

Say all of it.

Good. When can I have.

Tomorrow night, if you're good. Bad little
spiders get Fang down their throat. Good little girls
get spider candy. Very, very good little girls get this.

What is it?

It's a kiss, but you have to give me one first.
Make nice to Unca, because Unca loves you.

Stupid little spider, that's not a kiss. A kiss is
with your mouth open and your tongues touch.

Better. You get one kiss for one kiss. Want to
know how to get more?

Yes.

I'll teach you, but not tonight. Now go in the
bathroom and clean yourself off You're a disgusting
mess.

She walks naked down the dark hall to
the bathroom. Her room was hot, her tummy
prickly where the spider candy stuck, but the
hall is cold. The bathroom is freezing the stuff
on her tummy freezes to her skin she parts the
curtains stiff in the cold

snow.

Up to the window ledge, deeper than she's
ever seen it. Trees across the field black, twisted

like the legs of poor Spider dying in the cold.
The black web of Spider has caught Moon.
Moon bleeds her light onto the white field of
snow. Little Spider raises the window a crack,
scoops up snow in her hand. Her hand is wet
with cold red blood. Rubs at the sticky white
candy her tummy is red. Sticky with blood.
Needs to pee but her blood will pour out insides
pour out black flush away blow away across the
field of snow.

Walks back to her room. Spider is gone.
Dark empty and hot, curtains easy in the light
air of summer. Walks to the window and closes
that air out, snap. Curtains are limp and dead.
Crawls into bed, under the sheet it sticks to her.
Ma-Ma will have to wash it. *Ma-Ma has enough
to do without you*

  disgusting mess
    shivers under the blanket in the hot as
    Spider crawls under the door and
    grows as he crawls and
    crawls as he grows all
    round and black which is his body
    with two dots of light which are his eyes and
    one long red thing which is his Fang

    crouches on her naked belly
    binds her with his white
    clothesline
    stabs her with his red

all wet

Disgusting child
she's wet her bed
has quite enough to do without you
disgusting child
so you can just sleep
on the floor

know what happens to a dog that wets the floor?

Know what happens to a little spider that
What?
won't eat Ma-Ma's delicious dinner that she
slaved for hours over
Can't eat it. Can't chew it.
What a thing to say to your Ma-Ma
But you said don't bite so how can I
tell the truth
the simple truth is all we ask
Unca never said that

Oh but I did when she bit my finger
the little rat

Why did you never tell me?
You have a weary enough cross to bear
as it is my dear
with a daughter I fear
it is difficult to love.

But I do love her
because it is my Christian duty.

And mine to punish her I fear
 pretty good when punishment is due
so
What happens to a bad little spider?
What?
When she runs away from Unca on her eight
little legs?
What?
Web to bind her and

when she talks back to Unca with her dirty little
mouth?
 What?
Stick to gag her and
poison to still her
 that made her
all spiders
rats
 night-crawling things
 down her throat
to kill her

Goddamn you you bit me!

You bit me

You fucking little rat

Know what happens to rats?

Goddamn you do you know?

They live in the cellar

In the dark

Eat garbage

Eat poison

Scream

Die

How long must she stay?

Our Savior lay in His tomb from the afternoon of Good Friday until Easter morning.

Mother, let it be so. And can we hope that she, like our Savior, will be born again?

We can pray.

Then, Mother, let us pray.
This child is our cross.
Out of darkness let her be born
as the bride of Christ our Lord.

She had not remembered her bed was so hard. It bruises her naked skin, scrapes her when she moves. The raw chill in it rises from some deep black place. The black smell in it is old. Rotting. Wet her bed *disgusting rat* on floor sleeping. Lying in cold pee *what happens to a dog that goes on the floor?*

Wipe it up. Nothing to wipe with. No clothes no blanket no hands. Spider has no hands. Eight little legs to scurry from Rat *where?* There is one between her lips. Don't bite. Lips suck tongue soothes two little legs three four gags *don't bite candy in her throat spews out. Vile little rat* lies on her side curled up in the dark. Little rat is blind in the dark. Big Rat can see.

Let's play hide and seek. I'll be it.

What do I get if I win?

Candy.

What do you get if you win?

Candy too.

I don't have any candy.

You are candy. Sugar and spice and everything nice. That's what little rats are made of.

She hides under her bed with the door closed. Big Rat knows where she is. She can hear his teeth splintering the wood. The door will fall down.

Ma-Ma?

Why would she want to lock the door? What could she be hiding?

Mother, I fear she has much to hide. Have you

*seen her eyes? In the dark? They shine red like an
animal's eyes.*

*Such a secretive little thing. I confess I find her
a burden.*

Our cross to bear.

*Yellow teeth like chisels. They have made a hole
in the door. She sees his red eyes through the hole.
Big Rat can see in the dark.*

Come out come out wherever you are   stay still.

Come out before Unca loses his temper   still.

*Vile little rats hide under the bed. There's a trap
under there for rats. It's an invisible trap. Sooner or
later, little rat sticks her head into it. Snap! Like the
chicken's head I'll kill for dinner, right off. You know
what else?*

*All the bad thoughts in there. All the dirty, vile,
ugly, disgusting thoughts, they'll pour out onto the
floor. They'll make a black stinking mess on the floor
that nothing can get off. Ma-Ma will know. Do you
want her to know?*

*Good little girls sleep in their bed between the
sheets. They get candy. They get read to out of their*

Do you think we ought to let her have that?

*It's just fairy tales, Mother. It's innocent
enough.*

*They're pagan. They'll pervert her imagination.
And think of who sent them.*

*She doesn't have to know that. We can say I got
them for her.*

You were always a good father to her.

I try, Mother. Our Lord knows it's hard, but I do try.

book.

Read me about Hansel and Gretel.

I don't know if I ought to. They were bad little children. They ran away from home.

Their father was the bad one. He left them out in the woods.

What happened then?

You're supposed to read.

I know what. We won't just read the story, we'll play it. You be Gretel.

Who will you be?

Hansel. We're in the deep dark woods now, walking and

brambles in the meadow catch at her bare legs. Trace red veins on Unca's blue overalls bob along fast ahead of her. Into the deep dark woods.

Gretel was so poor, her clothes were all in rags. The thorns tore them right off.

Don't remember that part.

It's in the book, so you have to do it. Take them off.

What about Hansel?

I'm not Hansel any longer. I'm the Witch's candy house.

You don't look like a house.

I'm a good candy house. What's this?

The thing the candy comes out of.

*And what did Gretel do when she came to the
house?*

She was hungry. She nibbled on it.
She sucked on it. Go on, little girl.

What happened then?
*The Witch came out and caught them and kept
them in a cage in her kitchen for a long time. But we
don't have a cage. What shall we do?*

Just pretend.
*That's it. I'll tie one end of this rope around your
middle, and the other to this tree. Just like that. Now
you're in the Witch's cage.*

What about Hansel?
*He was a had boy. He ran away. The Witch ran
after him*

but the rope jerks her down. Dirt in her
mouth and she spits at the dirt and the white
candy-taste, fumbles at the rope, but it's tied
tight behind her back. Tied to a branch of the
tree too high to reach. *The Witch went away and
Gretel was in the cage. She was thirsty and hungry
and scared, waiting for the Witch to come back for
her. The Witch didn't come and didn't come, and
it was getting dark. Something was rustling in the
bushes. She could see its red eyes.*

*Do you think I have nothing better to do than
play with little rats? I work like a dog on this place,
and what thanks do I get?*

I want to go home.

And how is it, do you think, that you have a home to go to? What have you done to deserve it? You want to try working this farm for one day?

Want to go home.

That's what Gretel said to the Witch. Do you suppose the Witch let her?

Don't like this game. Don't want to play.

She doesn't want to play. When I've killed half my day to give her a treat. How would you like to spend the night out here?

Want to go home.

There are stray cats in these woods. Sharp claws to kill little rat. Fangs to eat her. Foxes, coyotes, wild dogs. Wolves and bears even. Snakes with poison teeth. What was that?

What?

Anything. Might have been anything.

Home. Please. Home.

Then you play with me. Finish the game. The Witch fattened Gretel up to eat her.

Not hungry.

Eat your candy. Or I'll leave you here for Cat.

Not hungry.

Father, what is wrong with that wretched child? Talk to her.

I'll do more than that. Your mother slaves all day in the kitchen, and you won't eat? Work up an appetite then. Go dust everything in the living room.

She's lax and clumsy. All she'll do is smear it.

Then I'll teach her better. I've spared the rod, I fear, and spoiled the child.

It's your kind nature.

Which I see I must set aside, and do my duty by
her. I'll watch her like a hawk from now on. Like a
cat

who walks lightly in the dark, cloaked in
black, sees but is not seen.

Do you want to hear the end of the story?

Tell me.

Gretel stuck chicken bones through the bars of
the cage, but the Witch was not fooled. She saw that
Gretel was nice and plump, and so one day she built
up a good hot fire in the stove, and she caught that
little girl by her two ankles

like this
and dragged her out
and threw her into the hot hot fire
and ate her all up

just like that

That felt funny.

Nice?

Maybe.

Good little pussy gets a nice tongue bath. Bad
little pussy gets

What?

Remember Fang?

Little Cat hunts. In the barn, the field,
the edge of the woods, by the pond and the
damp verge of the well, she stalks whatever

hops, crawls, scurries or flies. Daily she stands
beneath the nests of barn swallows, rapt, head
cocked for the first peep of the hatchlings. When
she hears it she returns to the house, drags from
the shed a stepladder twice her own height.
Back across the barnyard she goes, scattering
chickens before her, leaving parallel grooves
in the dust. She herself is being stalked, or will
be before the day is out, and she knows it, and
shivers with delight at the knowing, but she
does not look back or hide her trail. That would
spoil it. She tugs the ladder into the barn, stands
it up under the nest, and mounts, panting with
triumph. Only one egg has hatched. That's
good; more hunting here tomorrow. She cups
the fluttering thing in her hand, puts the head
in her mouth, bites hard with her sharp little
teeth. In her hand she feels a single slight
tremor. Then the bird is limp, but she gnaws at
it, mangles it, for some time before spitting it
back into the nest. Only then does she become
aware of the mother, swooping and crying
around and around her head.

She stands on the ladder hopefully, staring
into the nest which contains three more eggs.
Often Big Cat follows her in here, slips up close
in the throes of her killing, pounces before she
knows he's near. But he's not here now. In fact
she had not really expected him, for he likes to
hear about her hunting, and she has as yet not
enough to tell. She climbs down and, leaving

the ladder where it stands, walks out across the barnyard, blinking in the strong sunlight. The stupid squawking chickens tempt her. Once she caught one by the neck in her two hands, but she could not squeeze it hard enough, and when she raised the head to her mouth it pecked her cheek. Chickens are for Big Cat, and raccoons, bad dogs, and snakes. Once by the well she came upon a five-foot blacksnake, sunning among the loose stone and timbers, and she was fierce and brave, flailing at it with a two-by-four as it coiled and hissed, but not strong enough to hurt it. Big Cat came then and caught it by the neck, held the whipping body out to her, laughing as she cringed, then dropped it down the well into the black heart of the earth. When she too is Big Cat, she will kill everything that walks on the earth or flies over it.

It's hot today and the grasshoppers in the field fly fast, but she catches two and squeezes the juice out of them. That is something but not enough, still she is hungry, and then, easing through the tall scratchy grass with her eyes to the ground, searching, she has wonderful luck--a nest of baby rabbits, five of them, under a tangle of blackberries. She kneels, reaches in through the thorns. They rake her wrist and that is good, it's all good on this bright June morning as she pulls out the first of the five, cuddles the soft fur against her cheek, delaying the moment; then slips the head into her mouth

and bites down. She works with her teeth until
she tastes blood. A drop of her own blood has
welled up on her wrist. She licks that up as
well. Four more times she catches, bites, sucks
with her hungry mouth. It seems there is not
blood enough in the world to fill her. She kneels
over the drained puffs of fur, reluctant to go;
she might find a frog by the pond, or a toad by
the well, but those are just for squashing under
her foot. Not as nice as rabbits. Then

snap! The claws of Big Cat around her
middle. She wriggles and squeals, fairly caught,
knowing what will come next. He turns her onto
her back in the tall grass, pulls off her shorts,
and with his tongue and his fingers he strokes
her between her legs until she purrs. Then he
lies down over her, but not heavy, and slow and
then fast, sliding smooth in her sweat, rubs her
belly with his own belly. Finally he smooths
the sticky stuff down onto the inside part of
her legs and between her legs, and puts his
hand to her face to lick. He pulls his pants up
then, lies down on his back, settles her astride
his stomach. His stomach and chest are white,
covered with black curly hair which she strokes
with both hands, nicely, not tickling, for he
hasn't said it yet and he has to say it—

Good hunting, Little Cat?
One bird. Five rabbits.
Which makes how many?
Six.

*So how many chocolate kisses have I got for you
in my pocket?*

Six.

But what do I want first?

Kiss. She bends to his face and they kiss
with their tongues the way he taught her.

*Six kisses for greedy Little Cat. I love you, Little
Cat.*

There! That was what he had to say.

I love you, Big Cat.

We will hunt together forever.

Forever.

Six kisses. He unwraps them and slips them
between her lips, one by one.

In the winter, something else is out hunting.
Big Cat comes in grim-faced from early chores
one morning. *Go out and look.* Six white chickens
lie dead in the snow, two with their heads
off. Three or four of the twelve feet have been
gnawed off, and there are feathers scattered
everywhere, patches of dark red blood, a
twisting rope of guts. Little Cat shivers, crosses
her arms tight across her belly. Between her legs
she feels loose and moist and happy.

What did it?

Can't say. No tracks.

She sees that herself now. The only tracks
are Big Cat's own, where he walked around
looking. How can that be?

Who knows? There are things out there in the

dark, Little Cat, that can float like a mist on the top of the snow. Ghost foxes with real teeth.

He's staring down at her, smiling. She squirms at the wonder of it.

How do you catch a ghost fox?

You don't. Keep your poultry close, but fox can go anywhere. Into the house even. Into the room where a little cat sleeps.

Now, standing in the open doorway, she feels the cold. Shivers.

Close that door, child. Do you think we're rich, can squander heat?

She knows they're not rich. Ma-Ma tells her often enough. And can't afford to

just throw things away like that. You lost your doll, so you'll do without.

But Pussy Doll is not lost. Pussy Doll was murdered in her bed one night. She was fine when Little Cat went to sleep. In the morning her neck was broken. Her head was on backwards. Her eyes were blank sky-blue. She was naked, her chest and belly and thighs all gouged and bloody. Little Cat jumped out of bed and dragged the covers up over her. She made a lump in the bed. *Good little girls do not make their beds in that slovenly way.* The sheets must be soaked with blood. She took her black dress out of the drawer and wrapped Pussy Doll up in it and hid her under the bed, and later that morning when Unca was out in the field and Ma-Ma was in the living room with

her Book, she carried her down by the pond
where the ground was soft and buried her. The
next morning she was back. Little Cat smelled
her before she saw her, the sweetish smell of
something rotting in damp black earth. She put
her into her pillow case this time and tied it
shut, and she threw her into the well.

*It's Sunday, child. Why have you not dressed to
honor our Lord?*

Don't know.

Go and change at once.

Can't find my dress. It's gone.

*Father. Do something. Talk to her. Is the child
possessed?*

Well, Little Cat? Are you?

It was the fox. It killed Pussy Doll, just like
it killed the chickens.

*Yes. But you shouldn't have tried to hide her.
Why didn't you tell me?*

Don't know.

*Your mother doesn't understand about the ghost
fox, but I do. I saw where it dug Pussy up after you
buried her, and I found your dress. Here it is. I even
washed it out for you, so Ma-Ma wouldn't know.
We'll never tell her. It will be our secret.*

But when the fox murders Miss Kitty Cat by
gnawing her head off, it is not a secret, because
the head has been perched on Ma-Ma's Book.
The black fur is spiky with blood. Blood has
defaced the Holy Word of God. Ma-Ma screams

and screams.

> Catch it. Can't you catch it?
> *I believe I already have.*
> What?
> *You were the ghost fox all along, weren't you?*
> What?
> *Baby birds and rabbits weren't enough for you anymore. You killed my chickens. You killed Pussy Doll and Kitty Cat, blaming it on the fox. Little Vixen, you've been bad. I'm going to have to punish you pretty good.*

> It wasn't me. I didn't do it.
> *Lying makes it worse. Take your pants off. Take your panties off. Lie down on your back. Spread your legs.*
> What are you going to do?
> *You shed blood, you pay with blood. Remember Fang?*

Little Dog's name is Foxy. In the field with tail a-wag he stalks grasshoppers, flinches when they buzz off under his silly black nose. In the barnyard with tail stiff he stares at the chickens, paws the ground, drops his chest and raises his silly black rump, but the rooster, who has not come to play, stalks and routs him. Big Dog's name is Fear.

> *Do you hear it, little Vixen?*
> What?

The Hound in the woods. Baying.

I don't hear anything.

You won't last long, then. The Hound is black from tail to head, has long white teeth, has blood-red eyes that can see you in the dark. It can hear you breathing. It can smell your sweat. The Hound is yours and you are the Hound's. It wants you and you only, and one night soon it will find you.

Why? Me?

You have to ask? You, who killed baby rabbits in their nest?

I never.

And lie. I caught you sucking their blood. Now you will know what it is to be hunted.

Take your gun and shoot it.

I? Little Fox, you slaughtered my chickens. You killed Miss Kitty Cat and cut her head off and put it on your mother's Bible. You are a wicked little fox.

I never. Did that.

Also you lie. Hear the Hound baying?

Yes.

You're lying. The Hound is creeping closer very quietly. Beware the Hound when you don't hear him.

I don't hear him now.

But you see him, don't you? Down there in the woods, look. His eyes like red embers.

Yes.

You're lying. He's passed out of sight. Hiding in the barn, maybe. Waiting for some little vixen to come bird-hunting.

Unca, get your gun. Please. Kill, kill, kill him.

If you were a good little Vixen I might.

What is good?

Truth is good. At bedtime you must tell me every bad thing you did all day. Then I will punish you, and you will be safe from the Hound all night.

But can't you just kill him?

No one can do that. He's the Black Dog of the Underworld. Satan's familiar. At best I can keep him at bay. If you make me want to. What bad thing have you done today?

I spilled milk on Ma-Ma's Book. Clearing the table, right after you left. All over it.

You're lying, Little Vixen. I'm going to punish you for lying. Spread your legs.

Don't go. Unca, please don't go. What about the Hound?

What will you do nice for me if I stay?

Anything.

Sorry, Little Vixen. But you lied, you see. Maybe tomorrow. If the Hound doesn't get you tonight.

She pulls the covers over her head and curls up tight, and the cold strikes into her bones, though it is warm in the room with the window shut. Maybe she sleeps; and moves restlessly in

her sleep, so that the spread falls away, as she
dreams of the Hound's red eyes. She's running,
stumbling over rocks and roots in the dark,
and always, however she twists and turns in
her tracks, the eyes are ahead of her. She falls
headlong, scrambles to her knees and

red light washes her room from eyes like
saucers pressed against the glass

and

teeth click rattle on glass

bays and bays

Father, what is that dreadful commotion?

Daughter had a nightmare, I think.

*Well she might. But I thought I heard a dog
barking.*

Foxy, must have been.

*Not Foxy. It sounded big and fierce. What was
it, Father?*

You must have had a nightmare yourself.

I spilled milk all over Ma-Ma's Book. I
knocked the pitcher onto the floor and it broke.

*I know you did. I'm going to have to punish you
for that.*

But I told the truth. I was good. So you'll
stay?

*Maybe. Kiss me nice, like I taught you. Maybe
Hound won't come tonight.*

*I swear she's doing it on purpose. I tell you my
Bible is ruined. What's gotten into the child?*

*It's odd, isn't it? Always at table. Always the
Holy Word. You'd better keep it somewhere safer*

until I can
> *Spare the rod and spoil the child.*
> *I'm afraid there's nothing else for it.*
> *But my Bible stays where it is.*
> *Then I fear that Daughter will have to be*
excused.

She lies curled tight, clutching her stomach. Hound is in the room with her, inside, gnawing from within.

The room is dim, the wash of light silver. No sound. She sits up, knees wrapped in her arms, listening to the nothingness which is Hound, whose silence is his presence. Swings her feet to the floor, walks with her courage in both hands to the window. Moon hangs in the top pane, the full moon of October who lights the way of the Hunter. Glass is cold against hands and nose. Hound bites hard in her belly. How long since she's eaten? She must eat this night or die.

She is wearing her flannel pajamas, once pink, worn smooth at hip and shoulder, inches too short at wrist and ankle, for they are poor and cannot afford to replace a perfectly good pair of pajamas. She slips on her sneakers — why, to go down to the kitchen? Anticipating far-searching. Walks down on fox-feet, on the edges of the treads, contained in her silence, shrouded in her garment of no color. With her hand on the refrigerator door, she sees the light that will transfix her, a beacon for the red eyes

of Hound. Who truly, she knows now without
seeing or hearing or smelling with her foxy
nose, is in the house with her. He is standing
alert in the upper part of the house, at the head
of the stairs barring her way back. She is all in
a cold sweat, off which the mist of her fear rises
and spreads. In a little while it will reach the
eyes of Hound, haloing the moonlight in the
upper hall. The nose of Hound, a sour brassy
broth of starvation and terror. The fur on the
back of the neck of Hound. The sound caught
in his throat will carry through the timbers
of the house, through the floor into her feet,
binding her there, rising into her heart. Freezing
her wildly pounding heart as Hound descends
the stairs, slowly, slowly, lapping her fear as
he comes; growing large on it, strong, fierce,
and happy, until, in the room with her now, he
sucks the last of the white frost which is Vixen
into the black hole which is Hound.

Unless she goes now. She gags the scream
in her throat with both hands, wrenches her
feet loose. Runs for the back door, opens, out.
Silvery in the barnyard, moon is her friend,
Hound's friend, and she runs. Barbed wire at
the edge of the field catches her leg, rips, she
tears free and runs staggering. Bramble and
tussock are Hound's friends, holding up her
blood trail to his nose. Tripping and catching
her for his jaws. Woodchuck hole seizes her by
the ankle, twists her down full-length on her

face. There she lies hidden where Rabbit hid her
children, the blood of Rabbit's children hot in her
throat, red in her eyes, and the grass all around
her shines red. Moon has fallen low in the sky
and borne in blood her own ensanguined twin.
Hound's eyes. Vixen runs. She will hide in the
well.

She has a friend in the well or a sister, she
never knew or can't remember, but there will be
someone there to welcome and hold her. Against
the cold of this October night which aches in her
bones, there will be a clean bright fire. Her friend
will bind her wound with a white cloth, give her
fresh white bread and milk and rich broth, rock
her to sleep; and in that dark country, enfolded
in silence, she will sleep forever.

It is too dark to find the well with her eyes,
though the moon has risen high and silvery
and lonely. But if she closes her eyes and walks
slowly, it will call her home. For she is Vixen,
and with her long nose she can smell water. With
her sharp ears she can hear it murmuring against
stone, calling. Now it is a black hole at her feet, a
soft black cloth to warm her. She

white bird
screams
staggers back
arms flailing
talons of
cold silver
eye bright gold

wind from his wings
hurls her back into the world where
she runs sobbing with rage
back through the field, leg on fire, cramps
doubling her, through brambles and across fence and

where is Hound?

No sight or sound or sniff of him.

The house is dark and still. Across the
barnyard she slips on her fox-feet to the kitchen
door. At first she thinks it must be stuck. It has
never been locked. But it is locked now against
her. She clutches herself. A cold wind is rising.
It blows a cloud across the face of the moon,
blows the moonlight out. What remains is the
luminous track of a bird, a circle of white light.

At its still center stands Vixen.

After a time, when the bird is gone and the
moon again shines, she circles the house and
comes to the apple tree in back. She is forbidden
to eat the apples because they are poor and need
all of them to sell, and so instead of picking the
low fruit she could reach from the ground, she
scrambles up into the tree. No one will miss
an apple from high up near the trunk, if she
wedges the core tight into a crotch, or even the
three she has eaten when she sees, approaching
from the house, the eyes of Hound.

No, it is one eye, not red. Unca with a
flashlight.

Any foxy little thief in the apple tree
better climb pretty high and hide pretty deep.
But it smells like Hound. She crouches still
and small in the branches, gut curled tight
around what she has
Vixen, are you up there?
stolen.
You never learn, do you? You bitches. From Eve
on down. Come down here, little Bitch.

I better not have to come after you.

Now you're going to get it.

The light shines into her eyes. The tree
shakes under the weight of

Unca.

Look what you did to your pajamas. You think
you're going to get any more?

Squeezes her eyes holds tight hand on her
waistband rips away
look. Ruined them. I'm going to have to punish
you pretty good, little Bitch.
holds tight

Fang seeks as

it all *God!*
comes out *damn you damn you bitch kill you*
kill you kill you for
this
cheek on rough wood what she gets

stealing apples in the middle of the night
bad blood in her father's blood
blood of Eve
be good I promise
 promise
promise
from now on always
 good
little Bitch.

She follows him everywhere, wagging her
foxy tail. Chases Rabbit out of the brushpile
for him *boom* dead. Warm soft thing. Chases
Squirrel up the tree boom dead. Warm soft.
Chases Deer to where he waits boom but
Deer gets up runs on. *Stupid bitch you didn't*
run him close enough
sits up begs. Rolls over plays dead.

Run down to the house, Bitch. Fetch me my
tobacco pouch.

Where's my pipe?

You're lying. Of course I told you. Bad dog. Go

get it.

Where's my dinner pail?

You're not good for much of anything, are you, little Bitch?

Go to the house and get a bucket and a long rope. Dip me up some water out of the old well.

The well is a black hole with crumbling stone sides. She lowers the bucket, but it hangs on a taut rope, comes back up dry. Twice she trudges back to the house for more. At last the line slackens, but when she pulls on it, it stays light. One of her knots has failed. She has lost Unca's bucket.

I ought to make you go down there after it.
I'm sorry, Unca.
You didn't just lose a bucket, you know. You woke up what lives down there.
What's that?
You're liable to find out one of these nights. It gets hungry enough, it'll climb out after you.

What does it? Eat?
Whatever I scratch up to feed it. Kitchen leavings, rats, frogs, but I've got no time to hunt those things. That dog of yours, now. That ought to satisfy it.

No. Please.

*She's got to pull her weight. Tell me what else
she's good for.*

I could be the one to feed the thing. I could
catch frogs. Then you wouldn't have to.

*That's a thought. Five-six big ones a day it'll
need, you want it to stay where it is.*

Five the first day and six the second and five
the third. Then the frogs get scarce or smart.
They leap ahead of her hand, hide in the

*mud all over your pants. What have you been
doing?*

Nothing. Hunting frogs.

Girls don't do that. You stay out of that

pond. She takes two little ones to the well
and drops them in. Hears its hissing breath, way
down there in the dark. It's still hungry.

I can't get any more frogs. What should I
do?

*You've got that dog. That ought to last it for
two-three days. Maybe longer. If it eats like a snake.
If what it is is a snake. Last it a week or more.*

No, please. Isn't there anything else?

*A chicken would hold it. One of those big
Leghorns. A hardworking girl your age might have a
whole flock of those.*

I could work hard. What could I do?

*Course, you owe me pretty big already. You owe
me for those pajamas. You owe me for the bucket.*

*You owe me for every bite of food you put in your
mouth.*

I'll do anything. I promise. What can I do?
You know what a whore is?
No.
*It's what you're good for. What you are. Take
down your pants and get on your hands and knees,
Bitch. I'll show you how to make your way in the
world.*

Now can I have a chicken, please?
*You have big ambitions, little girl. That was for
the pajamas. Tomorrow's the bucket. After that we'll
talk about*

chickens missing. Three in the last week.
What's taking them, Father?
*Could be anything. Raccoon, fox, even a coyote.
Even that dog.*
Not Foxy. She never would.
*You keep her close, then. Keep your eye on her.
Dog can turn bad.*

But she's too busy to watch Foxy. She has
her whore work to do for Unca, which takes a
long time, because she's too stupid to be any
good at it and often she has to do it over again.
Then when she's earned a chicken she has to
catch it early in the morning before Ma-Ma's up,
carry it by the neck squawking and fluttering
all the way to the well, and drop it down. That's

why she's not there when
   boom from up by the house.
   Her heart stops.

   Foxy was bad. She was chasing chickens. I
thought she was a fox.
   Oh Foxy. Oh Foxy.
   You've got snake food now in plenty, anyway.
Drop her down the well.
   No, please. Thank you.
   Price of chickens just went up. You've got your
own keep to earn. If I don't buy what you've got to
sell, who's going to? You want to keep on my good
side.

   I'm sorry, Foxy. Poor Foxy. Poor Foxy.

   Seems it wasn't the dog after all. Another one
last night. Coyote, I believe it was. I'll get up early
and watch.

   Only Coyote is tricky. She knows somehow,
and stays far away from the barnyard, and no
more chickens are missing. The one Bitch takes
three nights later, she's worked long and hard
for. It's hers. So what happens is a mistake in
the dark
   boom sting
   blast of salty rain and
   run.
   She falls down and her chicken flutters away

out of sight. Nothing to take to the well. Her
skin burns, her arms and legs and the back of
her neck. All
    dark.

When she opens her eyes, the sun is rising.
Coyote is standing in front of her with the
chicken by the neck in her jaws.

Coyote is almost as big as a wolf. Her fur is
gray and rough and full of burrs. Her teeth are
long and white. Her eyes are yellow-gold and
pierce to the heart of Bitch, who scrambles to
her feet but does not run. Walks to Coyote's side
and runs her hand down her back.

Are you going to take that to the well?

Why?

To drop it down. For the thing that lives there.

Nothing lives there.

I've heard it. It's hungry. It will come out after
us.

I'm hungry too, and I can run very fast.

She devours the chicken to the bones. Goes
home with her face smeared with blood.

I caught our Coyote. Here she sits.

Daughter? Stealing chickens? Father, how can it
be?

I only know what I saw. Saw something crossing
the fence and heard the squawking, and I fired.
Thank the Lord I missed. My hand was guided, and
my footsteps also, Mother, for I was able to follow
her. What she's been doing goes beyond mortal

understanding. Stealing chickens and throwing them down the old well.

Daughter? What have you to say for yourself?
Nothing.

If she were even remorseful. What are we to do with her?

It will require the guidance of the

Lord deliver you, Daughter, from the jaws of the Evil One.

I'm not your daughter.

Watch your mouth. Honor thy father and thy mother, that thy days be long on earth.

You're not my father.

The Lord has been pleased to place me in that humble role. Sharper than the serpent's tooth is an ungrateful child.

I'm not a child

nor a house pet. She moves out into the woods and fields.

One night in July, a close, moonless night, Unca slips naked into her room to reason with her. The covers are pulled up over her head. He draws them back, reaches down to shake her awake by her hair, because

I've taken all any man could take from you
nasty little bitch but
no hair on no head
sticky wet
Bitch is not my name. Whirls to the window

but the damn thing is stuck. From outside
where she lives she's laughing at him and he
drives his fist through the glass *kill you bitch* and
his wrist throbbing. Squeezes it with his other
hand, stumbles out into the hall and down the
hall to the bathroom just as Mother emerges
from their bedroom. He slams the door almost
in her face, snaps the light on, falls gasping
to his knees. There's blood everywhere, life's
blood gushing out of his hand and arm *Father?*
laughing at him cackling witch

 Father? What is it?

His bathrobe is hanging there on the door,
but if he lets go of his wrist long enough to put
it on he will bleed his life out. If he doesn't,
Mother will see him

 never satisfy a woman with that

lunges for the robe as she pushes the door
open and the hook into his teeth and his mouth
fills with blood rips it down covers himself
sprawled on the floor

 Father

 Get out get out get out.

Not all of it is blood. Some is red paint from
the brimming bowl which Coyote placed in her
bed.

When Unca is out on the tractor is the best
time. She can keep her eye on him then, and
hear the noise of the engine and the no-noise.

No noise means run, and Coyote is the fastest
dog alive. In his cloddish boots he can never
catch her, but running means dropping the
boards she has taken from the barn, so stealth is
better. She gets the hammer and saw and nails
out of the tool room, and the tarp which is so
heavy she staggers under it. And collects rope,
for sleeping on the ground is not safe. Unca she
can hear coming, and see, for unlike Coyote
he is blind in the dark and carries a light, but
there are other things stalking the woods, or one
Thing, and it moves silently, and it can see with
its red eyes, and it has no scent. It has killed
Deer by stabbing him in the neck with its one
long fang. Nightly it gnaws him, until Deer in
the twilight, from across the clearing, is a splash
of white flowers or a drift of snow.

She works hard, building a sleeping
platform twenty feet up a white pine. Worries
even so about the Thing's long reach. The rope
is to explore the well, which she believes to be
dry. That would be the place. It would never
find her there, if only, and she twists this in her
mind and worries at it, she would not have to
leave the rope, or the ladder she might make,
hanging from the top of the well to climb up
again. If only she knew someone. If she had a
friend to watch for the Thing, and draw her up
again when it goes away. She could take food
down, which she steals now with Ma-Ma right
there in the kitchen, backing her off with her

yellow wolfish glare, and water, and her friend pull up the ladder. She walks out to the road sometimes, where people go by in cars, but she hides in the bushes. People shoot coyotes. Unca shot her sister and hung her on the fence to dry in the wind.

She has no friend and no sister and she is lonely, so sometimes, when the tractor is in the far field or the pickup truck is gone, she slips back to the house. She wanders from room to room searching, for there are things she remembers, a book of stories and a doll with long brown hair, a black cat and a little tan dog, which she would like to find and keep with her. There are traces moreover of someone who once lived here, shiny black shoes the size of her own feet and a black dress which she strokes. and cuddles against her cheek. But though she looks everywhere, even in the dark place beneath the house, she discovers nothing of her own. The search so wearies her that once she lies down for a moment on the little girl's bed, and drifts off, and wakes to find the Thing standing over her. The Thing is an Ogre ten feet tall. It has bound her hand and foot to the bedposts. It has a long red thing in its hand with which it stabs her again and again and leaves her torn and bleeding. After that it's a long time before she returns to the house, and then only for a little while, for her fear is a thick mist about her.

She carries fear with her everywhere. The

Ogre has found her tree and marked it with a
splash of bright blood. He is twenty feet tall, can
pluck her off her platform without raising his
hand above his head. So she has no place of her
own now to go home to, but must lie down in a
new den each night, curled up under the creek
bank or in the tall grass of the field. Each night
he hunts and harries her. Winter comes, with it
snow, and she leaves tracks wherever she goes.
And so she comes to think that, friend or no
friend, she will have to go into the well. Of the
pieces of rope she has collected, some are thin
and frayed. So even if he knew where she was,
he would not be able to follow. The rope would
snap under his great weight and he would fall
and die. Then it would be Coyote's turn. She
would rip him apart with her teeth and eat him
down to the bone.

Therefore she makes her plans. With a sharp
knife which she took from the kitchen and now
carries with her everywhere, she cuts the old
knots out of her ropes, the places too frayed to
hold even her, and ties them carefully together.
No telling if it's enough. It's as much as it
is. She coils it up and loops it over her arm,
working slowly and awkwardly, for it's a cold
day and her hands are stiff. Yesterday it rained,
then froze, and an inch of new snow fell on the
ice. She skids and falls, gets up and falls again,
and so approaches the well fearfully. It would
not do to fall in before she is ready. There is no

tree nearby to tie her rope to, but there are old timbers scattered around. She picks one which seems long enough and strong enough and with her shaking hands, with her fingers which she can no longer feel, she ties the rope around its middle. Now she must drag it into place across the well mouth. But to do that, she will have to go very near herself on the frozen ground, and so she is tentative about it, poking with her feet as she lies back away from the terrible black hole, and the whole thing slides in and falls down, carrying her rope with it.

She lies there for a little while staring at where it went, dry-eyed and empty. When she looks up, the Ogre is standing over her. He has a rope of his own in one hand and the red thing in the other. She scrambles to her feet. When he reaches out to catch her, she jumps backward into the well. Wolf's eyes glitter. Her teeth are long and white.

I'm going to have to punish you pretty good, little bitch.

Not my name. Touch me and I'll drive this into your heart. I'll throw you into the well. You'll rot down there.

Maybe you better come home. It's cold out here.

I'm keeping my knife. It's mine and I'm keeping it. Touch me and I'll cut your heart out and eat it.

He walks back up toward the house, Wolf
following with the knife in her hand. With every
step she swings it in a short tight arc. She could
slash between his legs, slicing his balls and
cock off, and shove them down his throat until
he choked and died. At that there is a letting
go inside her, a flowing from between her own
legs; a bright telltale stain at her crotch. She
puts her finger to it, sniffs and licks, and her
knees turn to water, for it is her blood leaking
away, the retribution of God, and she will die
where she has fallen. Unca glances back once,
grins wolfishly, keeps on going. She lies on the
frozen ground for a long time, her knife still
tight in her hand, her life emptying out of her,
thinking of the black hole out of which she was
born. And of going back into it. She would be
safe from him then. She stands with the earth
wavering under her, white light shimmering all
about her. The sky is deep blue. A bird circles
her, centering her where she stands, and its
wings are pale gold flames.

She is never without the knife. During the
day she wears it tucked into the waistband of
her pants, with her shirt loose over the handle.
When she bathes it sits in the soap dish, for
there's no lock on the bathroom door; so when
Unca comes in and stands beside the tub staring
down at her, it sharpens the space between
them. The lock on her bedroom door is on the

outside, useless. She never sleeps. She can see
in the dark with her golden eyes, on a still night
she can hear a mouse rustling in the field and
smell her blood when the owl takes her, but
she lies not on her bed but under it with the
knife between her and the wall. Once or twice a
night she may close her eyes to rest them. In a
moment a dry thrumming snaps them open, the
wind in the sinews of Coyote where she hangs
on the fence, or the staggering bone-clicking
dance of Deer in the wood. Then she rises and
trots down through the field, following her ears
and then her eyes, for she is hungry always,
her sides caving in, she is skin, sinew, stringy
muscle and long supple bone; but not so thin
as Deer, whose bones when she runs them
clattering to earth are dry. They taste of old
iron, the flavor of starvation.

At last she grows weary. She wanders
around the house yawning, hardly knowing or
caring that Unca's eyes never leave her. Her
hand on the knife handle is flaccid. It drops
away though she is standing within his arm's
reach, and she turns one day, in the middle of
the day, mounts the stairs, falls onto her bed,
and sleeps. When she wakes she is naked and
cold. Darkness presses down on her and into
her, filling her. She is only empty night. She is
in the well, falling away into the black heart
    black ice pulsing

zigzag cracks race through it
at every beat
cold red fire anneals it
fiery web of
Spider who bound by her web
dances circling
freezing
burning
Spider Rat Cat Vixen Bitch Coyote Wolf
dance
seven sisters
in the shadows the eighth
labors to be born
cold salt rain in her face.

*You stupid little bitch. Think you can just lay
there*
sleep yes sleep
like you were doing me a favor
windowsill piled high with snow
 glass webbed with frost
gray light
like you were special
sleep
you look at me when I'm talking
stupid little bitch
 *think that hole between your legs is all you
need?*
sleep is all
wake up and smell the coffee bitch
not my name

every bitch in this sorry world has got what
you've got
    Ursus Major
    roll over bitch
    Great Bear
    warm your ass
    north-pointing
    snarls into the pillow at the
    crack and *crack* and
    on your knees bitch
    dreams
    you give me a pretty good ride
    what will be born of
    now bitch now bitch now
    now
    quickening
    in spring when
    birds fly north pale gold flame
    golden eyes
    talons for killing

It is the coming of the new ice age. Glaciers
creep south from the pole. Hungry ghosts of
the Great North ride south on the shrieking
wind. Snow drifts to the top of the downstairs
windows. The woman sits at the table with her
Book open before her, the man with his hands
almost in the fire. Neither lamp nor fire nor
the Holy Word of God can dispel the cold gray
light. Upstairs, Bear dreams of
    remember Fang?

birth

What is Fang?
This.
What is it for?
Stupid bitch. Take your pajamas off. Stand here and fuck yourself.

Bites deep. Coils inside her, poisoning.
Through her belly throat mouth
   flicking red out of her mouth

   hands behind your back
   bitch

arms melt into her body

on the bed
on your back spread your legs
wider
bitch

no legs
empty below where
Snake's head stabs
she coldly coils writhes
eyes black as fire

now

born

old.

She bothers me, Father. Have you looked at her eyes? They look
Knowing. I wouldn't want to tell you what I suspect she knows.
Cold. What's got into her?
What hasn't? And I caught her up the apple tree again.
Can you do anything with her?
I fear she's grown too old to be any use. To me or any other man.

What happened when Eve ate that apple?
What?
Little heathen. After all your mother read you? She got God's boot up her ass. You know the tragedy of human history?
What?
She had Adam so pussy-whipped, he bent over for the other boot. If it was me in that garden, things would be different. They're different here and now, anyway. Little Miss Snake-in-the-Grass, you can twitch your tail right out of here.

Go? Where?
You'd starve to death on the road. You're old, used up. But there is the

well. A long way to walk in the hot sun.

The throat of Well is twilit. His belly is dark.
His breath is cold, rising from a deep place and
bearing with it a scent she almost remembers.
An animal scent? It smells like Home to her.
It is time to go Home. As Wolf teeters on the
brink, heart pounding, Falcon's scream hurls her
onto her back on solid ground. In a little while,
when she can again breathe and look around
her, she discovers that she's holding a small
cloth satchel. She opens and paws through it. A
few clothes--socks, underwear, a spare pair of
jeans and a shirt--and two crumpled five-dollar
bills. That's it. But enough to tell her which way
to go. She takes one last look back up the hill,
then sets off down through the woods toward
the road.

Chapter Six

Early one May morning, Constance receives a phone call from her mother, who says: "Your friend is awake and dressed, eating bacon and eggs in the kitchen, and she'd like you to come as soon as you can."

So she hangs up the phone with her hand trembling, the receiver clattering into the cradle, and walks through her house like a stranger, bumbling into the furniture. And the skirt she wants is not in the closet where she hung it, nor out on the clothesline, nor on the shelf in the hall closet waiting to be ironed. After awhile she forgets about the skirt, wanders the house trying to remember what she has to do—cancel her appointments, water the plants, feed the fish— as if she were going a long way and staying a long time. Someone has hung up the skirt in the closet in the last ten minutes when she wasn't looking. She puts it on along with a sweatshirt with loons on the front which Brother gave her, does some things but not some other things,

and is almost to the door when she remembers
she will need shoes. And it would not do to hit
someone with her car. She backs out with the
stiff care of one not too drunk to know she is
drunk, and she had better not be stopped, for
never could she walk a straight line, or hold a
balloon with her shaky hands to blow into it.
She drives wondering: *did I feed the fish, and if
not and I'm gone for a long time, will they eat each
other? And is it Wolf? Or is it Laurel? And did I
call my clients, and if not will they hate me forever?
And what of what I never even thought of doing? Is
the coffee pot on? Will the house burn down? One
will freeze and one will burn. Is it Falcon?*

It is Wolf, though when they draw back to
arm's length from a long embrace beside the
kitchen table, Constance hardly knows her. She
looks gaunt. Her eyes are deep and dark, the
eyes of one who has known all and suffered all:
fought through the whole of a black and bitter
war.

"Dear Wolf." Her voice cracks. Her heart is
broken, she is dying of heartbreak. "What did
they do to you? What of the others?"

"They did what they did before. All of it.
We suffered all. We are terribly wounded. The
others are in Old Woman's house in the wood,
sleeping. But for her we'd have died."

"And you have come?"

"For one last time, to walk on the earth and
under the sun. To say goodbye."

"But . . . Wolf, my darling, who will be here then? In this body, if not you?"

"Laurel. Laurel will be here."

"No. There's no need. You could all share, as before. Only knowing each other now, being friends, sisters. The strength and wisdom of all of you, in one body—she could do anything. Be anything."

"I wish we could. Constance, I love being alive, being Wolf, running swiftly under the stars. But Unca and Ma-Ma are still down there, still alive—if you can call it life, and terribly strong. And Little Girl is with them. And, my dear friend, they torture her every day. We must go back down through the well again, and get her away."

"Through the well? But won't it all happen as it did before? And again, and yet again?"

"We are stronger now. Armed with knowledge. And together."

"Are all of you together strong enough? Against the Ogre?"

"Not . . . simply standing side by side. But there was something Old Woman said. I don't understand it altogether, and it frightens me, but I believe it points the way. She said I would eat my sister Coyote to the last bone and drop of blood. And so, if in that way we become one.... "

Constance stares at her. Her knees turn to water and her heart to ice in her chest.

Then, for the whole of that one day, they walk together in the woods and fields. At twilight, Wolf says that she must go.

Constance says, "There is one more thing you must know. Perhaps I delayed telling you until now because of hoping you would change your mind, though I knew you could not and would not--with Little Girl so needing you to come. This is what Falcon said a year ago last March, when you went into the well for the first time. He said that Ma-Ma and Unca would die. One in fire, one in ice. And so, you see, your triumph is foretold."

"In fire and ice. Summer is fire and winter is ice. I think it will be a long time, almost a year, before Laurel wakes again. What else did Falcon say?"

"That it would be a time of great sorrow and great joy, but, dearest Wolf, I feel only the sorrow."

"The joy will come when Laurel is reborn, with the lives of all of us inside her."

"But I don't know Laurel. I only know you and the others, and I love you so, I don't know how I can live without you."

"And so, dear friend, yours is the harder task after all--to wait and keep faith. Goodbye, my love."

"Darling, goodbye."

They hold each other tight, until Constance knows that there is no one there. Then she and

her mother lay the body of Laurel to rest for her
long sleep. She sleeps through summer, the time
of burning; through autumn, when apples ripen
and rot; winter, when the homeless freeze; and
into spring, when young trees bloom.

The house stands where it always stood, up
the slope at the top of the field, in plain view
from the woodlot. At the bottom of the field
the well descends. Bear in the woods lies on
her back with her four paws in the air. Bitch
tumbles on her belly and all round about her
like a puppy. Coyote joins in, rolls Bitch over
and darts away, sly Vixen slips between her legs
and all three go down in a wriggling heap; it
grows to a gray shaggy height, for a second is
Mount Wolf, dissolves into four, rises as Mount
Bitch. Around a pine, Cat stalks Rat, pounces
with sheathed paw, and between the paws
Rat turns, burrows under the soft belly, bares
her long teeth . . . and licks. Snake, wrapped
around a low limb, weaves her head to the tune
of Spider's weaving, which is Snake-charming.
Falcon, circling the wood, weaves all together.

When it is time, they walk, trot, slither, and
ride to the well. It takes them no time at all.

It smells of cold water and iron. They stand
in a circle around it looking down, and see
themselves looking up, and the ones below are

changed. Wolf can see through the gray hide of
Well-Wolf, red tracery of blood, white frame of
bone. She can see into her golden eyes, which
say *I am dying. I am starving. Come to me. The
only food for Wolf is Wolf.* She looks up lest she
be drawn in before her paws and her tail and
her pounding heart are ready, meets the eyes of
Coyote, and she knows what Coyote has seen.
Each has seen. If she draws back. If she hesitates
even, she will feel the teeth of Well-Wolf at
her throat. She does not spring, for there is
no power in her legs, but she is in the air, in
a rushing darkness, in cold water though she
never seemed to strike water. She is sinking,
kicking her way down with her lungs bursting.
The well is bottomless. She will breathe water,
water will fill her and she will drown in the
dark and drift lifeless in the dark forever. She
draws the killing breath. Well-Wolf rushes in
and they are one, breathing. In less than no
time she is down and out, standing dry with
the others in a twilit wood. It is a winter place,
for the trees are bare, and nothing grows from
the forest floor; a place of blight which has
twisted the branches into frozen writhings. The
air is heavy, neither warm nor cold, no scent of
life in it nor breath of wind whispering. Sky is
cloudless, the color of slate. Flat gray light leaks
out of it. There is no sun.

Then Wolf breathes and shakes herself, and
in that moment it all changes. Sky is the thin

blue of early spring morning. Trees in spring
leaf cast long shadows. A cold wind blows,
carrying on it a smell that is sour and old, and
that is Ma-Ma. A smell of blood and lust, and
that is Ogre. Beneath those, fainter, something
flowery, clean, young, and frightened. And that
is Little Girl.

Wolf looks around at the others. They all
know what the wind has told them, and know
where they must go, but none of them move.
They could stay here after all. The spoor from
the house is faint. The wind will shift in time
and grow warm, and it may be, in this quiet
place, that it will always be spring. If they go
to the house, the Ogre will kill them all and
devour them to the bone. It is true, they all
know it. If they stay here they will live. If they
go they will die, and how will that help Little
Girl? If they stay, they can plan. Spirit her out
with a trick.

They mill about a little. Flowers have sprung
up all around them, snowdrop and crocus, the
harbingers of spring. And surely that is a sign
that they must stay, though the rotting meat
spoor of Ogre is harsh in their nostrils. Now
another smell, strong and very near. Old frog
and Old Woman. She is standing among them,
though none saw her coming, and her eyes
gleam with a dark and terrible laughter. None
of them, with their sullen heads hanging, can
meet her eyes.

You think you can stay here? Look about you.

Once she strikes the ground with her staff.
The flowers wither, infusing the air with a thick
funerary reek. Twice she strikes and the trees
split open and bleed. A third time and the sun
goes out, a blast of thunder hurls them to the
ground, and they lie in a choking red rain.

None may shelter in this wood. Go to your own
place.

They are standing in a tight group at the
top of the field, staring up at the house. The
curtains are drawn. The door is shut. This is a
place where cows give blood, headless chickens
peck with their bloody wounds. Shadow Vixen
darts and snaps among them, teeth ever meeting
in empty air. In air too thin to carry sound,
Shadow Wolf howls. Coyote howls. Cat hurls
herself against the window, falls back bloodied,
again leaps and falls. Bitch whines and scratches
at a door which never opens. Above the door,
Spider weaves of empty air. Bear paces, head
down and swinging, caged. Rat twists, gnawing
her own tail. Snake writhes as the beak of
Rooster stabs and stabs at her eyes.

How can we pass?

I am afraid.

But Wolf has stared through the ribs of
Shadow Wolf.

They are ghosts. They cannot harm us.

And she leads them across the barnyard to

the house and pushes the door open. Inside,
in the kitchen, the reek of Ogre is strong. The
door to the cellar is ajar. Ogre is down there,
and Little Girl too. Wolf can hear her crying.
But when she follows halfway down the stairs,
she senses that the cellar is empty. The scent is
old. The crying is a lingering echo. It is too dark
to see, but she smells a place where there is no
wall. A tunnel. That is where Ogre has taken
Little Girl. Wolf's legs are stiff with fear. The
hair on her neck bristles. One step at a time, for
she will not turn her tail to that place, she backs
up the stairs to the kitchen.

*They're down there. That's where we will have to
go.*

But Cat has been exploring.

*Ma-Ma is in the other room. Reading her Book,
alone.*

They follow Cat. Ma-Ma is sitting there at
the table in her dark blue dress, her hair dull
brown with no gray in it. They form a circle
around her, with Spider between Vixen's long
ears, Rat perched on Wolf's neck, Snake coiled
on Bear's back, and stand staring at her. She
reads on, unheeding. Cat leaps to the table and
lies down on the Book.

There is a small tremor in her now, a flickering in her eyes, yet still she seems to read,
as if the words were imprinted in red or in
white on Cat's black fur. Wolf watches. They
all watch. Cat is long and black to them, with a

real tail twitching and a real snarl in her throat,
but what if Ma-Ma truly is reading through her,
and when she comes to turn the page will raise
it through the body of their sister? They would
be ghosts themselves then, Shadow Cat and
shadows all, powerless to touch her.

But no more than the corner of the page
will turn. Cat's strong black paws are holding
it down. And they breathe again. Stand silently,
hearts pumping real blood, while the clock
strikes twelve times and Ma-Ma tugs and
twitches at the page. At last, as the twelfth note
dies, she stands up, her hand resting idly on
Cat's back. The hair bristles under her hand.

*Haven't I told you? Never bother me when I'm
reading. Go play.*

Cat leaps to the floor, rejoining the circle
of her sisters. It is cold in this room, though a
fire is burning, and dim, though a lamp is lit.
Ma-Ma sits back down, turns the page. Wolf
says:

Do you know who we are?
Of course, dear.
And why we have come?
To worry me, I'm afraid.
*We are your daughter, and we have come to save
our lives by taking yours. Are you ready to die?*
*Don't talk nonsense, child. Are you going to
make me call Father?*
*Summon him then. If he will come, it will save
us a long chase. But I do not think he will come.*

Father.

He will never hear you. Call louder.

Father.

A third time.

Father.

Your father has abandoned you. You are alone here with us. Bear, strip her.

Bear with her great claws rakes Ma-Ma back and belly, leaving her naked and white with long red scorings. Her breasts are dry pendulous dugs. Her pubic hair is a winter field, her vulva a dry well.

Now look what you've done to my dress. You will pay for it, young lady.

Spider, bind her.

Spider with her sticky web weaves her fast to her chair.

Out of my way, child. I've better things to do than fool with you.

She has forgotten that she gave birth to us. Rat, remind her.

Rat burrows her head into the well and with her long teeth gnaws and gnaws. When she backs out, a trickle of black blood follows her.

It is true. How many times have I told you? Never, never this side of the grave can you pay me for the pain of your birth.

She starved us. Coyote, take what she never cared to use.

Coyote with her strong white teeth slices, gnaws, worries the dugs from Ma-Ma's chest.

No milk flows from the wounds and little blood.

We are poor people. You cost us more than you can ever repay.

She never touched us. Bitch, take what she never used.

Bitch with her strong teeth bites off, one after another, Ma-Ma's ten fingers.

Always underfoot. In the way. Standing between me and the light.

She never listened to us. Vixen

with her sharp snout and clever little teeth makes deep holes where her ears were, and into each hole, from the pile of ten which Bitch made, she sticks one finger.

Your racket will drive me mad. A child is to be seen and not heard.

But she did not care to see us either. Cat

twists her claws into each eye, and into each socket she sticks one thumb.

Out of my sight, child. Such an ugly child.

Nor had anything kind to say. Snake

strikes through Ma-Ma's clenched teeth and with her sharp fangs bites her tongue. It swells until it fills her mouth and bulges out of her mouth like a red ball for a child to play with, or a red apple for a child to eat.

And now. And last

Wolf with the fire in her eyes sets the Book alight. The words on the page burn in the air with their own flickering red fire

The *Lord will smite them with madness*

as Ma-Ma's hair catches
and blindness
as she writhes in the fire
and astonishment of heart
as it consumes her
leaps to the sofa
the curtains
the clock a pillar of flame
quick
and they run, and watch from the barnyard
as the flames rise and take the roof, the
windows explode, the house burns to the
ground. And as they watch, Shadow Wolf stalks
to Wolf's side, Coyote to Coyote and all to all,
and each of the nine is one. Vixen in her hunger
snaps up a chicken, and it is flesh and blood,
and she eats as she watches and is satisfied.
Snake drives her venom into Rooster's heart and
watches as he flops away and dies.

The sky darkens and rain falls, raising a
great hissing cloud of smoke and steam. When it
is time, they approach the cellar hole, which is a
charred pit open to the sky. Whatever was in the
house that could not burn is down there, stove
and refrigerator, crockery and kitchen tools,
sinks and bathtub, the brass pendulum from
the clock, the television, and Ma-Ma's bones. A
greasy stench rises out of the pit, melted rubber
and plastic and roasted flesh.

Sister Wolf, I don't want to go down there.
Sister Coyote, nor do I. But there is the tunnel at

the bottom of the wall. That is the way they went.

I wish the Ogre had been in the house when it burned.

Little Girl would have been there too.

What matter? You think he won't kill her if we get close?

Sister, he killed all of us many times over. Well Wolf was dead. Shadow Wolf was dead, yet they were there when I came for them, and I feel their strength in me. Is it not so?

It's so. But the stairs are gone. How will we get down?

We will jump.

Ah. And how will we get back up?

We will not he returning by the same way.

Then, if I have to go into that place once only, I am ready.

They have all heard and all are ready. Wolf takes Rat onto her neck and leads them down, raising where she lands a noxious cloud of ashes. Breathes Ma-Ma deep into her lungs and chokes on her as the others land all around her and gray stinging grit fills her eyes and ears and mouth. They are a few breaths from dying in this underworld, and if they die, Ma-Ma will be their terrible queen. Blindly Wolf lunges for the only way out, which is down into the dark places of the earth.

The way of the tunnel is down, its color a blackness even Cat's eyes cannot penetrate. They bear the stink of ashes with them, cloaking all other smells. At first they stumble on roots, and in that connection to the upper world, to sun and sky, find some comfort. But soon they pass beneath the realm of living things, all but white webs of fungi glowing faintly from walls of damp stone. The floor is of stone, too steep and too slippery to climb back up, the roof brushes the tips of Wolf's ears, and the cold strikes into their bones.

How could the Ogre have come this way? He is ten feet high.

Only when it suits him. He can take any size and any shape.

Then how will we know him?

By his stink. And we will know Little Girl.

How can we defeat him?

By becoming one.

I am afraid of dying.

I, also. What do you smell?

Ashes. Cold stone.

What else? Ahead.

The Ogre's stinking boots. What he killed by stamping on it, and it clung and rotted there. He's not far ahead.

What else? Faint.

Very faint. Flowery. Like a single apple blossom. So he does have her. She's with him still.

You doubted it?

In this darkness I doubt everything.
Your ears as well? What do you hear?
Wind. Words of mourning I cannot make out.
What do you see?

I see . . . what in the world above would be
moonlight shining on one apple blossom, a mile
away. But which here is the end of the tunnel.

All of the far-seeing ones among them can
see it now, and soon even Spider and Snake
can see it. They pass through the darkness of
a moonless night, through the time of quarter
and half and full moon, a whiteness glimmering
all around them. And their eyes tell them what
their paws already know. Down here, in the
lower end of the passage, walls and roof and
floor are studded with bones. This is the domain
of the Ogre.

This is his domain: a place of strewn white
stone, boulders higher than Bear standing. In
crevices which hold a little earth, clumps of
gray moss grow, or patches of yellowing grass,
or stunted leafless trees. A cold wind swirls
about them. They huddle close under the flat
gray sky.

Which way?

And though Coyote spoke silently into the
mind of Wolf, which way? echoes and shrieks
about them, is sucked into the tunnel and
through the tunnel and eddies in Ma-Ma's
bones. And she smiles a white smile, knowing
they are lost and will die. For the Ogre in his

own country can hear their thoughts, and hide from them in any shape, ambush them from behind any rock, but they can see no distance at all, and hear nothing but the wind, and though the stink of the Ogre is strong in their nostrils, it comes from everywhere and nowhere.

Which way?

Any way. We must only seek, and what we seek will find us.

And so they set out, stumbling across the stony field. They walk for an hour or a day or a year, their path all mazy turnings, and the landscape and the light remain ever the same. They grow thirsty, but there is no sight or scent of water. Stone skitters and clatters under their paws, bloodying them. Their spoor is of blood and pain, weariness and fear; but the Ogre's spoor is black for anger and red for lust, and strong whichever way they go. Then Wolf, leading, sees something. It is the body of Little Girl, naked and mangled, wedged between two rocks.

No. It is Barbie Doll. Her vulva is ripped open and her breasts gnawed off; fingers stuffed into her ears, thumbs into her eyes, and her tongue, a fat red thing, bulges out of her mouth.

How did he know?

He knows everything.

This is what he will do to Little Girl. Should we turn back?

There is nowhere to turn.

Do you smell her? Apple blossoms?
Withering. I smell mostly fear.

They are all staring down at Barbie Doll,
not watching around them. There is a new
sound suddenly, a rapid buzzing. A flicker
of darkness, and Spider cries out in her voice
which makes no sound, her light weight falls
from Vixen's neck, her eight legs writhe on the
stones. Ogre in the form of Wasp has stung her
with his poison. Her body swells, her life oozes
out of her and dries up in this desert place she
has come to, and she dies.

Wolf stands with her paws shaking, cold.
Now it has begun. What they came for has
begun. It is their time.

Rat. You must eat her. Eat all of her, and lick the
stones where she lies.

There is a stirring among the others, but
Rat, young as she is, is the sister of Wolf and
of all of them, and she does what she must do.
When she is finished, nothing of Spider remains.
Spider goes with them.

They travel on. Wolf speaks to Rat, riding on
her neck.

Do you understand? What will happen next?
I did what you told me.
Yes, and now Spider is safe. That is what you
must remember.
Safe? She's dead.
How do you feel since you ate her?

I don't know. Different. Larger.

Because you are Rat and Spider together now. In need you could spin her web. If you bit the Ogre, he would feel the sting of her poison.

I'd like to do that.

Only, Little Sister, the two of you together are still small. Not strong enough to kill him.

Then how can we help?

Sister, you will help as Spider has. Do you understand?

I have to die?

As each one of us will.

I don't want to die. I'm afraid.

As each of us is. But we will all be with you.

And? After?

As you ate Spider, so Cat will eat you, and carry you along with us inside her.

But I won't be Rat any longer.

No. I don't know what you or any of us will be in the end. But we will kill the Ogre, and we will be something large.

If I saw him coming in time? Could I run?

But there is no running, for the Ogre comes swiftly as a black bird, snaps Rat's neck, and is gone.

Cat?

And Cat knows now, and eats Rat to the last whisker.

Do you understand?
*I understand. I heard. I don't want talk. I want
to be left alone.*

They travel on through that stony place,
and after a time it seems to Wolf that they are
descending into some great shadowed valley.
The sky may be darker, or perhaps her eyes are
growing dim. The wind's keening is darker,
with a new sound under it. Little Girl crying.
Where?
The way the wind swirls? Anywhere.
I meant, where is Cat?
She is no longer with them. She has slipped
away to die alone. Wolf's breath catches in her
throat. If Cat is lost, then Spider and Rat are
lost. And it requires all of them.
*Bitch, your nose is best. Can you backtrack to
where she left us, and follow her trail?*
*I will try. But there is nothing here to hold a
scent.*
But in the event, backtracking is easy. Any
of them could do it by eye, for their blood is red
on the white stones.
Here she turned aside. Or something else did?
Something else?
*This is not altogether the spoor of Cat. It has Cat
in it, but it is different. New.*
She is new. She is Spider-in-Rat-in-Cat.
They go only a little way, following Bitch's

nose, before they come to her body. It has been
crushed flat, for the Ogre, from the sight and
the smell, stamped again and again with his
filthy boot after the first killing blow.

Vixen?

I would prefer to eat chickens. Even apples.

But her hunger is sufficient. She devours Cat
to the last claw.

Vixen? How do you feel?

*That I can see in any dark. I look into the
darkness inside, and I see only fear. It is a red flame
which burns cold and gives no light.*

Cat is safe now.

But she is not Cat.

*And you will not be Vixen, nor I Wolf, but we
will give our strength, our wits and our night-seeing
to something large.*

*That is cold consolation. Sister, he will come for
me as Hound, as he always came. And I must stand
and face him, for if I run, I will run so far before he
catches me that you will never find me.*

*I think you are very brave. Walk along beside me.
Perhaps . . .*

*But she cannot say what she thinks: If he comes
as Hound, then maybe I could kill him, since I am
Wolf. And then I and the others would not have to
die.*

*Vixen hears the thought but says nothing, and
then what she alone can hear.*

Sister, what is it?

Hound. Baying. You cannot harm him. Stand away.

His eyes are coals from the furnace of hell, his teeth the white bars of the gates of hell. He is a great rushing blackness, and when he passes, Vixen lies with her blood pooling on the stones, her head almost ripped from her body.

Bitch?

My sister. I cannot.

She is dead, Sister. Would you leave her there for carrion birds? When you eat her, you will take all that she was into you.

When I do that, I will be marked to die.

Yes. Drink your sister's blood before it dries.

Would it be . . . a good thing to do? Would I be good?

You would be good. Good dog.

And so she drinks and eats as she must.

How do you feel now?

I feel sad. I thought that if only I were good enough, he would love me. But I can see into the dark now, and I know there was no love in him.

Yes. How else do you feel?

Angry. Why die now, when I am just learning to live? And afraid. What will it be like to die?

You will be alone, I think, but only for a little time. Then you will be with your sisters.

But I will never again be Bitch. Never, never.

No. Part of something large. What do you hear?

Footsteps. Ahead. Something large. The ground is shaking.

They are walking a narrow, twisting way between standing stones. A few yards ahead the path opens out a little, and when they come to that place they see him. He is ten feet tall, white-faced and black-eyed, and his teeth flash white when he smiles. In one hand he holds a great red club. Under the other arm, Little Girl, naked, her face shining with tears, her eyes pleading. Coyote and Wolf bristle and lunge at him, teeth snapping on air as he brushes them aside and brings the club down. The shock of it topples stones all around them, sucks light out of the sky and turns the world black. When they can see again he is gone, and none of them can bear to look at what remains of Bitch.

Coyote?

We can never kill him. Never, never. Didn't you see? We are all dying for nothing.

Falcon foretold our triumph. One to die in fire, one in the cold. And Ma-Ma is burned to the bones.

And where is Falcon now?

Wolf searches. The sky is empty.

Yes, and where is Old Woman? She saved Bear and me. She drove the Ogre back with one word, but where is she now?

Our fate is in our own hands, Little Sister. Eat, as you must.

*As she must, Coyote devours Bitch to the last
drop of blood.*

Who are you now?

*Spider-in-Rat. Rat-in-Cat. Cat-in-Vixen. Vixen-
in-Bitch. Bitch-in-Coyote, and much good it may do
me. Sister, I love being Coyote. I am not reconciled.
With no hope, I must try to trick him and get away.*

Try, dear sister.

They touch noses. Everything passes
between them.

When the Ogre comes he is twelve feet tall,
his mouth is smeared with the blood of what
he has eaten, and he is laughing with the joy of
killing. The eyes of Little Girl, doll-sized under
his arm, are blank with terror. Coyote leaps into
a narrow place between two stones. The Ogre
raises his club, smashes first one and then the
other. They shatter like glass, leaving Coyote
exposed, too stunned to move. The club remains
poised over her head for long seconds, mocking,
before it descends for the third time.

Wolf looks around her. Only Bear and Snake
are with her now, and neither has spoken this
whole time, and she cannot read their eyes.
With sorrow she eats her dear sister to the last
tooth, and laps the blood from the stones. Now
it is her own time, and her bowels have gone
slack, her knees have turned to water, her heart
hammers in her throat and there is a great
ringing in her ears. She will have to wait for the
Ogre to come for her here.

But the path ahead leads on down into the valley. Even with Cat's night-eyes she cannot see it, nor smell it with Bitch's nose, but there is a place of final meeting they are going to, the Ogre's Place. She knows it with the sensing of all of them.

Bear? Great Sister?

I am here.

When I am dead and you have eaten me, go on. Down, always, to the lowest place in this valley. Tell Snake. She will carry all of us at the end.

She knows. Lead ahead, Little Sister.

So Wolf goes on, her heart overflowing with sorrow at leaving even this barren place, for the white stone in the twilight gleams with its own pale light, and has a deep and terrible beauty. Her tears flow, and where they fall, small white flowers spring up behind her.

They come at last to where they can see, far below, a grove of dark trees, with black sawtoothed mountains rising beyond them. That is the place. They walk faster now, Snake coiled on Bear's back. In a little while, Wolf can see with Cat's eyes something white in the grove. Then that it is a house. Then Unca's house. Roof, shutters, walls all white. The first trees are very near now. The house is built of bone.

The Ogre steps into their path. He is fifteen feet tall, and he holds Little Girl with one hand closed all the way around her waist.

Wolf. Bear. Snake. You may not enter here.

His eyes are dead black coals, his voice a rumble of thunder. Wolf knows he is afraid.

Do you want to die as Ma-Ma died? Give us Little Girl and we will kill you quickly.

He shifts his grip to Little Girl's ankles and dashes her brains out on the stony ground, and then he eats her in one gulp, headfirst, and licks the blood from his lips. Wolf leaps. It seems to her that she is a long time in the air. She feels her teeth meet in the Ogre's throat before he snatches her away, hurls her to the stones, stamps the life out of her.

Bear. Snake. You may not enter here.

But he turns and walks away into his wood, with his great red club on his shoulder. Bear eats Wolf to the last gray hair.

Hold tight to my back, Little Sister. We will see what we see.

They walk in among the trees, brooding evergreens which hide the sky. It is dark, but Bear can see with the eyes of Cat. It is a long way, the house a white glimmer receding before them, but she trots along without tiring on the strong legs of Wolf.

Then suddenly with Bitch's nose she smells the Ogre very close. With Vixen's ears she hears him breathing. But it is too late. From behind a tree by the path he springs and drives her to her knees with a blow of his club. She staggers up roaring, rakes with her claws, and she lays his belly open before the second blow kills her.

Snake. Go back and save your life. The way to the upper world is open to you.

Snake coils, hissing. When the Ogre turns and walks away, she swallows Bear whole. Goes on slowly, her belly bruised on the hard ground. It is too cold for Snake, but she is not Snake only, harboring the warmth of the others inside. At last, in the center of the woods, she comes to a clearing, and in the center of the clearing stands the house of bones.

Snake. You should not have come so far. Now you must die like the others.

She sees only his boot beside her head, and drives her venom into the bare flesh above as the club comes down. The blow splits her belly wide open. Out of it the woman springs, Laurel, naked and full-grown. The Ogre jabs at her belly with his club. With the speed of Cat she snatches it, with the strength of Bear she snaps it across her knee.

The Ogre steps back, his eyes glittering with fear. He diminishes, as Dove leaps away into the air. Above him, the scream of a hunting bird. Falcon stoops in a flash of white and gold, Dove falls as Ogre, and the ground shakes under him.

Go away. There is nothing for you here. Little Girl is dead.

Her desire is to kill him where he stands, but she is not yet ready. In the time it takes her to swallow Snake, he hobbles away into the house and slams the door behind him.

Now, with Snake coiled with the others in
her belly, she is whole. Still she is empty, and
the name of that emptiness is Little Girl. Little
Girl is dead. With the eyes of Wolf she saw
him kill and eat her. In her terrible despair she
grows cold and quiet. Then she feels in her belly
a flicker of fire, and that is anger. It grows until
she is cold and hot at once. Cold aims her. Heat
looses her.

The door is built of the thigh bones of
women, and the knocker is a skull. She opens
the jaw and snaps it shut with such force that
the teeth fall out, and listens, but there is no
sound from within. She batters at the door
with the strength of Bear, but it does not shake.
This way is held against her. She walks around
the house. On each side is a narrow window
set deep into the wall, tightly barred with the
arm bones of women and curtained within.
The curtains are yellow, brown, gray, red and
white and black, for they are woven of women's
hair. She tugs at the bars, but they are set too
close for a strong grip. No light shines through
the windows. It is dark inside, in the place of
her enemy, whose prey she greatly resembles,
who if he defeats her will feast on her flesh.
Strengthen his walls with her bones, and live
inside her. How many came here like her, in
their innocence thinking to defeat him? But gave
up body to his body, bones to his dwelling.
Then her knees shake, and she is afraid. And

even if she desired to enter, there is no way in. She walks back into the edge of the woods, and sits facing the house with her arms around her knees, watching. She watches for three nights and three days.

When she stands at the end of that time she is lightheaded, having eaten and drunk nothing, but her mind is clear. The Ogre has not come out. It's he who is afraid. Wolf tore his throat. Bear ripped his belly. Snake poisoned him, and Falcon struck him down from the height of the trees. He is hurt and sick, and hungry, for he has not been out hunting. And he must hunt always. That she remembers, from the years when she was the hunted. *Seek, catch, rend, devour, without rest.* Now his house is besieged. Moreover he has no weapon. She took his red club from him and snapped it like a twig across her knee. With Bitch's nose she breathes deep. She can smell him in there, the sour reek of starvation. With Vixen's ears she listens. She can hear him gnawing his own flesh. With Cat's inner seeing she looks. His lips are spread in a thin snarl, his eyes dark and dull. He is dying. She has only to wait.

If you leave him alone to die, Little Girl will die with him.

She looks up. Golden light flares off Falcon's wings, dazzling her. Falcon's eyes are fierce and bright.

Little Girl is dead already. He dashed her brains

out and ate her.

She is alive, but she will die if you do not save her.

What must I do?

Go into the dark place where he lies, and kill him with your hands.

I tried. I did try. There was no way in.

There was no way in for Bear. Are you only Bear?

I am nine, and the nine are one.

Then you will find the way.

Alone again in the edge of the clearing, she stands quietly looking at the house. She thinks with the wit of Coyote, and in a moment the way is clear. She goes to a window and sends the part of her which is Spider in through the bars to look. On the inside of the front door is no lock, but a simple latch. The Rat part of her squeezes through, climbs to the top of the window, and gnaws away the curtain. Hair, golden and gray and brown, auburn and black as midnight, falls away in showers, and now the whole of her can see. The latch is the bones of a woman's hand, the five fingers blocking the door. With the part of her that is Bitch, who with her mind can stop a clock from across a room, she flicks the fingers back and the door creaks open. She walks around to the front, with the strength of Bear wrenches it off its hinges, and enters. Her feet are Cat's feet and make no sound.

He is nowhere on the ground floor of the house, has never lived there. She paces to the last door, opens, descends. And the treads are damp bones, slick under her feet, but her feet are the clever paws of Cat. It is dark, and the air is close, the floor littered with bones and other things, but she is Rat, and with her whiskers twitching she can find her way. With the fiery eyes of Wolf, she makes a dim red light. The Ogre is there, lying naked on his bed in the corner. His face is white and his eyes black, but he is diminished. His name is Unca.

His lips twist into a thin smile, he licks his dry lips and stares and stares at her, and his cock rises, for she is naked, her hair falls loose almost to her waist, and she has grown tall and beautiful. His voice is rusty, harsh as Raven's voice, but it is his own. She knows it, and is glad of that.

You came back for what you always did want? Come and get it, then.

I came for Little Girl. Where is she?

You're too late. I ate her.

Then I will rip her out of your belly.

I was joking. She's around here somewhere.

I saw you eat her. Now you will give her up to me.

You'd threaten a helpless old man? Good girls don't talk like that.

Do you still not understand?

She walks up to the side of the bed and

stands looking down at him. He is still erect. He hooks a hand like a claw around her waist and draws her down to him, and his arm, hurt as he is, is terribly strong. She puts her hands on his shoulders, and bends toward his face.

I knew you wanted it. That was all you ever wanted.

And he opens his mouth for her kiss, his red tongue flicking between his teeth. With the speed of Snake she strikes, and drives Snake's venom into his lip.

You crazy Bitch. What did you do that for?

Not my name.

You know what I said I'd do if you bit me. I'm going to get up off this bed and punish you pretty good.

Try, then.

I can't move. I'm cold. Cold. What did you do to me?

Poisoned you. As you did me. Here's something else you taught me.

She picks up rope, which he keeps there to bind his prey, and with the clever hands of Spider she ties him to the bed.

That was just for fun. It was a game we played. You begged me to play that game.

The game is ended. Now where should I begin?

Laurel? Is it you, all grown up? Let me look at you. You're so beautiful, Laurel.

With your legs? You chased me down and caught me, always, no matter how fast I ran.

With the strong jaws and sharp teeth of Bear and Wolf, Coyote and Bitch, Vixen and Cat and Rat, she gnaws his legs off at the thighs and eats them.

Now you will never chase anyone, ever again.

This is going beyond a joke, Laurel. You're going to feel pretty guilty about this.

And when you caught me you slapped, hit, poked, prodded, stabbed.

She gnaws off his arms at the shoulders and eats them.

Nice girls don't do things like this, Laurel. And you always were a nice girl.

Next, with your filthy cock you raped my body and spirit. You stole my childhood.

There's no proof of any of that, you know. Your word against mine, and who's going to believe an ugly little girl?

You wanted your cock in my mouth? Then you shall have your desire.

And she bites it off and eats it, and his balls also.

Castrating bitch.

It wasn't much. Half a bite at most. Have you ever satisfied a woman?

You've changed, Laurel. You're grown cold and hard and bitter. Dried up, you might say. Now why is that, I wonder?

Never as cold as your pitiless heart.

She rips it out of his chest and eats it.

Why am I getting the feeling that you're

*resentful? But there's little misunderstandings like
that in every family. Why don't you tell me about it?*

*Your stomach. Because you were insatiable.
Devoured me every day of my childhood, and it was
never enough.*

She rips it out of his belly and eats it.

*Laurel, now really. Don't you know you're going
to get in trouble if you don't quit this? Quit it right
now and I won't tell a soul, I promise.*

Cross your heart and hope to die?

Cross my heart. That's a good little girl.

*But Unca, aren't you forgetting something? You
haven't got any heart, or any arms to cross it with.
And how would you tell anyway, once I've eaten
your tongue?*

*Always the joker. You were, I swear, the funniest
child.*

*But first, I think, your eyes. Which left me no
secrets. Invaded my soul. Are looking at me with
lust, I believe, this very moment.*

*Well really, Laurel. If you go around naked like
that, aren't you kind of asking for it?*

She gouges his eyes out and eats them.

*And now your ears, which never heard when I
sobbed and pleaded.*

*You always were a crybaby, Laurel. Always
boohooing about some fool thing or another. And if
you don't mind my saying so, I can't really see that
you've grown out of it.*

She gnaws his ears out of his head and eats
them.

And your tongue. With which you carved the heart out of me daily. Shredded my soul and left me bleeding my life out on the ground. But then I'm forgetting--you can't hear me now, can you? Is there anything else you'd like to say?

I'm afraid you've gone too far with this, Laurel. I'm going to have to punish you pretty good. Remember Fang?

Fang is broken and rotting in the woods. And I am tired of hearing my name on your foul lips.

With the long clever snout of Vixen, she plucks his tongue from his mouth and eats it.

What now? Head, lungs, rib cage?

She eats all that remains.

When she has done that, she stands still for a moment. The room is quiet and dark, for she has let the light go out. She searches with the senses of all of them, but there's nothing there. It's a hollow place like a tomb that she's standing in. Where is Little Girl?

Then she feels a quickening, and she knows. She is with child. Little Girl is safe inside.

Chapter Seven

One April morning Laurel woke in a room
which at first was strange to her. She rose from
her bed and looked at herself in a long mirror
mounted on the door, and her body too was
strange. And the sunlight streaming in through
the window. There were clothes laid out on
a rocking chair, underwear and an old green
sweatshirt and blue jeans, and socks and a pair
of black canvas shoes on the floor. She put them
on without knowing she knew how, and they
fit, so perhaps they were hers, but she could not
remember bringing them to this place.

She stood looking around her. The wooden
floor was bare except for a braided oval rug,
blue and green and gold. The walls were clean
white, hung with small bright art prints with
women in them—bathing at a basin, reading
a letter, playing on a beach, combing a young
girl's hair. The quilt was golden sun, blue
sky, white birds; silver river, and green things

growing. She made the bed, desiring to leave everything in order, though she could not have said where she would be going or when or even why, and walked to the window. It was halfway open, the curtains, yellow and white flowers in a green field, rustling a little in a light wind she felt was from the south. Though how could she even think she knew that? The window opened out onto a wide porch; beyond that an expanse of lawn, an apple tree not yet in bloom, then a rail fence, fields, woods, and a pale spring sky. No people anywhere in sight. But someone was moving quietly about in another part of the house. Why then was she not afraid? Because it was Constance she heard, her friend and healer. Only how did she know that? And this was Constance's room, a safe place where she had slept long and deep.

And dreamed. Dreamed. Ma-Ma and Unca were dead, and she herself was changed.

She turned back into the room, walked to the door and opened it, her hand knowing what her mind for a moment did not, the glass round and cool in her palm, the light resistance revealing to her a little of the strength in her wrist and arm. She was in a hallway which led to an outside door, so she went that way, went out onto the lawn and to the tree and stood with her hands resting among its branches, looking about her at the world.

It was there that Constance, not knowing she

was awake, came upon her. Laurel's back was to
her, and she was glad of that, for she was able
to stand quietly, breathe deeply, calm herself a
little. Then she called from across the lawn, and
Laurel turned.

It seemed to be Laurel, though she looked
both older and younger. This woman, whoever
she was, stared unsmiling at Constance for an
unnerving length of time. Her hands rested
lightly on the tree, and she did not move at all.
She might have been part of the tree, rooted
there.

"Laurel? Is it you?"

"Yes."

"May I come closer?"

"Yes."

As she approached, Constance saw lines of
sorrow and weariness, of strength and joy and
the living of life, etched deep into Laurel's face.
Then, from closer still, she saw it was a trick
of the dappled light. Her face was smooth as a
young girl's. Only it was not a trick of light. The
lines were real.

"May I hug you?"

"Yes, love. Yes."

The voice was light as a young girl's, dark
as an old woman's. They held each other. The
scent of Laurel's skin and hair was familiar and
strange, apple bloom with something fierce
and wild under it, and in her arms a terrible
and gentle strength. Constance began crying

suddenly and could not stop, shuddering in the arms of her dearest friend and stranger.

"Not so good. I was supposed to be the strong one. Welcome back. Welcome home."

"Am I home?"

"I think the whole world will be your home. Once you've walked around it a little and got your feet under you. And the upper air. I think you can fly."

"Has Falcon been here?"

"He's been away for a long time, then early this morning we saw him circling the house. I should have known you'd be waking. Laurel, what of the others?"

"The Ogre murdered all of them, and he murdered Little Girl. They are all alive and well, in me."

"Thank God. I'm glad."

"Constance, I killed the two of them. I burned Ma-Ma alive in her house. I followed Unca a long way to a terrible place and killed him in the cellar where he was hiding from me. They're dead."

"You did what was necessary. It was what you descended to do."

"I can't tell you—I can't make it clear how hard it is for me to believe that they're alive in this world. A mile or two from here, just as they were when we went to their house. I suppose Unca is watching one of his filthy videos this very minute."

"Let's go in and have breakfast. Are you
hungry?"

"Now I am."

She hadn't known how hungry. She ate
ham and eggs and potatoes and toast until she
felt she must be feeding all of them, the whole
crowd in there, with Bear getting ready to
hibernate again.

"We might take a walk now."

"Indeed, I need to."

But she had not been prepared to go the
way that Constance led her, straight down the
field toward the fenceline. Or to see Constance
spread the wire, scramble through, and stand
looking back at her from Unca's Place.

"What are you doing? I'm not ready to go
there. I don't think I'll ever be ready."

"Can you trust me this far? Come over here
with me, and we'll sit and talk. Then you can
decide whether or not to go farther."

"It's not much of a fence. You ought to have
electrified chain link, ten feet high."

"Actually it was your stepfather's fence. Now
it's yours—and all that lies beyond it. Come
over, Laurel, and claim your inheritance."

"What do you mean?

"You're saying they're dead? In real life?"

"And are you surprised? I told you of
Falcon's prophesy. Did you think he would lie,

or be mistaken?"

"You told Wolf. One would die in fire and one in ice. Did they? Constance, did they?"

"I don't like talking with this wire between us. Come over here beside me."

Laurel bent the top wire down and stepped over it. "Now tell me."

"They died as Falcon said they would. In fire and ice. Your mother in the house when it burned, your stepfather last winter in the cellar."

"Then I killed them. Somehow in real life I killed them."

"You didn't, my love. You were asleep the whole time."

"I slipped out and did it in my sleep. You don't know what powers I have."

"I have some sense of it. We talked about what Falcon said, Brother and I, and how we might best protect you. We thought of locking the room, but then it would have been just our word that it was locked. Brother talked to some people--have you ever heard of a camera with a time-and-date stamp?"

"I don't know. What are you talking about?"

"They stamp the time and date of the exposure on the film. And there are cameras with automatic timing devices, and there is infrared film which can see in the dark. How long would it take you to get from my room, travelling on foot at night across the fields, to your mother's house? Immobilize her somehow and set a fire? Get your stepfather and his pickup truck away and hide both of them? Because, dearest, he and his truck were gone when your mother was found, which is why everyone believed and still believes that he murdered her. How long would it take even you to do all that, walking in your sleep, and return with no trace of soot or smell of smoke anywhere about you?"

"I don't know."

"Could you do it in an hour?"

"No. Of course not."

"Yet you were photographed by an automatic camera every hour from the time you went to sleep until after your stepfather died."

"There's some trick. I must have done it. You're saying it was coincidence?"

"It was not coincidence. Mystery rather. Synchronicity. Destiny or destination. Laurel, I believe you have been where the planes of existence come together, the veils are lifted, where time and space are no more. It is hard to explain what I understand dimly, at best, in my dreams. You went into the deepest places of the underworld?"

"Yes."

"But not in your body. That stayed here. To light a match requires the use of fingers."

"I can start fires with my eyes."

"From two miles away? And can you now?"

"No. Maybe not. I've lost that?"

"It was a talent, let's say, which went with an earlier stage of your existence. Which you have now outgrown, or assimilated rather into other talents you don't yet know about."

"So I couldn't have done it?"

"No, dearest. You couldn't have done it."

"I'm a little lost. Where's the house from here?"

"On the second ridge. You can see it from the far slope of the first one."

"How do you know? You never came here when you were younger, did you?"

"No. It was forbidden."

"Why? What did your parents know about us?"

"Only that you kept very much to yourselves. But Mama's a seer, and she sensed it was a place we should not go."

"Did she never think of trying to help me?"

"You'll have to ask her yourself what she thought. You might want to do that when we get back. But, Laurel, there was nothing she could have done. You went to school every day, when it was cold you wore a coat. There was no evidence that anyone else could have seen."

"Yes, they would have seen to that. When we
get back from where? Where are we going?"

"It's your day. Your place."

"Why am I dreading this so?"

"Dearest, for too many reasons to list.
Because you don't believe they're dead, and you
fear they will spring on you and drag you back
into the country of your childhood where no
one will ever hear you screaming."

"You're quite vivid. I thought that was why I
went into the well—to be done with all that."

"I'm afraid that's not the way of it, darling.
You have to go down again and again, all the
days of your life. Only now, because you've
been so very brave, you will come to know that
there's nothing down there that can harm you."

"Let's go then."

They walked across a miry pasture and up
the long slope of the ridge, through a belt of
oaks still in bud, and then, across another field,
they saw no house. Only a tall stone chimney,
standing alone against the sky on its hilltop.
Laurel stopped and stared. In a little while her
hand sought her friend's and she held on tight.
When at last she set off again she walked fast
on her long legs across the field, Constance at
first stretching to keep up. Then, deliberately,
she lagged back, five yards and ten and fifty

by the time Laurel climbed the hill and stood
unmoving, staring into the hole at her feet.

She did not look up when Constance came
and stood beside her, nor speak for some time.
At last she said, "It's exactly as I saw it. All
that's missing is Ma-Ma's bones. Tell me what
happened."

"It burned one night, a hot, still night, in
early August. Brother saw the red glow in the
sky before dawn when he went out for chores.
He called the volunteer fire company in town
and drove over himself, just in time to see the
roof cave in. It had been burning for hours, long
past saving by the time the fire truck got there.
The firemen hosed it down, Brother said, more
because they were there and it was exciting
than for any practical reason. They didn't know
your mother was in there until well on in the
morning. They'd assumed, since your stepfather's truck was gone, that they'd left together
on a trip. Except Brother knew that wasn't so,
because the stock was still there. He was the one
who milked and fed the cows."

"And did they discover how it was that she
came to be trapped inside?"

"A day or two later when it had cooled
down, an arson investigator came, and he found
out."

"She had been tied to a chair and left there
to burn."

"Yes. Do you want details?"

"By all means."

"They found the remains of the ropes. Nylon melted into her wrists and ankles."

"That would be Unca's style. He had no great fondness for women. Do they know how he started the fire?"

"Put a kettle of gasoline on the stove and turned on the burner, they think. It would take a good while to heat up enough to vaporize."

"And Ma-Ma sitting there all that time, knowing. Because he'd have been sure to tell her. I wonder if he at least left her Bible open in front of her so she could read. What would he have chosen for her, I wonder? The 23rd Psalm? Hardly that. Or the Song of Solomon? The irony might have appealed to him. Or maybe just something about fallen women and whores. Constance, why am I so heartless? Why don't I feel anything?"

"Because it's not yet the time for feeling."

"What happened next? Quite a hullabaloo?"

"Oh yes. Law enforcement people of all sorts for a short time, until they became convinced that we didn't know your stepfather at all and had no idea where he might have gone. News people for longer, and a man who said his name as if we ought to have recognized it, and was going to write a bestselling true crime story and make us all famous. I had to restrain Brother from throwing him down the front steps."

"They didn't know about me?"

"They knew your mother had had a daughter who dropped out of sight two years ago, but there was no connection they knew of between the two of us. So it never occurred to any of them to ask if you might be right there in our house."

"Then what? What about Unca?"

"They never did find either him or his truck. He must have hidden it in deep woods or deep water, they think, and maybe gotten away by hitchhiking. When he came back in the Winter, he walked. And nobody knows where from--or why, or anything about it. What he intended, whether he jumped into the cellar hole or fell. Tried to get out, or came there on purpose to die."

"What do you think?"

"I would like to think he came there to die. He had no coat on."

"And you feel that his desire to die would redeem him?"

"That his heart melted a little at the very end? It's too large a question for me."

"Except that I know the answer. His heart did not melt. His very last words were of punishing me, and that was his way of doing it."

"Then, my love, we must see that he does not succeed. We have work ahead of us."

Laurel did not answer. She was looking across the cellar hole, to what had been the back of the house.

"The apple tree. Was that burned to death too?"

"Let's go look."

On the side nearest the house, Constance snapped off brittle blackened twigs. "It's dead here." She walked around. "Living on this side. See the buds?"

"I should be glad. Life renews itself. But I have bad memories of this tree."

"We've been here long enough for now, maybe."

"Who found him?"

"I did. Out for a walk in the snow, and then I saw Falcon circling the house. I knew right away. He'd been there, they think, for as long as a month."

"Let's go down to the well."

"All right."

But Laurel, who had walked so fast up the hill to the house, now dragged her way down the pasture, and did not seem to know just where she was going. It was Constance finally who took her arm and pointed: "More to the right. Over there." They walked to it hand-in-hand and stopped, at Laurel's slight urging, ten feet away.

"I'll have to have it boarded up. It's dangerous."

"Yes, it is. There was some talk of searching

it when your stepfather was missing, but nothing ever came of it."

"They wouldn't have known how to look. Or they weren't the right ones to look. It's my well. And he's down there, all right. Both of them. Which I suppose is another way of saying that they're in here. Constance, I'm cold. I don't feel comfortable at all."

"Poor darling. Did you think you did all that to be comfortable? No, you did it to live."

"But what if they come back to life stronger than ever, and take over again? What am I going to do?"

Constance stood beside her looking up at her; but Laurel's eyes were fixed on the well.

"Do you feel able to walk closer?"

"Why should I?"

"It would tell me that you're ready to begin our work."

Laurel glanced at her, walked gingerly to within three feet of the edge, and sat down cross-legged, facing it. "So?"

Constance sat down beside her. "So tell me how you see your inner country. Describe the landscape that is you."

"I was going to say a barren place, but I suppose not really. A lush place, meadows and forests and birds singing, but it's been damaged. Scorched and parched, and there's a kind of pall in the air. The sun isn't shining clearly. A chill.

I've heard that's a sign of ghosts."

"Yes, and is there any dwelling in this country? Your particular home, where you go to sleep at night?"

"Hard to see. It might be your house, but that can't be right."

"It can, because that house means shelter and safety to you. Now where is Ma-Ma?"

"She's in the house. That's where the chill is coming from. She's sitting in the middle of the living room reading her damn Bible, paying absolutely no attention to me or anybody, with a white mist of cold all around her."

"You said, paying no attention to anybody. Who else is there?"

"You and your brother and mother, of course. It's your house."

"So you have friends to help you. Now what would you like to do about your mother?"

"When I went down the well before, I tied her to her chair and burned the house around her. Just like Unca."

"Is that what you want to do again?"

"No, of course not. Burn our house?"

"What, then?"

"Throw her out. I want her gone forever."

"You can't do that, my love. She lives in that country. But what you can do is move her out of the way, drain her power, even use her for some good purpose. All that cold in the living room,

like a furnace running backwards. What's she
good for?"

"Air conditioning? There's never been a day
in hell that hot."

"Insulate her, then. Put her inside
something."

"Maybe one of those big chest freezers?"

"Excellent, and then?"

"Drag her up to the attic. Enough cold will
leak out to keep the shingles from curling up in
the summer. In winter she can stay in the root
cellar. Pass the time with the potatoes."

"You see. Now when you feel your
fingertips tingling with cold, you will know
what to do. But where is Unca?"

"Not in the house. In a cave somewhere.
You can find your way to it because everything
that grows along his track is blighted. There's
a big rock blocking the entrance, and I can hear
him huffing and puffing and rattling around in
there. Maybe he'll get strong enough one day to
break out, and then he'll be loose."

"Will you go to the cave if Brother and I
come with you?"

"Yes. I did kill him once."

"And so you can again, if it should come to
that. Picture the three of us walking along that
blighted track, and tell me when we're there."

"Yes. All right."

"What's it like?"

"Pretty. The cave opens into a clearing in the woods, but there are bones in the clearing, and no birds singing."

"They're afraid of all that anger. Diabolic energy in there. You're strong enough to fight it, but it's not good to have to. It's wearing, it distracts you from your creative life. You were made for better things than to be a perpetual prison guard. So what shall we do about Unca?"

"You say he can't be killed or exiled, and I can tell that you're right. I feel empty, tired out. All I can think of is that I wish you weren't."

"You're exhausted at the prospect of being a jailer. Never being able to turn your back on him for a minute. So why not just let him out?"

"Let him out? He'd pillage the countryside. Rape, loot, burn, my God. You think he's reformed?"

"Not at all, but I think, with the help you have at hand, that you can render him powerless. How might you do it?"

"Cut his hands and feet off."

"Excellent, love. And as it happens, Brother brought along his big cleaver. Would you like to hold it ready while Brother rolls the stone aside?"

"What if he attacks us in that moment?"

"But you killed him singlehanded, unarmed and alone. And now you are armed and have friends."

"All right. I'm scared, but I guess I'd better."
"Tell me."
"Brother's moving the stone. It's cool and
dim in the cave. I don't see any bones. I don't
think there was anything to eat in there. He
was lying on the floor, now he sees us and he
gets up, but he's slow and clumsy. I swing the
cleaver, it's light in my hand, and his right hand
flies off. Now his left. Now I cut his feet out
from under him and he falls so hard the earth
shakes. He's cursing me. He says he's going to
punish me, but he can't, can he? What can he do
with no hands and no feet?"
"Crawl on his knees and elbows out into
the clearing. And you said he was already weak
with hunger. How will he keep from starving?"
"He'll be hungry all the time. Weak. But I
think . . . he used to hunt birds and animals—
hawks and crows, rabbits, coons, anything that
moved. Maybe if he grew very humble, and
quiet, and asked them to forgive him, they
would bring him things to eat."
"But if not, if he were raging, they would be
afraid to come near."
"So he would grow hungrier and weaker
still."
"Thus you are triply safe. No feet to chase.
No hands to strike. No strength to harm. Love,
has anything changed? The sky?"

"It's brighter, clearer. Deep blue. Constance, look!"

They both look. Falcon is circling them. They are standing in the center of a wheel of golden light.

That night she dreams. In her dream, and upon waking from her dream, she rises naked from her bed and bathes herself with cool water. She draws on the white gown which is laid out ready for her, ties a green sash about her waist, and walks barefoot onto the lawn in the early morning. Her feet leave shining tracks in the dew, and in her tracks white flowers spring up. Beside the blooming apple tree, she stands under a deep blue sky filled with stars. The sun rises, its rays touch the apple blossoms, and they turn red and fall as drops of blood. Where they fall red flowers grow. She walks about gathering them, and when she has gathered them all they are nine. They are bright and beautiful, but their stems have sharp thorns which stab her hand. Their perfume mingles with the scent of her blood. Where blood touches them they turn black, the sweet reek of decay rises to her nostrils, and she hurls them away. They fall in a circle around her. They are Spider and Rat and Cat, Vixen and Bitch and Coyote, Wolf and Bear and Snake, all bloody and torn. All dead.

Her tears flow into the ground, and a bare

black tree springs up. From its branches grow long thorns. She plucks one off and drives it into her heart, her blood spurts out and mingles with the blood of the nine. Falcon circles above them, his shadow a golden wheel. It touches Spider, and Spider stands on her eight nimble legs. Touches Rat, Rat shakes blood off her fur, death out of her body. Cat stretches and purrs. Vixen leaps. Bitch wags. Coyote grins. Wolf howls. Bear growls. Snake coils. Each meets her eyes, and the light that passes between them makes the spokes of the wheel. They dance around her, slowly at first, then faster, faster, until they merge into a white wheeling radiance. Faster still they wheel, Falcon soaring golden above them, drawing them into the sky. They all rise into the light. At the center of that circle Laurel stands, tall in the first morning of the world. She is a straight young tree, blooming.

ABOUT THE AUTHOR

Ed Moses, the author of four novels
and a memoir, lives a quiet life in rural
Pennsylvania.

Books by Ed Moses
One Smart Kid (1982, Macmillan Pub Co.)
Nine Sisters Dancing (1996, Fithian Press,
    reissued by River Boat Books in 2024)
Pilgrimage with Fish: A Fishing Memoir
    (2004, New Rivers Press)
The Big One (2020, Daniel and Daniel
    Publishers)
What Love Can Do (2021, River Boat Books)